Dalton's Pit

James Fay Jr.

ISBN-13:978-1546426165
ISBN-10:1546426167

Dedication

To those who wait for us on the other side, especially my dad James Fay Sr.

Contents

1. On the Farm — 1
2. Where Am I? — 47
3. Lucky Dogs — 69
4. Ultra Violet — 94
5. The Corporal — 112
6. Best Friends — 164
7. Visiting the Past — 199
8. Ultimate Sacrifice — 234
9. Entering the Game — 263
10. The Reunion — 285
11. Hannah — 322
12. Full Circle — 353

Chapter 1

On the Farm

The sun started disappearing behind the barn a bit earlier; summer was coming to a close. Billy Dalton, as he often did, was hanging out under the front porch with his little sister Hannah when his mom yelled, "Kids, supper time." It was late September in Spring Hill, Kansas just about 30 miles outside of Kansas City. Spring Hill was a small town with a population of only 6,000 back in 1978. Billy and Hannah had just begun the 6th grade at Spring Hill middle school a few weeks earlier. Billy didn't have all that many friends to speak of and most of the time simply kept to himself. He could usually be found alone fishing a frog out of the nearby creek or playing with a stray animal he befriended on his way home from school. Every afternoon he would walk the mile stretch between home and school with his younger sister Hannah. They were in the same class

Daltons Pit

although Hannah, born in December, was 11 months younger than Billy. Billy was always closest with Hannah, despite having 3 older brothers. Ever since they were toddlers Billy had always looked out for Hannah. He called Hannah "Pip," short for pipsqueak, because she was so tiny.

The two of them would walk home from school every day, do their homework together and then usually end up under their front porch playing games or telling stories to each other. They even had a hidden spot under the porch they kept secret from everyone else. They called it "Dalton's Pit." It was a 3 ft. by 3 ft. stretch that was hidden by some old tires their father had left under there years ago when he ran out of insulation for the siding. They would crawl under the porch, move the tires over and slip into this little opening and pretend like they were the last survivors on earth. The little crevice contained a small white treasure box which held their most valuable keepsakes. Billy had a few of his magazines about dogs, a rabbit's foot and some cool-looking rocks. Hannah kept her diary in there which listed all the animals Billy had found in the creek on his many excursions out back. It was their own little clubhouse and they made sure to keep it secret. Whenever they wanted to get away from the family

On the Farm

madness, they would sneak away under the porch and hide out in the pit. One of Billy's biggest passions was that he loved to go exploring, especially in the woods around the back of the house. Afterward he would come back to Hannah and share his findings. He would often snatch up a frog or salamander from the creek and carry it back in his pocket to the pit just to show her. Their house itself was not much to speak of. It was an old brown farmhouse built in the 1920s with weeds growing out from everywhere. It had a huge oak tree in front that would fill the yard from front to back with leaves every fall. There was a tire hung from the tree's lowest branch and a wraparound porch surrounding the house that creaked with every step you took. The yard itself was massive and littered with a dozen or so spare parts from cars that their dad had been working on the past few years. Their dad loved to tinker with cars, especially ones left for junk. Just to the right of the house, beyond the littered lawn, was a dirt path that led all the way into the yard where the barn and chicken coop were.

Billy's father, Big Ernie Dalton, stood about 6'4' and had a stomach that protruded about 2 feet beyond his big, long horned belt buckle. He always wore his black

Daltons Pit

10-gallon cowboy hat and was never without a toothpick hanging from his chops. Ernie owned and ran the local gas station about 1/2 mile down the road from the house. Every morning, 7 days a week, he would get up before dawn and work a 12- or 14-hour shift at the station.

On the rare days when he wasn't working, he'd usually end up at Farley's Pub and spend all day and night drinking with some of his cohorts. Spending time with his children just wasn't his thing. He figured it was his job to bring home the money and his wife's job to raise the kids. Often he would stumble home around 3 a.m. after a night of drinking and expect his wife Florence to recook his dinner or even be available to him for his manly cravings. Flo, a loyal companion, always acquiesced to whatever Ernie desired.

Each night when Ernie came home from work, Flo was sure to have his meal ready and a bottle of whatever he fancied on the table. Ernie would walk in wearing the same worn down overalls with his hands full of grease. He'd give Flo's rear end a slap and yell, "Let's get to it, woman; I'm hungry". She would always laugh it off and say, "Coming, dear." She was a very simple woman, content with her lot in life. It was as if she lived in a

On the Farm

bubble that protected her from outside reality. Ernie needed her and she needed him. They were perfect together. Flo was your typical middle aged southern mom, never without a smile and always in the kitchen cooking up a storm for her family. Soaking wet Flo must have weighed about 95 pounds. She had this incredible mane of red hair and was loaded with freckles from head to toe. She grew up in the back woods of Kentucky with only her mom and sister and never made it past the 4th grade.

Due to her humble beginnings, Flo always greeted the many house guests with her incredible smile and gullible innocence. She married Ernie Dalton at the very young age of 17 and they started their family right away. At age 18 Flo gave birth to the first of their 6 children, a boy named Travis. Then they had a girl a year later named Charlotte who passed away of pneumonia only a few days after coming home from the hospital. She was only two weeks old when she died. A few years later the twins Austin and Cooper were born. Then Billy and finally Hannah. Although he would never admit it, losing Charlotte contributed to the start of Ernie's heavy drinking. It also contributed to the incredible bond that Flo now had with her daughter Hannah. She catered to her Hannah and made sure she was always happy and

Daltons Pit

content. It made sense since living through the loss of a child would make any parent a bit overprotective.

As far as role models go, Billy didn't have to look any further than his oldest brother Travis. Travis, who also worked at the gas station with his father, had graduated from high school six years ago. He pretty much ran the gas station along with his dad. Travis was a bit of a legend around Spring Hill. He was the star running back on his high school football championship team. He even had dreams of playing football in college and perhaps even professionally. He was blessed with his father's size and was as big and solid as an ox. He set a state record back in 1972 as a senior by scoring six touchdowns in the Kansas State championship game. Everyone in town knew Travis Dalton, the all-state running back.

Since graduation, though, life was never the same for Travis. Unfortunately, he took after his mom and did not have a strong aptitude for learning. His IQ at best was around 85 and it was widely known throughout Spring Hill that the only reason he survived high school was because of his ability on the gridiron. There were always Division 1 scouts at his games checking him out, but as soon as they saw his high school transcript, they

On the Farm

backed off. After graduation he signed up to play for a local Division 3 college program. Only two months in though, he dropped out after the realization that he couldn't fake his way through another 4 years of schooling. Now 6 years removed from high school, he was no longer the center of attention in town and by all accounts at the age of 24, his 15 minutes of fame were long over.

Travis however, always had a heart of gold and would give the shirt off his back to anyone who needed it. Everyone in Spring Hill loved him and many would often come by the gas station just to say hello and reminisce about his high school playing days. The station itself was on the way home from school for Billy and Hannah, so they often stopped in and hung out on their walk home. They would sit in the office and do their homework while Travis worked on the cars. When things were slow Travis would show Billy how to take apart an engine, fix a flat tire or do a simple oil change. Although Billy was not cut out for that type of work, he was always curious about how things worked and being the student he was, always paid close attention. Sometimes he and Hannah would even wait for Travis to finish his shift so he could drive them home. They would then sucker him into treating them to a milkshake at Sprinkles Ice Cream

Dalton's Pit

shop on the way home. Hannah always had a strawberry shake while Billy had vanilla.

Billy was in awe of his brother Travis. He viewed him as this incredibly larger than life superhero who was always there to protect him. He could do no wrong in Billy's eyes. In fact, a few years back in the 4th grade, Billy had to do a report for school on whom he admired most. He wrote all about his big brother Travis. He told of his football games and what a big star he was. He also talked about the walks home from school and the trips to Sprinkles. Travis was so proud of Billy's report that he had it framed and hung it in the gas station window for all to see.

There was never a dull moment at the Dalton farmhouse. Always someone coming in and someone going out. Often it was Travis's high school friends coming over to reminisce about football and have a few beers out back in the barn. Sometimes, though, it was the thing Billy feared most, his twin brothers and their disheveled crew of delinquents. Austin and Cooper were seniors at Spring Hill High School. The brothers were aptly named after their father Ernie's favorite car, the Austin Cooper Mini (ACM) pickup. The ACM had just come out in early 1961 and Ernie fell in love with it. So,

On the Farm

when the twins were born, he decided he would name them after the car.

Austin himself was also very well known around Spring Hill. Unfortunately, it was not for football like his brother Travis, but instead for a rather extensive rap sheet for a kid of 17. Austin took after his mother, having long orange hair and the same freckled body from head to toe, although quite a bit larger than hers. He earned the nickname "Red" as a young child because of the hair. As he got older his crew started calling him "Dead Red" because sooner or later someone would wind up dead if they hung out with him long enough. It could also be because one of his favorite things to do was to blow through red lights while driving around town with his brother Cooper. Another one of his hobbies was playing mailbox baseball. He, along with his brother, would drive up and down the residential streets smashing mailboxes with a baseball bat as they drove by. The name Dead Red eventually was shortened and then he was simply known as Dred. A fitting name for someone who everyone dreaded being around. He had already had several stints in the county jail, including a 3-night stay for graffiti and vandalism just this past summer. The moniker **DRED** was spray

Dalton's Pit

painted on every street corner in Spring Hill, including the front steps of the police station. Austin couldn't understand why he always got caught even though everyone knew who Dred was. Either that or he really didn't care. It seemed as if every weekend Flo would get a call from the sheriff because Austin was up to something new. Austin, the older twin by 15 minutes, thoroughly enjoyed seeing people, animals or anything breathing suffer. When he was 12 years old he used the family dog Bugsy as target practice with his BB gun. Bugsy was an older dog who had been with the family for 10 years already. He used to walk around very slowly and was an easy target. One night the dog was so badly injured and bleeding that Ernie had to carry him to the local vet, Dr. Clifford. After Dr. Clifford patched Bugsy up, he convinced Ernie to allow him keep the dog. Bugsy had some other medical issues and living with Dr. Clifford made a lot of sense. He ended up saving Bugsy's life that night and the dog remained with the doctor until he passed away 3 years later at the age of 13. Austin didn't care, he just simply moved along to his next torture victim. The only Dalton who loved Bugsy anyway was Billy. Billy became very friendly with Dr. Clifford after he adopted Bugsy. He visited the dog and Dr. Clifford every Saturday afternoon for the next 3

On the Farm

years until Bugsy passed away. Cooper, on the other hand, was a born follower. He was thin as a rail and limber as a monkey. Always climbing trees or hanging out on top of the barn smoking pot with Austin. He loved being in the woods and fishing in the river just outside of town. A bit of a daredevil, he would try almost anything for a laugh. Whenever Austin dared him to do something crazy, he always did. He spent most of his life it seemed, with a cast somewhere on his body. Usually it was an arm or leg from jumping off the barn or diving off the bridge in town head first into shallow water. Cooper also had a nickname; his friends called him Newt. This was due to a ridiculous tattoo of a frog he got on the back of his neck. One night when he and Austin were out drinking with their friends, Austin dared him to get the tattoo. Cooper, never backing down from a challenge especially from his brother agreed. Usually Austin goaded Cooper into doing things just to show his superiority, other times it was just for kicks. Their relationship was an odd one for sure. It was as if Austin was a maniacal dictator and Cooper his loyal soldier. One morning a few months back the twins were involved in something that could have significantly altered their lives' path. If it wasn't for Travis intervening, they might have gone to jail for a

Dalton's Pit

very long time. Sometimes in life you're just in the wrong place at the wrong time. Austin seemed to have the uncanny ability to make this a habit. The path of a person's life is usually dictated by just a handful of what appeared to be insignificant decisions. It's not until years later when we realize just how important some of those decisions actually turn out to be.

It was early June, the last week of junior year. The day started out like any other normal morning. Austin and Cooper had just arrived at school about 15 minutes before their first class was to start. At this point classes were pretty much over for the year. Everyone was coming in just to get their final grades and hang out for a few hours before being released for the summer. The boys pulled into the parking lot behind the school, parked the car and began walking casually to the front entrance of the school. Cooper was now a few yards ahead of Austin and talking with someone as he entered the building. Austin lagging as usual, noticed Jenny getting off the bus on the corner and decided to wait for her. Jenny was a neighborhood girl who Austin grew up with and always had a thing for. She was his exact opposite. She was thin, smart and blonde. She looked like a Breck girl from the commercials on TV. The kind

On the Farm

of girl who could roll out of bed without any makeup and look absolutely amazing. As she approached the school, the second bell rang, indicating there were only three minutes to the start of class. Austin as usual, though, had other things on his mind. He scampered away from the front entrance of the building and approached Jenny. Jenny looked up and saw him.

"Hi, Austin. The third bell's about to ring, shouldn't you get inside?"

"Actually, Jenny, our first class has been cancelled, they just announced it. Some of the kids are in the back hanging out. Come on, I'll take you."

Jenny was a bit skeptical. "Are you telling the truth, Austin?"

"Of course, would I lie?" Austin replied.

Jenny knowing full well that Austin wasn't the most trustworthy person, gave him a skeptical look.

"Come on Jenny, you can trust me" he said with a smile He convinced her to walk around to the back of the school and as she expected, no one was out there.

"OK, so I lied. Hang out with me. Just for first period.

Dalton's Pit

There's nothing going on anyway; you already know you got straight A's. Tell them you didn't feel well. You're such a good student they will definitely believe you. Come on, Jenny live a little. Plus, I need your advice on something. Trust me, Jenny, no one will question you. You always do the right thing."

Jenny smiling said, "Ok, but just this one class. I have to go into second period to speak with Mrs. Kramer."

The third bell rang and the school doors shut. Cooper was sitting in class wondering where his brother was. He was right behind him five minutes ago. *What could have happened in only five minutes?* he wondered. Meanwhile Austin and Jenny were standing in the cement courtyard just behind the school talking. Just to their left was the outdoor track and far to their right was the high school baseball field. Behind the field on the third base side were weeds as far as the eye could see. Austin convinced Jenny to walk with him to the bench near the third base dugout to talk. Jenny had known Austin since she was five years old, so she didn't think anything of it. They walked over and both sat down on the bench. Jenny put her book bag down on the grass. "So what's this all about, Austin?"

On the Farm

"So Jenny, here is my problem. I really like this girl, but I don't know how to tell her. I need your advice. How would you want a boy to tell you that he likes you?"

Jenny now smiling, said, "Well Austin, it depends if I like him or not. Tell me, who is the girl? Maybe I can put in a good word for you."

Austin realized he had crossed over into the point of no return. He mustered up his courage and leaned across and kissed Jenny right on her lips. Jenny was startled. She pulled away and got her

ankle caught in the strap of her book bag and fell directly on top of a rake lying in the grass. While still holding on to Austin, she accidentally pulled him down on top of her and his head hit her square in the face, causing her nose to start bleeding. He also accidentally ripped her shirt sleeve on the way down. Austin immediately got up and apologized to Jenny and helped her to her feet. Just as that was happening, Coach Fisher had come out of the back entrance of the gym and witnessed the whole thing. He thought he saw Austin attack Jenny against her will. He immediately ran toward the baseball field and after Austin.

Dalton's Pit

Coach Fisher ran full speed in Austin's direction. "Hey Dalton, *freeze*."

Austin panicked, ran into the weeds behind third base and disappeared. Undeterred, Coach Fisher ran in after him yelling his name. Austin meanwhile was kneeling down only five yards away from the coach and was sure to eventually be caught.

Jenny was still a bit dazed. She began walking by herself back to the school toward the nurse's office.

Now about 50 feet deep into the weeds, Coach Fisher spotted Austin hiding. He chased him down and grabbed him by the arm, twisting it behind his back.

"Austin, I saw you attack Jenny. You think you're a tough guy. Try that with me. You're in big trouble, mister."

Cooper meanwhile was still wondering where Austin was. He excused himself from class to go to the restroom. As soon as he came out of the classroom, he saw Jenny with her face all bloodied up walking toward the nurse's office.

"Jenny, what happened?" he asked.

On the Farm

Jenny, still dazed, told him, "Your brother, the baseball field, Coach Fisher."

Cooper ran out back looking for Austin. He sprinted across the courtyard and towards the baseball field then to the weeds. There he saw Coach Fisher towering over Austin, twisting his arm behind his back.

"You like this, Austin? You like causing pain?" Coach exclaimed.

Cooper saw his brother was in trouble, picked up the rake lying in the grass and slowly entered the weeds behind the coach. He lifted the rake over his head and whacked the coach right in the back of his head, knocking him to the ground unconscious. He then flung the rake further into the weeds and helped Austin to his feet.

"Are you ok, Austin?"

Austin nodded his head. "Let's get out of here now"

They quickly exited the weeds, ran across the courtyard to the parking lot, jumped in the car and pulled away from the school. Austin was covered in blood. Was it his own? Coach Fisher's? Jenny's? He had no idea. He

Dalton's Pit

wasn't even sure exactly what happened. Did he hurt Jenny? The coach?

Cooper turned to Austin. "What the hell happened back there? Why was he twisting your arm?"

"I don't know. I guess he saw Jenny all bloody and thought I was hurting her."

"Yeah, I saw Jenny in school with blood on her face. What did you do to her, Austin?"

"Nothing, you jerk. I only kissed her and then tripped and fell on her."

"You fell on her? Bullshit, Austin. You always do this."

"Look man, I'm telling you the truth. I fell on top of her and she got a bloody nose and hit her head."

Cooper realizing what he may have done, said "Oh God, man. You think he's dead? Did I kill him? What if he's dead, Austin? What did I do? I don't want to go to jail."

Austin panicked. "I don't know, dammit. What do we do now? Let me think." After a short pause, Austin continued, "I know. Let's go talk to Travis. He was his star football player for years; maybe he can help us. We

On the Farm

have to get to the garage immediately."

The twins abruptly turned the car around and headed directly over to the garage. Travis was with a customer when he noticed the look on his younger brothers' faces.

"Ok, what did you do now? And why aren't you guys in school?" Travis asked.

Austin replied, "Travis, we need your help. We need you to come with us to the school."

"Tell Mom. I'm busy here. Can't you see I have six cars waiting?"

"Please, Travis. We need you. We can't tell Mom."

Travis looked over to Mel, one of the gas station attendants. "Mel, take over for a bit; I'll be back shortly, I have to go save my little brothers again."

"You got it, kid," Mel replied, shaking his head with a smile.

Travis wiped the grease off his hands and got in the passenger side of the car with an annoyed look on his

Dalton's Pit

face. "So what is it this time, Austin? What trouble are you in now?"

As he pulled out of the station lot, a nervous Austin explained to Travis about Jenny and what happened by the baseball field. Then he told him about Coach Fisher and that he could be lying in the grass dead.

Travis grew a bit angry and blurted out, "He can't be dead. He's the toughest guy I know. He's the coach. Don't worry, he's not dead. He can't be. Damn. You guys are so stupid," he quipped.

As soon as they made the turn onto the street by the school, they saw cop cars everywhere. Austin, seeing all the commotion, panicked and made a U turn on the street right in front of the school. Sheriff Jackson, who was standing out front, saw him and immediately jumped in his squad car and followed Austin down the street.

"Austin, pull over right now," Travis demanded.

"No, they are going to arrest me. But I didn't do anything."

On the Farm

"Austin, pull over. If you didn't do anything, you have nothing to worry about."

With the sirens of three cop cars blaring behind them, Austin attempted to speed up to avoid his inevitable arrest, when suddenly Travis grabbed the wheel from his brother and pushed him into the driver's side door. The car spun right and spiraled directly into the marsh on the side of the road. The car rolled down the 5-foot embankment, right into the weeds on a 90-degree angle. Travis jumped out of the car with his hands up and said, "Everything is okay, sheriff; just boys being boys here."

Sheriff Jackson drew his gun while ignoring Travis. "Hands up where I can see them, Austin. Get out of the car now. You too, Cooper." The boys came out with their hands over their heads and were immediately handcuffed. All the while Travis pleaded with the sheriff that it was just a misunderstanding.

"Not now, Travis; these boys are under arrest," the sheriff said as he put the two of them into the squad car. It wasn't until after they arrived at the station and were processed did Travis finally get a word with the Sheriff.

Dalton's Pit

"Sheriff, this is all just a mistake. What're the charges on my brothers?"

"There's no misunderstanding here, Travis. Austin is being charged with assault on Jenny Wilson and with the attempted murder of Coach Fisher. We can probably release Cooper after we sort all of this out."

"Attempted murder? That's crazy. You know us Daltons; we're a little nutty from time to time, but we'd never hurt anyone."

"Look Travis, this is out of your control. It was only a matter of time before your idiot brother did something stupid like this. We all know he is a bad kid. He belongs behind bars. And I'll see to it that he is there for a long time." He then turned to Cooper and said, "Son, you can go. Do yourself a favor and stop listening to Austin. One day you'll thank me for this advice, trust me."

"You're wrong, Sheriff. My brother wouldn't hurt a fly. I'm gonna prove it too," Travis replied.

Travis and Cooper walked out of the police station and headed back to the car. While sitting in the car, Travis debated what to do next and if he should inform his parents. Instead he turned to Cooper.

On the Farm

"Cooper, tell me exactly what happened."

Cooper explained to Travis that Austin never showed up to their first class and how about 20 minutes into class he went out to look for him and saw Jenny in the hallway with a bloody nose. He told him how she mentioned that Austin was by the baseball field with Coach.

"Then what?"

"Then I went out to the field and saw Coach standing over Austin twisting his arm behind his back, yelling at him. So I saw a rake in the grass and picked it up."

"What did you do, Cooper?" Travis asked as his eyes widened.

Cooper replied, "I whacked the coach in the back of his head and knocked him unconscious with the rake. I am really sorry, Travis. I didn't kill him, did I?"

Travis now realized the significance of what may have happened to the coach. Was he okay? Where was he?

"Wait, the sheriff said attempted murder. That means he must still be alive. Cooper, let's head over to Spring Hill hospital. He's gotta be there," Travis said.

Dalton's Pit

Travis had hoped he was there. He hoped he was okay. Coach Fisher was his mentor during his four years of playing football and Travis was his favorite player. He needed to get to him and fast.

Ten minutes later they arrived at the hospital and approached the front desk. Travis was holding his breath in hopes that the coach was there and that he was ok.

"Coach Fisher's room, please," Travis asked nervously.

"Patient's first name, please?" replied the woman at the front desk.

"Um, I think it's Hank or Henry. Yes, Henry I think."

The woman at the front desk scanned the patient log and said. "He's in room 17C, third door on the left."

Travis was cautiously relieved. "Cooper, you stay here. Let me go see him by myself first."

Travis nervously walked down the hall in fear of what he might see and knocked on the door, then opened it slightly.

On the Farm

The coach heard the door and looked up from his bed to see Travis. "Travis, my boy, good to see you."

"How are you, Coach? Everything okay?" Travis asked.

"Yes, I'm fine; just a small bump on the back of my head. They said they will be releasing me in about an hour or so. Hopefully."

"Coach, can I ask you what happened to your head? Austin didn't—"

Coach Fisher cut him off. "Travis, your brother is not like you. He is a bad kid. I saw him attack that girl and I had to chase him down. He is a dangerous kid and needs to be punished. He has to learn that there are consequences to his actions."

"Coach, how did you get that bump on your head? Did Austin do it?" he asked.

"No, he didn't. I don't know what happened. I was standing over him one minute and the next minute I woke up with a bump on my head. I must have fainted and hit my head. I haven't been feeling that well lately. I am on some new medication and occasionally it makes me dizzy."

Dalton's Pit

"So Austin didn't do anything to you?"

"No, he couldn't have," Coach replied.

"Ok thanks, Coach. So, you're feeling fine then?

"I am fine. But that girl. She isn't fine. Your brother is going to have to pay for that."

Travis, somewhat relieved, walked toward the door and said to the coach as he was leaving, "Glad you're okay, Coach. I'll see you soon."

Travis walked out to Cooper who was pacing frantically in the lobby. He explained to Cooper that Coach had no idea that he was hit in the head and that he was fine. Cooper let out a big sigh of relief. They then walked out of the hospital and got back into the car to deliberate their next move.

Cooper commented, "Should we go talk with Jenny? She didn't seem too upset with Austin when I saw her in the hallway. Maybe she can tell us what really happened. Austin swore he didn't mean to hurt her."

"Good idea, Coop. It's worth a try; let's go."

Travis put the car in gear, pulled out of the lot and

On the Farm

arrived at Jenny's house a few moments later. As they approached the house, they saw her father standing outside in front. Travis got out of the car and Jenny's father immediately started walking toward Travis, yelling.

"Get off my property, Dalton, before I call the cops. Your brother is in big trouble. He is going away for a long time."

"Look, Mr. Wilson, my brother says he didn't do anything. Can I speak with Jenny?" Travis asked.

"If you don't get off my lawn right now I am calling the sheriff and have you two arrested as well. You're all garbage, the whole Dalton family."

Jenny was listening behind the front door. She opened the door slightly and peered out. Cooper saw her and asked, "Jenny, can we talk with you for a second?"

"That's it, I'm calling the cops," said Mr. Wilson.

Jenny came out from behind the door and onto the front lawn. "No, Dad. I want to say something. Austin didn't do anything wrong. He tried to kiss me and when I pulled away I tripped over my book bag and I pulled

Dalton's Pit

him down on top of me. It was an accident."

"Jenny, get back in the house. Let me handle this."

"No, Dad. Austin didn't mean to do this to me. He was actually very sweet."

Travis turned to Jenny. "Jenny, would you be kind enough to tell that to Sheriff Jackson? Austin is in big trouble right now and you're the only one who can save him."

"Is that really true, honey, or are you protecting that kid?" Mr. Wilson asked.

"It's true, dad. He did nothing wrong," she replied. "Yes, I will go with you, Travis."

Travis and Cooper drove Jenny down to the police station to speak Sheriff Jackson. Jenny verified that Austin didn't mean to hurt her and said it was completely accidental. Travis also got the coach to confirm that Austin never hit him as well. After listening to both Jenny and Coach Fisher, Sherriff Jackson had no alternative but to reluctantly let Austin free. The sheriff did, however, warn Travis that the next time Austin got

On the Farm

in trouble, he would throw the book at him, stating "It's only a matter of time."

It was only a few minutes before 5 o'clock. The Dalton boys exited the police station and got back in the car when Travis turned to his brothers and yelled, "Why can't you guys smarten up? And they call *me* stupid. Next time you two knuckleheads won't be so lucky. Never ever run away from the cops. You hear me? okay, Austin?"

Austin just nodded. Disaster averted. Unfortunately for Austin this was where the legend of Austin Dalton began to grow.

They arrived back home as if nothing happened and somehow their parents never found out. *This time*. After dropping them off, Travis went back to the garage and finished up his days' work as usual. There's one thing to be said about Travis: He may not have been the brightest person, but he always had your back, no matter how bad you messed up. Especially if you were family. You could count on him to be there when things started to get messy. That was a good thing since getting messy was commonplace in the Dalton household.

Dalton's Pit

Three months had passed since Austin's latest brush with the law and not much had changed around the Dalton farmhouse. Billy was spending more time under the porch and out of sight from his twin brothers. Quite often when their dad was working and Travis was out, the twins would hang out in the barn with a bunch of their friends. Usually to drink beer and smoke pot. They would get high and then use the BB gun for shooting practice on the animals. Sometimes they even used it on Billy and Hannah. Billy and his little sister starting spending so much time under the porch to avoid their brothers that they would even eat their dinner under there on occasion.

At the young age of 11 Billy Dalton was already an extraordinary young man. He not only excelled in school but was the top student in his class. His middle school had recommended many times that he be skipped a grade, since the material being taught was mostly beneath him. He always declined the offer because he wanted to remain together in the same grade with Hannah. He didn't feel comfortable leaving her behind despite his eagerness to excel. Instead he would broaden his scope of knowledge by disappearing up to his room to read about topics that other 11-year old's had no interest in. Every weekend like clockwork while

On the Farm

on his way to see Bugsy at Dr. Clifford's he would stop off at the local library and sit for hours on end just reading magazines and books. The more he hung around with Dr. Clifford the more he knew what he wanted to do when he got older. There was nothing Billy loved more than animals. In fact, his best friend, other than Hannah, was Etta the family cow. When he wasn't at the library or in his room reading, Billy was in the barn hanging out with Etta or under the porch playing with Hannah. That was his routine, his life growing up.

Besides Hannah, Travis was the only other person Billy spent any time with at all. Travis would always visit him in the barn and wrestle with his little brother. He would retell the stories of his football games and Billy would always listen. As for Hannah, there were many days when she just wasn't around to play with. She was born with a medical condition called Microcephaly. This is a disease which causes a person's head and torso to be much smaller than that of a normal person. It is a form of dwarfism that could lead to significant heart troubles as well as life threatening seizures. The doctor let the family know she might only live to be about 30 years old. When Hannah was younger, her smaller size was

Dalton's Pit

less noticeable, but at this point she was a full foot shorter than most of her classmates. Despite her appearance, however, she was always happy and always smiling. She also did well in school, but her condition prevented her from doing most of the things that 11-year old's do. She was never able to run with the other children in the school yard. The boys in class never talked to her. During recess she was usually in the classroom doing her work or when she didn't feel well, in the nurse's office. Her life was school, then home for treatments and then on good days, hanging out with Billy under the porch or in the barn. Hannah was never one to let her handicap get her down though. She never expected any preferential treatment either. She was adamant about doing everything by herself.

One afternoon at lunchtime recess, Billy was being picked on in the schoolyard by the class bully Peter. Peter was this huge Polish kid with big hands and a small brain. He was left back a grade and was already 5'10" while still only in the 6th grade. Peter's dad was a prize fighter who eventually became the town drunk after Peter's mother left him a few years back. Being brought up only by his alcoholic dad meant he had no boundaries at home whatsoever. He spent much of his

On the Farm

school day picking on the rest of his classmates. That day in the schoolyard Peter was in classic form. That day's victim unfortunately was Billy. Peter was calling him names and pushing him around a bit. That seemed to happen more often lately since Billy was not one to fight back. He would usually just walk away and take the abuse in stride. After all, Peter was twice his size.

That day ended quite differently than most other days in Billy's childhood. When Peter started in on him, a crowd of kids gathered around and formed a circle to watch, as kids always do. Hannah, who also happened to be in the schoolyard at that time, saw this from the other side of the yard and walked over.

"Hey, you big jerk, leave my brother alone," Hannah snarled.

"Hannah, don't worry about it; he's only joking around," Billy responded.

"Aww, what's the matter, Billy? You need your baby sister to fight your battles? You stupid loser," Peter replied.

Hannah yelled, "Shut up, you big jerk. Pick on someone your own size."

Dalton's Pit

"Look who's talking, you midget. You're a freak just like your stupid brother. How tall are you anyway? Two feet?"

At that moment, something came over Billy like never before. Perhaps it was his pride or maybe just his instinct to protect his little sister. *It's one thing to make fun of me,* he thought, *but now he's making fun of Hannah.* With his heart pounding, Billy took a deep breath and closed his eyes. He clenched his fist and swung with all his might. He hit Peter square in the face and knocked him backwards into the brick wall. Unfortunately for Billy, Peter didn't go down. Just as Peter was about to swing back, one of the teachers, Mrs. Bradshaw stepped in front of Billy to break it up and *wham.* Peter punched Mrs. Bradshaw right in the chest, knocking her down to the ground. The entire schoolyard was gathered around watching in disbelief. They saw everything. The other school monitors in the yard ran over and helped Mrs. Bradshaw to her feet. Then they escorted both Peter and Billy to the principal's office. After hearing from multiple students who were eyewitnesses to the event, Peter was immediately expelled from school while Billy received only a two-day suspension. The following Monday when

On the Farm

Billy returned to school, his class gave him a standing ovation. They were all thrilled that Peter the bully was finally gone. Equally as important as having Peter gone, Billy had gained the respect of everyone in the class. Maybe they wouldn't think he was weird anymore. He realized that standing up to Peter wasn't as hard as he thought it would be. He also realized that if Mrs. Bradshaw hadn't stepped in front of him, he would have been demolished by his immense counterpart. It didn't matter though, because he was no longer afraid. It took protecting Hannah for him to find the strength within himself that he had all along. Hannah was so proud of Billy she was beaming. In one split second decision, Billy may have redirected his life's path. Talk about life's seemingly insignificant decisions. That one punch certainly didn't take years for him to realize its importance, that's for sure.

Two weeks later, on a Friday afternoon, Billy was by himself under the front porch playing. Austin and Cooper were hanging out with some friends and he overheard a disturbing conversation. Usually the twins would talk about what they were going to do that weekend or who they were going to mess with. That day, however, the conversation took on a completely different tone. Austin, Cooper and two other friends,

Dalton's Pit

Tyler and Harlan, were planning a break-in of the local Foodway store where Tyler worked. Tyler usually locked up with the owner Mr. Danby on Friday nights and knew where he kept the petty cash box when the store was closed. The plan was for Tyler to unlock the back window just before they closed up so that Cooper could climb through the small 2 x 2 window. Once in the store he would come around front and open the door for Austin and Tyler while Harlan looked out for the cops. Billy got really nervous about what his brothers were planning to do, he knew he had to get to Travis right away. Billy's parents had been out of town for the day with Hannah, seeing a special heart doctor in Kansas City and could not be reached. Travis meanwhile was still working at the gas station, so as soon as his brothers went inside Billy took off to find Travis. He ran the half mile to the gas station in less than 5 minutes. When he arrived at the station he saw Mel the gas attendant.

Billy was out of breath when he said, "Have you seen Travis?"

"Hey Billy, you just missed him. He'll be back in a few hours. He had to pick up a part for this old Chevy we're working on," replied Mel.

On the Farm

"I need to speak to him right away. Can you reach him?"

"Afraid not, Billy; sorry kid. But if he calls in for any reason; I'll let him know you're looking for him.

Billy was in a bit of a panic, so he decided to go see Dr. Clifford, thinking maybe he could help. Unfortunately, by the time he arrived, Dr. Clifford had already closed up shop for the day. Without many options left, Billy headed on back home. He thought maybe he could talk to Cooper and convince him not to go along with the plan and explain to him that he could get in trouble or arrested. It was already 5:30 p.m. by the time Billy arrived back home. The Food way was closing at 6 p.m. and his mom and dad wouldn't be home until around 8. Billy had very little time to convince Cooper to back out of this bad idea. When he finally got back to the house, he saw Cooper sitting on the front porch alone. Austin was nowhere in sight. It was the perfect opportunity to talk some sense into him. He ran up the front drive to the porch. He proceeded to tell Cooper why he shouldn't go out tonight and how Austin was going to get him into trouble. He pleaded with Cooper up and down not to go. Austin who was listening to the

Dalton's Pit

conversation from the front hallway, opened the screen door and stepped out onto the porch. Without saying a word, he aimed his BB gun directly at Billy's face. Billy just stood there, motionless with fear. Austin then pulled the trigger hitting Billy square in the face about an inch below his left eye. Billy immediately dropped to the floor covering his eye with his hands. Austin seeing his brother writhing on the floor in pain, then kicked him in the stomach and snarled, "Don't you ever mess around in my business again, you little shit, and if you tell Mom and Dad, I'll kill you. Let's go, Cooper, *now*."

Cooper followed Austin to their pickup truck and they sped away. Billy was left on the floor of the porch crying with blood gushing from just below his eye. Lucky for Billy the BB missed his eye but it did give him a large gash and a welt the size of a golf ball just below it.

It was 5:45 p.m. and Mr. Danby and Tyler were locking up the store. Mr. Danby looked over at Tyler. "Tyler, let's go. I want to get home a few minutes early tonight; it's Mrs. Danby's birthday. Look, I bought her this beautiful locket." He pulled a small box out of his pocket, opened it up and placed it on the counter to show Tyler. Then Mr. Danby began to count the money

On the Farm

from the register, putting some in his pocket and some in the petty cash box hidden underneath the counter. Tyler then walked to the back of the store and gently unlocked the small window above the walk-in freezer. He quickly returned and said, "All locked up, sir, ready to go."

"Ok. Let's go then. Have a good night Tyler. See you Monday."

They secured the front door and Mr. Danby pulled away, heading home to celebrate his wife Marjorie's 50th birthday. Tyler said goodnight and left afoot in the opposite direction. As soon as he turned the corner, Tyler bolted down the street, sprinting about two blocks to where the boys were waiting.

"Ok guys; it's time. Old man Danby is gone. He left early for his wife's birthday or something. Let's go."

Austin replied, "Take it easy, man. Let's go over the plan one more time. Did you make sure the back window was unlocked?"

"Yes, we're all set."

Dalton's Pit

"OK Cooper, here, take this mask just in case someone spots you climbing through the back window." He handed him a black ski mask he had in his pocket. "All you have to do is climb in through the window and open the front door for me and Tyler. Can you handle that?"

Cooper nodded as he grabbed the ski mask from Austin's hand. "Me and Tyler will be waiting by the front entrance. Harlan, you stay on the corner and keep a look out for the cops. okay, let's go."

At 6:15 p.m. they returned to the wooded area behind the store where it was mostly weeds and marsh. The sun was just about to drop behind the houses across the way. A large dumpster was strategically placed by Tyler just below the back window. Cooper donned the black ski mask his brother brought for him and was still carrying the BB gun Austin had taken from the house after he shot Billy. Austin and Tyler started walking around the front while Cooper hoisted himself up onto the dumpster and through the unlocked window. He climbed down from above the freezer with the BB gun in hand. As he walked into the front counter area where the petty cash box was, he heard a click and someone yelled, "Freeze!" Panicked, he lifted the BB gun, but before he could cock the trigger, a single gunshot was

On the Farm

fired, piercing his chest. He fell to the ground. Upon hearing the shot, Austin and Tyler, who had been standing at the front entrance waiting to be let in, took off and ran into the weeds off to the side of the store. Harlan, stunned at what was happening took off and disappeared down the road. As the sound of police sirens in the background started to get louder, Austin, for the first time in his life, looked scared to death. Just a few moments later, Sheriff Jackson pulled into the front parking lot, got out of the car and pulled his gun. He then inched up to the store entrance with his gun cocked and aimed it directly at the door. He could see the silhouette of a man holding a gun who appeared to be crying.

Sheriff Jackson peered into the front entrance of the Foodway.

"Drop the gun and come out with your hands over your head. *Now.*"

"Ok, don't shoot me, Tom. I'm coming out," a voice replied.

Mr. Danby then walked out with his hands over his head, crying like a baby. Uttering the same thing

Dalton's Pit

repeatedly, "I thought it was real; I thought it was real. I am so sorry. I thought it was real."

Mr. Danby had returned to the store because he'd left his wife's gift on the counter when he was showing it to Tyler. He was about to leave when he heard the window open in the back of the store. He quickly pulled out the old shot gun he had hidden under the front counter. Seeing a man in a black ski mask with what appeared to be a rifle in his hands, he immediately fired. He killed Cooper with one shot right through his chest. Upon hearing Mr. Danby tell his story, Tyler got scared and took off through the weeds in back, running as fast as he could. Austin, however, still in disbelief watched as they carried his brother's lifeless body into the ambulance that had just arrived. In shock, Austin finally disappeared into the night through the back woods. Still numb to what he'd just witnessed, Austin returned home and climbed up into the loft in the barn out back. Austin thought to himself, *"What do I do now? Mom and dad will be home soon. Travis is going to kick my ass. What do I tell them? I know, I'll tell them I had nothing to do with it. I'll say I was hanging out with Tyler and I had no idea where Cooper was."* There was only

On the Farm

one problem with that. What about Billy? Where was he? He had to find him fast to make sure he didn't spill the beans; otherwise, his story would fall apart and his life as he knew it would be over forever. It was about 7:30 p.m., both Mom and Dad and Travis were sure to be home within the hour. Austin carefully sneaked back to the house in hopes of finding Billy. He searched the entire house and even under the porch and no Billy. *Where is this little shit?* he wondered.

He let out a yell, "Where are you, Billy? Come out, I want to talk to you. I am sorry I shot you before. Come out, let's talk."

Nothing, not a sound. Austin realized what was at stake and started getting real angry. "Get out here now, Billy; if I find you, you're dead."

Billy was sitting quietly under the porch in Dalton's Pit, not moving a muscle with dried blood still all over his face. Austin, completely frazzled, returned to the barn one last time to find Billy. Just at that moment he heard a car pull up the front driveway. He peered over the 4-foot chicken wire fence surrounding the chicken coop. Mom, Dad and Hannah walked up the front yard and approached the porch. The phone rang inside. Flo

Dalton's Pit

About 50 yards away Austin stood watching, hidden behind a large oak tree. The only one who knew he was there was Tyler. And just like that he was gone.

Chapter 2

Where am I?

He felt like he was on a roller coaster, spinning sideways then up and down. The lights were so bright he couldn't decipher exactly where he was going or what was happening to him. *This needs to end and end quickly,* he thought. Somehow, though, after a few moments he calmed down somewhat and began getting used to the ride. His fear and nausea quickly changed to curiosity and mild excitement. He wondered exactly where this ride was taking him. Was he in a tunnel? Hearing faint music in the background, the lights seemed to be simmering down a bit. All throughout the short journey, he noticed a faint shadow swirling about just ahead of him. It seemed as if it were directing him somewhere, leading him through the tunnel. After a few more moments, it all started to take shape and he could see more than just the shadow. Then just like that the lights went out, total darkness.

Dalton's Pit

He woke up in the middle of a large wooded area. To his left he saw a river that bent all the way around the corner and seemed to go on for days. To his right were trees as far as the eye could see.

Where am I? he marveled. Jumping to his feet he assessed his surroundings. He looked down and noticed a stain of blood right in the middle of his shirt.

How did that get there? he wondered.

Walking a few steps in each direction he began mulling over his next move. He looked to the river and saw an old raft that was pulled onto the embankment along the shoreline. It was almost as if someone had left it for him. Realizing he did not want to walk through the woods for fear of what he might find, he examined the raft just to make sure of its sturdiness. He wanted to make sure he could float down the river on it without drowning since he wasn't a very good swimmer. Reluctantly he set out down the river in search of something remotely familiar.

Where am I? he pondered. *Where is everyone?*

He floated downstream for several hours without having any questions answered. Around every turn

Where am I?

was the same thing, more trees, more river, more silence. The water seemed to go on forever with no end in sight. Although the water seemed a bit rougher than earlier. He sensed something was coming. He had that eerie feeling like he was about to uncover something truly majestic. He could also feel the change in the air. Usually when the water got choppy like this it could only mean one thing. Waterfall. Was there a huge waterfall around the next bend? As he approached the next bend in the river, he peered out and just as he thought, there it was. The drop looked like it had to be about 40 or 50 feet. The raft was moving way too fast to avoid the inevitable, so he held on for dear life. Reaching the edge, the raft went tumbling over and dropped all the way down to the river below. He remembered hitting the water and crashing through the surface before falling off the raft beneath the water. After that, nothing.

The morning breeze whistled through the open window of his bedroom. Now fully awake he jumped to his feet encompassed by familiar surroundings. With a smile, he said to himself, "Wow, what a weird dream. I was in my bed the whole time."

Dalton's Pit

He got up, took a quick shower and headed on down to the kitchen for some breakfast.

"Mom, where's breakfast? Mom?"

No answer, nothing but silence. He walked in and around the house, searching for anyone or anything. Nothing, no one home. Still very confused thinking maybe he'd had too much to drink the night before, he wandered outside. To his surprise, he noticed a young girl swinging from the tire which hung from the large oak tree out front.

"Hey, you over there. Who are you; where are we?"

He ran out the front door, down the porch steps, approached the girl and said, "Now I got you. What's going on here? Who are you?"

The girl, who couldn't have been more than a teenager, just smiled and said, "Hello, it's so good to finally meet you. I've been waiting for this day for such a long time now."

"Meet me? Why? Where is everyone? Where's Mom? Where's the rest of my family?"

Where am I?

"Don't worry, I will explain everything. They are fine," she replied.

"Well then where are they? Tell me now."

She just smiled and said, "Follow me."

They walked past the large oak tree and then past the chicken coop and all the spare car parts lying in the grass. They continued until they reached the front of the barn. She turned to him and said, "Are you ready, Cooper?"

"Ready? Ready for what? And how do you know my name?"

"Shhh. Are you ready to enter?" she asked.

"Ready to enter the old barn? What's the big deal about the barn? What's the joke? Is Austin going to tackle me down to the ground or something when you open the door? You had better give me answers now," he replied.

"Cooper, I've been watching you for the past 17 years, ever since the day you were born. I know everything there is to know about you."

Dalton's Pit

"Watching me?" he replied. "Why were you watching me? And where the hell are we?"

"My name is Charlotte. I am your older sister," she answered.

"Nice try, I only have one sister and her name is Hannah. What's the joke, kid?"

Charlotte just smiled and again asked, "Are you ready, Cooper?"

Suddenly it hit him like a ton of bricks. *Charlotte? Mom had a baby she lost years before I was born named Charlotte. This girl couldn't possibly know that. Unless...*

Trembling, Cooper looked around. "Am I dead? Is that what you're telling me? That I'm dead? This is ridiculous. What's going on? Where's Austin?"

"Cooper, I am your sister Charlotte. I died 23 years ago when I was only 2 weeks old. We've never met before but I have been watching you since the day you were born."

Cooper hadn't noticed the red hair and freckles until that minute. She looked just like his mom. How could

Where am I?

she be grown now? She looked like she was 16 or 17 years old. Could this be real? Was this another one of Austin's sick jokes? But how?

Just as he was going to ask her, she answered his puzzlement. "Cooper, I chose to be this age when I came here to meet you. That's how it works. Because I was so young when I died, I could pick any age I wanted. This is what I would have looked like at 17 years old. Not bad, huh? We're now the same age, Cooper. That's how I planned it."

Charlotte said once again, "So are you ready?"

Cooper nodded. "Yes. But for what?"

"For this." She opened the barn door and walked on in. Cooper followed her in and immediately froze in his tracks. There were no animals, no hay, and no loft. Instead it looked more like a portal into another world. There were people all over the place. There were beautiful waterfalls to the left, an open field of green grass to the right. Children were playing together, eating ice cream and cotton candy. There were sweethearts walking hand in hand. The colors were so vivid and amazing he just stood there in awe. The sun was shining so brightly and tranquility was everywhere.

Dalton's Pit

He then quickly turned back to look at the barn door and it was gone. To say that Cooper was in disbelief would be the understatement of the year. He just kept looking around and wondering if he was dreaming and where he was exactly.

Charlotte then took him by the hand. "C'mon, Cooper. Let me show you around. I would like you to meet a few people. I am sure they can't wait to meet you."

As they started walking down the path together, some things appeared very familiar to Cooper, but he couldn't quite place them. Then it hit him, it looked like Spring Hill but maybe 30 or 40 years ago. Everything looked brand new and perfect. No litter, no weeds, everything was immaculate. Even the bridge downtown he used to jump off looked like it was just finished being built. Cooper marveled at just how clean and pristine everything was. Throughout all his amazement, though, Cooper wanted more than anything to talk some more with Charlotte. He seemed extremely eager to get some more clarity on his current situation. He noticed some benches along the side of the road and asked Charlotte if they could sit for a while and talk. As they approached the benches, Cooper turned to Charlotte and asked, "Charlotte, is this heaven?"

Where am I?

"Not exactly, Cooper," she replied.

"Well, what is it then?"

"This is the place we go before we get to heaven. It's sort of like a weigh station that prepares you for heaven. Nice, isn't it?"

"I don't understand," he replied.

"This place is here for you to reconnect with some of the people you knew back home. We come down here to meet with you and make you feel comfortable. After you spend some time here you eventually go up to heaven."

"I am confused. Have you been here all this time?" he asked.

"No. I was here for a while and then I went up to heaven. I was chosen to come back for you. To be your guide, if you will."

Cooper was now totally engrossed. "Charlotte, tell me about when you arrived. How did you die? Do you remember anything? Who came to meet you? Do you remember Mom and Dad?"

Dalton's Pit

"Well, when I was born I came down with a bad case of pneumonia. At that time Spring Hill Hospital wasn't the best hospital to be in. Well anyway, they were in such a rush to get Mom and me out that day, that they missed my diagnosis. I came home with Mom and Dad and a few days later my fever went way too high. Then, by the time they brought me back to the hospital, it was too late. I died in the ambulance on the way over. I do remember, though. You see, when you first come here you get to review your entire life on earth. Since mine was so short, it wasn't that hard to remember. I remember Travis also. He was always trying to hug and kiss me. He was so big. He wouldn't remember me though. He must have been a great big brother. Am I right?" Charlotte asked.

"He was. But I should have listened to him more instead of... never mind."

"Instead of Austin? I know."

Cooper just looked at Charlotte with a shameful grin and nodded.

"Don't worry, this is just the way it was meant to be. You have me now. I am your family. C'mon, let's go. I have some people for you to meet."

Where am I?

Cooper's grandfather William Dalton was the person who met Charlotte back when she arrived 23 years ago. He was the senior vice president of a highly successful chain of banks and a very educated man. He was murdered way back in 1929. It was only a few days after the stock market crash that caused the Great Depression. During the days, right after the crash, life was very tense for many, and people were in severe panic mode. Unfortunately, so many people had lost most of their life savings and as a result, weren't thinking very clearly. William had just opened the bank that fateful morning and was immediately attacked by a mob of angry patrons. They used to call it "a run" in those days. Anyway, that morning after he opened the bank, over 100 angry people broke through the front entrance and tore up the place, demanding their money. He tried in vain to calm the crowd and almost succeeded. However, as he turned away to enter the bank vault, he was shot in the back by one of the bank's patrons who had lost everything.

Cooper's dad Ernie was just a kid when his father died. Ernie's mother Olivia had to raise him alone and lived to the ripe old age of 75. Cooper was only 7 years old when his grandmother Olivia died and he remembered her vividly. He always loved going to visit his grandma's

Dalton's Pit

house. Whenever his mom and dad went away or had a party with all the Daltons, the children got to sleep at grandma's. She always spoiled her grandchildren with her specialty, the world best apple pie. To this day the smell of apple pie always reminded the Dalton children of grandma's house.

We all have certain sights or smells that take us back to our childhood. It may be something that completely left our consciousness for a time until it was abruptly thrust upon us. Then just like a wave, the forgotten memories come crashing back in on us.

When Cooper and Charlotte finally stopped walking and talking he looked up and saw something he hadn't seen in quite some time. Grandma's house was just sitting there in all its majesty.

Cooper, now staring said, "I thought they tore this place down? How...?"

"They did," Charlotte replied.

As they started to walk toward the house, Cooper noticed his grandmother sitting in her rocking chair on the front porch. She was a big woman who could never

Where am I?

be mistaken. She always wore her blue house dress and slippers and would rock back and forth for hours. She would sit in that chair and wait for her grandchildren to walk home from school every day. It was as if he'd gone back in time. This time, though, she wasn't alone like she always was. There was a man sitting in the chair next to her. That must be his grandfather William, he figured. He vaguely recognized him from the pictures around Grandma's house. Cooper just stood there dumbfounded with an ear to ear grin on his face. Before he could muster up a sound, Olivia said, "I have a nice apple pie just about ready to come out of the oven, Coop. Why don't you come in and sit down and meet your grandfather?"

Over the next few hours Cooper learned more about his family than he even knew possible. His grandfather told him stories about the Great Depression, about how they came to settle in Kansas and about his father when he was a child. For the first time in his life he felt free. Free from the pressures of life, free from Austin. It was as if a great burden had been lifted off him. He was at peace.

On the walk back, Cooper still had so many questions for Charlotte.

Dalton's Pit

"Ok, so I get it; I died, but I'm not in heaven yet and you're my big sister. My grandparents are here and I am sure all the other people who died before me as well. But how did I die? I don't remember anything. Why did I die? I was only 17."

"All these questions will be answered in time, Coop. Or is it Newt?" she said with a laugh.

Cooper groaning said, "Newt? You know about that? My tattoo? How? I prefer Coop."

"Me too; I'll call you Coop."

They spent the remainder of their walk with the sun on their shoulders talking about their grandparents, what heaven was like and their family back on earth. As they approached their home, Cooper was amazed at the house. He hadn't noticed it before. There were no weeds in front, no car parts, and no fallen leaves. The porch didn't even squeak when he stepped on it. They sat down on the porch and continued their conversation.

"Think back, Coop, what is the last thing you remember?" Charlotte asked.

Where am I?

"I remember sitting where you are sitting and seeing our little brother Billy run up to the house. He looked out of breath and wanted to talk to me."

"Do you remember what happened next?"

"He was trying to convince me not to do something. I really don't remember what."

"Think harder, Coop."

Cooper rubbing his head, said, "Yes, I remember. He was trying to warn me about Austin and that he might get me in trouble or even arrested." His eyes then opened wide. "Austin shot him with the BB gun." Then like a tidal wave it hit him. Austin was the reason he was dead. He remembered the plan with Harlan and Tyler. "Wait... I remember," he exclaimed.

"I remember climbing through the window holding the BB gun. I remember seeing Mr. Danby. I remember the sirens and Mr. Danby crying. Mr. Danby shot me. Now I remember, I was shot because we broke into the Food way. Mr. Danby thought I had a real gun and he shot me."

Charlotte reached across and put her hand on Cooper's

Dalton's Pit

hand and smiled. "I am sorry, Coop."

"But wait, what about Austin? It was his idea. Why is he not here and I am? That's not fair. He should be here. It's not fair."

"Cooper, you don't understand yet but you will. Everyone has their time. And there is always a reason why you were chosen to come here exactly when you did. It was just your time."

"But I had so much more to do. Now it's over. It's not fair."

Charlotte hugged Cooper. "It's okay, Coop, there was a reason; there was a plan."

Cooper realized that his sister had only had two weeks on earth and here he was complaining about having only 17 years. He started to feel a little guilty. He looked up at her and said, "I'm sorry, Charlotte. I am sorry you died so young. I am here for you now. We have each other now, sis."

"Listen, Coop, when I got here the only person waiting for me was Grandpa. He was all alone and needed me.

Where am I?

We waited another 17 years in your time before Grandma arrived. Now we are a family. Everyone will cross over at some point or another and we will all be together again. It's only just time that is separating us, nothing else. One day soon we will all be here together forever. Does it really matter who comes first and who comes last? It took almost 40 years for Grandpa to get Grandma back and now they will be together forever. What's better than that?"

Cooper gave a smile, wiped the tears from his eyes and gave Charlotte a hug. "It's late, sis; let's go in and call it a night."

"I agree, Cooper; you have a big day tomorrow."

Cooper had no idea what she meant but given the day he had today he wouldn't be surprised at anything that would happen tomorrow.

The next morning Cooper woke up in his room like always, but not really sure where he was. Was he dreaming this whole thing about Charlotte? Maybe he was home all the time. Maybe he was in a coma or something. So many thoughts crossed his mind. Now

Dalton's Pit

fully awake he crept down the steps not knowing at all what to expect. Maybe Mom? Maybe Charlotte? He walked around the kitchen and living room and found no one. He walked out front to see if Charlotte was by the swing. No Charlotte. He came back in and searched the entire rest of the house and nothing. Suddenly he heard rustling noises in the yard. His heart was beating like a marching band drum. He came around to the front porch and slowly crept around into the yard. Sitting there was Bugsy wagging his tail a mile a minute.

"Bugsy? Come here, boy," he said.

Bugsy rushed over to Cooper and licked his entire face as they both fell to the ground. They shared a playful hug and then Cooper sat up. He remembered just how mean he was to Bugsy. How he and his brother used to shoot him with the BB gun. Why would Bugsy be happy to see him? It didn't make sense. When they were alive he would avoid him at all costs and now he was happy to see him. He looked down at Bugsy and it was clear the dog was trying to tell him something. He was barking and trying to lead him somewhere towards the back of the property. Cooper was curious and followed Bugsy all the way to the back of the yard to the barn

Where am I?

Cooper remembered yesterday and what happened when Charlotte opened the barn door. He was now expecting to see the same beautiful sights he saw yesterday.

This time; however, when he opened the barn door all he saw was the same barn he'd had as a child. The hay, the loft, even Etta the cow was there. Why was he in the barn? Bugsy was still standing by his side. He looked down at him and he seemed to be pointing with his paw up to the loft. The same loft Cooper used to climb out of back when he was alive. Now even more curious he climbed up to the loft and out onto the roof. Sitting there was Charlotte with a smile on her face.

"Are you ready?" she said.

Cooper was completely confused, but said, "Sure, I am ready."

"Ok then, let's get started." With her left hand, she made a waving motion in the air and just like that she moved all the clouds away as if she were erasing the blackboard in school.

She proceeded to open this large life-like screen in the sky. Like one you would see in a drive-in movie theatre.

Dalton's Pit

She then clapped her hands together and just like that Cooper's entire life flashed up on the screen. He saw everything. The good and the bad. He saw his birth, his first day of school, he saw Grandma's house and the apple pie. He saw some not so good stuff also. He saw himself driving around town with Austin smashing mailboxes, he saw himself shooting Bugsy with the BB gun. He also saw the fateful night of the Foodway robbery attempt. He watched his entire last day on earth from a totally different perspective. It was like being in a movie theatre, watching a scripted scene that you've seen so many times before. Each step of the way he realized how many opportunities he'd had to alter the final scene. Unfortunately, there was only one take in this scene and it was his last. He saw Mr. Danby shoot him. He saw himself being carried out into the ambulance. He saw Austin watching from the weeds alongside the Foodway parking lot. He saw it all. He just sat there after it was over and cried his eyes out. He was sorry for putting his family through this. He was sorry for his mom and dad. How could he do this and leave them? He felt their pain. He even watched his own funeral. He saw his mom crying. He saw his dad tackle Mr. Danby. He also saw Austin hiding 50 yards away, crying behind the tree. He felt sorrier for his family than

Where am I?

for himself. Especially Austin. He didn't hate Austin, he loved him. He knew it wasn't Austin's fault, rather it was his own. He was now starting to understand that it was just his time. The sadness, the anger all left his body. It was his turn now to wait for them just like Charlotte waited for him. As he turned to his left, Bugsy, who was still by his side, licked his entire face and then buried his head in Cooper's arms.

"Can I ask you a question, Charlotte?"

"Anything, Coop."

"Do we know when our family members will come join us? How did you know when I would arrive? I want to see Austin. I want to tell him it's okay and that he should not blame himself. I want to know when he will be here."

Charlotte replied, "We don't know exactly when, but just before they're scheduled to arrive we are told to come down here to greet them. Just like when I came down here to greet you. Until we are informed we just have to wait."

Dalton's Pit

What about Hannah? Will she still be sick when she comes here? I hope she will be able to walk better when she arrives."

"Everyone is healthy here. There are no disabilities. Our existence on earth is quite different than our existence in heaven. You will learn. As time passes by, more and more will make sense to you."

"Well I guess time is what I have plenty of now," he replied.

"That's true, now let's use some that time wisely, Coop. C'mon, let's go get some apple pie."

"That sounds like a great idea, sis. That would really hit the spot about now."

Chapter 3

Lucky Dogs

Billy had just finished up with his last patient, a six-month-old puppy named Duke who had gotten into the garbage to feast on some chicken bones. Duke ended yet another fourteen-hour day at the office for Dr. Dalton. This had become the norm for Billy over these past few years since his graduation from veterinarian school. Billy didn't mind working late most of the time, but this week was a little different. It was the beginning of Christmas week. Every year during Christmas week Billy would travel to New York City and visit with his sister Hannah. It was the one week every year when Dr. Clifford made sure he was available to cover for Billy and the office.

Billy graduated several years back in 1995 from Colorado State veterinarian school, finishing at the top

Dalton's Pit

of his class. Always the planner, Billy, now 28 years old, already had much of his future scripted out. He met the lovely Karen Gilbert in his first year of medical school a few years back. She was a spunky outspoken little blonde never without an opinion. She was also a very controlling person who needed to take the lead in most situations. Given Billy's quiet and easy-going demeanor, it seemed like a good match. They married just a few weeks before their graduation. Hannah was the only member of the family who knew of the marriage. When Billy told her, he had asked her to keep it a secret so that he could surprise the family when he returned home after graduation. Billy and Karen had been living together for the past two years in an apartment they rented a few blocks from the University.

Karen came from a well to do family up north and her father had been able to help them financially to get settled early on. Their plans after graduation were to move up north to Boston where Karen's family lived and start their veterinarian practice together. They both felt it was a good place to start a family as well as begin their practice. Billy and Karen had flown up to Boston a few

Lucky Dogs

weeks before graduation and with the help of Karen's father, rented a beautiful two-bedroom apartment in the heart of the city. They also found a small office where they could begin their practice together. It was nothing fancy but they didn't figure to be there very long anyway. Their plan was to build a clientele and hopefully within the next two years be able to open up a bigger office right downtown. Everything was set and the morning of graduation, Karen and Billy

couldn't wait for their future to begin. Billy was just about ready to head to the ceremony when he received a call from his mother Flo.

"Billy, I wish we could be there today," she said. "I hope you know that. But Hannah really isn't feeling that well and with all that's going on here I didn't think taking her out would be a good idea. I love you, son."

Billy already knew that his family would not be coming to his graduation. But he also knew that it wasn't for the reasons that his mother stated.

"That's okay, Mom, I love you too. I understand. I will see you in a month, after I get settled in Boston. I have

Dalton's Pit

someone I would like you to meet. Can I speak with Hannah?"

Hannah came to the phone. "Billy, I wanted to come today. I begged Mom, but she kept making excuses. I feel fine."

Billy replied, "Don't worry, Pip, I will see you in a month. Karen and I will come down to the house to see you guys. I can't wait. Maybe we can all hang out under the porch. We can show Karen Dalton's Pit."

"No way, brother. That's our place. Nobody, not even your wife, can know about our place."

"I know, Pip. It's ours and nobody else's. Love you, kid. See you soon. Take care of Mom."

Billy hung up the phone and headed down toward the school for the last time. Karen's entire family was there. Her parents, her sister and even her grandmother was there. Karen's dad Roger was an executive vice president with a major food chain up in Boston and had an ego the size of Mt. Everest. He would constantly boast about himself and all his accomplishments. One

Lucky Dogs

of his favorite pastimes was putting other people down whenever given the opportunity. Karen's mother Doris was a prissy woman who always seemed annoyed. Whether it was too hot or the chairs were uncomfortable, she always had a complaint about something. She was too good for everyone and scorned the less fortunate. She was a real drag. Needless to say, Billy didn't really care for the Gilberts. Karen's younger sister Heather was clearly the black sheep of the family and did not follow the family mold, that's for sure. She wore ripped jeans and a Rush t-shirt to the graduation. She had dark black hair, 6 earrings in her left ear and a tattoo of a rose on her left wrist. She was Gothic before it was even a term. She said whatever she felt like saying and fought constantly with her parents. Billy was scared to death of her. He had only met Heather once before. A few years earlier at the age of 17, Heather had run away from her parents and ended up staying with Billy and Karen for a few days in their apartment near school. One night when Billy came back early from class without Karen, he walked into what he thought was an empty apartment. As he entered his bedroom he plopped himself down on the bed just to relax. Just then Heather

Dalton's Pit

came out of the bathroom wearing nothing but a towel and stood in his bedroom doorway. Billy stuttered uncontrollably as Heather approach the bed with a devilish look in her eyes. In a quick panic move he was able to wiggle his way free and run out of the apartment before anything escalated. He decided that since nothing happened he wouldn't tell Karen anything about it. He made a few excuses and spent the next two nights in the library, pretending to study all night until Heather left to go home. He never said a word to anyone. When he greeted his in-laws after the commencement, Heather had that same devilish look on her face and kissed him on the cheek while grabbing his waist. Billy didn't want or need this stress in his life and quickly walked away.

After the graduation ceremony concluded, Billy and the rest of his new family flew home to Boston. He was very excited, especially since his apartment was on the opposite side of town from his new in-laws and far

away from his sister-in-law. Plus, after spending a few days with the Gilberts he was happy to get away from all the pompousness.

Lucky Dogs

They quickly settled into their new apartment, started working on the office renovations and had set a grand opening for about two weeks later. Since money was tight Billy again reluctantly accepted money from Roger Gilbert for a second time. This bothered him very much to be indebted to a man like Roger. Somehow he knew that Roger would hold it over his head for the rest of his life. The following two weeks were spent fixing and cleaning the office in anticipation for the grand opening. They even had a few customers already. Karen had many friends back home with dogs and had already secured a full week's worth of appointments. Everything was set.

And then the phone call. The call that would rearrange Billy's entire life. It is often said that when we make plans, God laughs. *Well,* Billy thought, *He must be laughing His head off right about now.*

The night before the office grand opening, Billy received a call from his sister Hannah. Billy's mom had taken a few too many pain killers and was found unresponsive on the kitchen floor. By the time paramedics had arrived it was too late; she died of an overdose. Flo had

Dalton's Pit

never gotten over Cooper's death years earlier. She had become addicted to pain killers over the years and was never able to regain her zest for life. This was the real reason she did not go to Billy's graduation. The real reason she rarely left the house anymore, let alone Kansas. Like ships passing in the night, just like that she was gone. The bigger problem, though, was that Flo was Hannah's primary caregiver. Billy's father Ernie was no longer in the picture and neither was Travis, who had moved out west to California after he got married years ago. Billy had a difficult decision in front of him. Who would take care of Hannah? He knew he had to talk this over with Karen but wasn't sure how she would handle it. He also knew that Hannah couldn't come up to Boston. Given her condition and her doctor's schedule it wouldn't work. Deep down he already knew that he had no choice but to return to Kansas to be with Hannah.

The next conversation Billy had with Karen was their last. She had no intention of leaving Boston and her new practice. She wanted no part of the Midwest and to quote her "those hillbillies" were not her kind of people. Billy on the other had no intention of staying. This was

Lucky Dogs

the woman he was to spend the rest of his life with? He couldn't comprehend why she didn't understand why he had to leave. Billy had a revelation almost instantaneously. This was not the woman he wanted to spend the rest of his life with. In fact, he was so turned off by his wife's actions, he was about to tell her all about the night her sister Heather propositioned him. Then, with the words just about to fly out of his mouth, he thought better of it. After all, that wasn't Billy's style. He figured let the next guy tell her when it happened again.

The partnership and the marriage was over after only three months. Billy caught the next flight home for his mother's funeral.

After the funeral, the next thing Billy needed to do was to get settled with a job and a place to live. All throughout his high school and undergrad years Billy worked in Dr. Clifford's office helping him in his practice. Once Dr. Clifford heard about Flo and Billy's plans to return, he immediately offered him a partnership in his practice. The plan was to work side by side for two years and then Billy would take over and

Dalton's Pit

buy out the business when Dr. Clifford retired. This was a logical move for Billy since he knew most of the clients and had a good relationship with so many within his hometown. He agreed and started working immediately. He also moved back into the old brown farmhouse to look after Hannah. He knew he needed to be on site for Hannah as much as possible. Billy soon realized just how much he missed his little sister and the old house, although things were quite different for them. Hannah still had good days and bad. Some days she was able to do anything a healthy person could do. Other days she would not be able to get out of bed and needed around the clock attention. Things went well their first few months together. They even, on occasion, sat under the porch and reminisced about the old days. Dalton's Pit was still there; although, they were now a bit too big to fit in it. The actual keepsake box, or time capsule as they called it, was still there as well. Still in the box were Billy's old pictures and books and Hannah's diary. They would talk about the things they had planned when they were little and how maybe one day they would open a retreat for unwanted and abused animals. Sometimes pretending is a good thing.

Lucky Dogs

Dreams don't always come true, but there's no law stopping you from pretending they do.

As luck would have it, a few weeks later, Billy learned that the three-acre lot directly behind their barn was put on the market. It was mostly just a wooded area, though it had a stream flowing through it from end to end. Billy used to play in those woods as a child. He would sit by the stream and catch a few frogs or lizards and then bring them back under the porch to show Hannah. The land also had a large house on the opposite end with a fenced in area where his neighbor used to keep his livestock: chickens, pigs, cows, among others that used to roam around in the large yard. However, since the owner had passed away a few years back, the land was dark and desolate. Billy and Hannah used to talk as kids about owning a shelter for animals. Well here was their chance. The fact that it was connected to the house was an even bigger bonus. Billy bought the land from the previous owner's daughter for a few thousand bucks. She was thrilled to get rid of it and Billy was more than happy to acquire it. This childhood dream became Billy and Hannah's side project. When he wasn't working with Dr. Clifford, he

Dalton's Pit

was tinkering with and fixing different structures on the land. On her good days Hannah could be found working in the yard cleaning and planting flowers, among other things. Billy had learned a long time ago how to be handy with tools from watching his brother Travis. He constructed an archway made of some fence logs adjacent to the old barn and put up a wire sign that read **Lucky Dogs Compound**. He couldn't wait to fill it with his four legged friends.

 Over the next several years he would spend most of his free time in the compound tinkering here and there. Then before they knew it Billy and Hannah had created an amazing oasis for unwanted animals. It had a large open field, a stream, a trail and so many other things that a dog would want. He even built an obstacle course for them to climb through or just run around in. He also built this incredibly large dog house. It looked more like a dog apartment building that spanned an entire side of the compound so that whenever it rained, the dogs could have their own individual space to keep dry. Over time the compound grew to house about 200 animals of which about 90% were dogs. Once completed, though Billy needed to find a new project. So oftentimes

Lucky Dogs

he would drop a few dogs off at the local hospital to spend time with sick children or the elderly.

It is said that the joy dogs bring to people in need of comfort is very therapeutic. What started out as a noble gesture, quickly turned into a weekly commitment. Everyone in the hospital looked forward to the end of the week when the new dogs would arrive. Especially in the children's ward. Every Friday Billy would drop off 15 or 20 dogs to the hospital and come home with the prior week's dogs. After a while it got to the point where he had several hospitals and nursing homes booked on a weekly basis. As a result, it eventually became too much to handle all by

himself. So, he hired a few local college kids to help with the transporting and eventually had three vans traveling continuously throughout the week. After the first year, he created a nonprofit organization called "**Lucky Dogs Inc**." After two years, the corporation covered hospitals and nursing homes in six states throughout the Midwest. As his company grew, so did Billy's reputation in the field of medicine. Lucky Dogs had billboards on many major highways and even had a

Dalton's Pit

few television commercials. The face of the company was, of course, Hannah Dalton. She appeared in the commercials and her face became synonymous with Lucky Dogs. Billy did all of this for charity and his love for the animals. Initially he didn't make a cent. He even won a few distinguished awards including the year 2000 Humanitarian of the Year in medicine for the state of Kansas. Throughout all his success though, everything took a back seat to Hannah. He always made sure she came first. Clearly the face of Lucky Dogs Inc., Hannah was featured in both commercials and on billboards. Things were going well for Hannah for the first time in her life. She was finally proud to look in the mirror. Unfortunately, things do not always stay the same in life. Change is inevitable for better or worse. It had been three years since leaving Karen and changing his entire life around for his sister. Hannah's condition clearly was beginning to worsen. As a result, Billy was no longer able to care for Hannah by himself. He thought of hiring a support person but that wasn't an option since Hannah needed to be around skilled professionals. Reluctantly he found a full-service nursing care hospital in New York that specialized in heart ailments such as

Lucky Dogs

Microcephaly. Bereft of options at that point he agreed to move Hannah to New York City for the care she needed. It's funny how things play out sometimes. Just a few years ago he'd given up his marriage and his life because he didn't want to move Hannah up North. Now he was staying in Kansas while she was moving up North. That's life, comprised of many unexpected detours.

In the early days of her stay, Billy would fly back and forth to New York every weekend. He took her all-around New York City. They took in Broadway shows, frequented St Patrick's Cathedral and they even visited the Statue of Liberty. He would wheel her around the entire city. Wherever she wanted to go Billy took her. Sometimes though, Hannah wasn't up to going out into the city. As her pain grew slightly worse over time she eventually spent most her time inside the nursing facility. All this while Billy continued to speak to many top doctors, all of whom had the same diagnosis. Unless she received a heart transplant it was only a matter of time. Even if she did, it may not even matter. Age 40 appeared to be a best-case scenario. Still Billy refused

Dalton's Pit

to accept the harsh reality. Life without Hannah was something he couldn't even think about.

It was December 23, 2001 and Billy's flight to New York was set for 8 a.m. the following morning. New York was still recovering from the tragedy of September 11th. Billy hadn't been to New York since then but had a few colleagues who had lost their lives that day. He had been in contact with Hannah almost every day the first month after September 11th. She was fortunate that the hospital was uptown and a few miles away from the attack when it occurred. Still he was a bit nervous to come back to New York City. Seeing the aftermath on television was one thing, but seeing it in person was another. To the people throughout America pain, was felt and tears were cried, but those who were at the scene endured life altering images that would haunt them for the rest of their days. Billy's good friend Jimmy Nelson was in World Trade Center 2 when the plane hit that morning. They had graduated medical school together and had still spoken a few times a year. He knew that Jimmy travelled to New York quite often but did not realize he was a victim until three weeks after the attacks. What a bright guy Jimmy was, such a

Lucky Dogs

shame. He was married and had a baby boy only one year before he died.

Despite all the gloom and doom surrounding his visit, Billy was still looking forward to seeing Hannah. He shut off the lights, locked the front door of his office and pulled down the gate. He then got in his car and headed out of the parking lot. He usually left a bit earlier on Fridays just to make sure he got home for Hannah's phone call. She called him every Friday night at 7 p.m. for the past three years since relocating back in '98. He never missed her phone calls and he always gave himself more than enough time to get home on Friday nights. Even though he was going to see her the next afternoon, he still wanted to make it home in time to hear her voice. The rain began to fall a bit heavier as he pulled out onto the freeway. He popped in his favorite Lynyrd Skynrd CD and set out for his 20-minute ride home. About five minutes into the ride he noticed a woman on the side of the road with her hazard lights on. Always the helpful one, Billy slowed and rolled down his window. The woman who looked to be in her late 50's or so was standing in front of an old beat up Chevy Nova. Possibly a 1978 or 1979 model. The car was

Dalton's Pit

smoking from underneath the hood and the woman who stood alongside it appeared to be a bit overwhelmed.

Billy said to the woman, "I see you're having some trouble with your car. Maybe I can help."

The woman replied, "This old car has given me a lot of trouble lately. It was my husband's car before he passed away last year. I should just get rid of it already, but I just can't seem to let it go."

"Let me take a quick look for you." Billy pulled up just ahead of the woman onto the shoulder and got out of his car and then popped open the hood. The radiator seems to be dry. Don't worry, my brother taught me a few things when I was a kid. Let's see what I can do," he said.

"Thank you so much, young man; you are too kind," she replied.

"There's no reason for you to stand out here in the rain. Please, sit in the car where it's dry and let me try to fix her up for you."

Lucky Dogs

"Thank you so much; my husband always took care of these things," she added.

Billy spent the next half hour working on the woman's car and then finally snapped the hood closed. Now drenched to the bone he knocked on the window.

"You're all set, ma'am. Start her up."

She started the engine and revved the gas. A relieved smile appeared across her face. She then reached into her wallet and pulled out whatever she had on her. It looked to be about $50 and she handed it to Billy.

"Don't be silly, this was my pleasure. I couldn't possibly accept your money. By the way I noticed you have an emblem on your trunk of a purple violet. The detail is amazing. I'm just curious if it has any meaning to you?"

"Actually yes, my name is Violet and my husband had it specially made for his car. He said that when he was on the road it was like I was always with him."

"Wow, Violet, sounds like you are a very lucky woman. He must have loved you very much. It's rare these days

Dalton's Pit

to find that. Believe me I've looked. Well anyway, take care of yourself; it was a pleasure to meet you."

"It was a pleasure to meet you as well. How can I ever repay you for your kindness? I don't even know your name."

"My name is William Dalton, but most people call me Billy. I'm from the area. Don't worry about it. You can pay me back by helping the next person you find that's in need of help just like you were."

"You have my word, Mr. William Dalton. I will never forget you," she replied. She pulled away and gave him a wave and a smile. There's an old saying, "you have never really lived until you've done something for someone who can never repay you." Billy genuinely believed that if you pay it forward, somehow it always comes back to you. It seemed like a good way to live life. Most people who do a good deed for someone tend to have a motive behind it and expect something back in return. Not Billy, though. He genuinely enjoyed helping people. As a result of his good deed Billy arrived home late and missed Hannah's call. Unfortunately, he

Lucky Dogs

couldn't just call her back. It's wasn't that simple. She had a certain timeframe to make her call and if she missed it that was too bad. But that was okay. He would see her tomorrow afternoon anyway.

Hannah had a rough go of it over the past few years with two heart surgeries and numerous procedures. When she first arrived in New York City back in 1998, she was much more independent than she was in recent years. But with her health deteriorating she often needed around the clock medical attention. Her prognosis was what it was. It was just a matter of time. It was highly unlikely she would ever find a heart donor. The problem was that since she was so tiny it was almost impossible to find a donor with a perfect match, given her age and size. Anything short of a child of say five or six who had a parent willing to donate their heart to her, the chances seemed bleak at best. The reality they faced was that most parents willing to donate their child's organs would prefer to give it to another child with their whole life ahead of them. Not a 32-year-old woman who had a life expectancy of 5 to 10 years at best. That just didn't make any sense and Billy knew it.

Dalton's Pit

Despite all her trials and tribulations Hannah was still always upbeat and smiling. She believed that whatever God had in store for her life, it was for a good reason. She always looked forward to her Friday night phone calls with Billy and his Christmas trips to New York. Once or twice a year she even spoke with Travis as well. Travis moved to California after Cooper died. He had gotten married about 10 years back. He and his wife Ivy had three children and he ran a local body shop just outside San Diego. He also was the head coach of his 8-year-old son's pee wee football team The Mighty Mites.

Travis and Ivy had spoken to each other for several years before they actually met face to face. Ivy worked for the auto wholesaler that supplied Travis with the car parts he needed at the garage. They spoke several times a week for 5 or 6 years. Since the company's order and billing department was in California, they had never actually met. Then when Ivy heard about Travis's brother dying, she decided to pay her respects and come to Kansas for the funeral. The first time they ever met was at the gravesite. They were immediately drawn to one another and within 18 short months were married. Travis then moved to California to start a

Lucky Dogs

family. Sometimes when things are stagnant in life, the best remedy is a change of scenery. Travis needed to get away from Spring Hill and find himself again. He needed a fresh start, so off he went. As for Ernie and Flo they split up two years after Cooper's death. It was too much for them to handle. Dad still blamed Mr. Danby for Cooper's death. One day when Mr. Danby stopped at the station to fill up his station wagon, Ernie lost control and tried to set him on fire by pouring gas all over his car and setting it ablaze. Ernie spent the next 10 years in a Louisville, Kentucky minimum security prison for attempted murder. Travis, who had just moved to California, offered to come back, but Flo convinced him to live his life and said that she and Hannah would be fine.

Since Ernie's release a few years back, he never reconnected with his family. He didn't even attend his wife's funeral. Rumor had it he was living in a mobile home trailer park somewhere outside Lexington. Flo's death a few years back all but ended any possible communication in the future between Ernie and his children. She just was never able to fully recover from Cooper's death. Then when Ernie went away to prison,

Dalton's Pit

she fell into a deep depression. She just couldn't function properly on her own again. Losing her son and then her husband was just too much for her to handle.

As for Austin, who knows? Still hiding out? Dead? He'd disappeared from their lives 19 years ago when Cooper died and had been missing in action ever since. The word on the street from a few of his old friends was that he was somewhere down South. Billy never expected to hear from him again nor did he want to. Billy's plane pulled into the gate at JFK international airport around 2 p.m. Eastern Time. He exited the terminal passageway into the airport lobby outside the gate holding his carryon bag. He was startled to see someone he hadn't seen in almost a year. Standing in the terminal with a smile from ear to ear was an unexpected surprise waiting to greet him.

Billy was so surprised he stumbled over his words. "What the…? How…? When did you…? I can't believe you are here." He gave his sibling a huge hug. "When did you arrive?"

Lucky Dogs

His big brother Travis lifted him up like a rag doll and squeezed tightly.

"I been waitin' a few hours already. My plane got here at noon. Me and Hannah wanted to surprise you. I talked with her last week on Friday and told her I was coming. I told her not to tell you."

"You came alone? On Christmas Eve? Where's the family?"

"The whole crew went to Ivy's mom's. I wanted to be here though, and Ivy didn't care none. It'll be like a family reunion. I can't wait to see Hannah. Maybe if you guys are good, I'll buy you both a milkshake." "Those were the days, Travis. Those were the days. I wish we could go back, brother; oh how I wish we could go back."

They headed on out to the baggage carousel for Billy's other bags and Travis put his little brother in a head lock and started giving him the business. Just like old times when they would wrestle in the barn.

Chapter 4

Ultra Violet

Violet Harrison was the woman Billy helped on the side of the road that night. Violet was actually much older than she looked. On her last birthday, she turned 67 years of age. Although she could have easily passed for a woman in her early 50's. In her earlier days, she was a newscaster at a local television station back in New Mexico. Prior to that she was a Division 1 college athlete in swimming. She even held the school record in the 200-meter butterfly for New Mexico State University. She met her husband Neal her freshman year at State. They married right out of college back in 1957. Neal graduated a year earlier than Violet with an engineering degree. It was love at first sight. They say opposites attract and in this case that statement couldn't be more accurate. Violet was a beautiful soft spoken woman who exuded class from every pore in her body. She was raised amidst very humble beginnings, however. Violet's parents had a small row house in a middle-class

Dalton's Pit

neighborhood outside Santa Fe where she grew up as an only child. Her mom and dad both worked, which was uncommon back in the fifties. Her dad was a laborer on a construction site while her mom hemmed dresses for the local haberdasher. Money was tight but somehow they made it work and did the best they could in raising Violet.

Neal, on the other hand, came from the better part of town. His father was a highly influential city official with contacts throughout the state. Soon after his graduation Neal's father got him a job designing wind turbines for the state government. Within 5 short years Neil became one of the most important minds in the engineering field. His designs for several projects earned him much clout not only in his field, but in the state government hierarchy as well. Everyone sought his opinion when it came to drafting new energy saving equipment. His notoriety led to many opportunities including opening his own company which he named Ultra Violet Interactives or UVI after his beloved wife. His company single-handedly constructed over 2,000 solar powered windmills in the New Mexico area. His invention saved consumers millions of dollars on energy

Ultra Violet

bills. To say Violet wasn't a poor old lady would be an understatement. Upon Neal's death, his estate was worth roughly 80 million dollars. Unfortunately, one night last August while Neal was working late, he fell asleep at the wheel on his way home and drove right off the road and into a ditch. He died on impact. Violet took his death very hard. He was all she ever had. The love of her life. Despite all their success and money, something had always been missing from Violet's life. She found out shortly after her marriage to Neal that she could not bear children. She had always dreamed of having a large family, a daughter to spend her life with and some grandchildren to spoil. She often thought about adoption but with Neal's work and the significant travel it just never seemed like the right time. Then one day it was just too late. Sometimes the days in life seem to go slowly but the years seem to fly by pretty darn quick.

Their house was nice but modest compared to others with their means. It was in one of the nicer suburbs just outside Kansas City. Violet herself never seemed too comfortable with money. She was brought up learning to do without. She felt after a certain amount she didn't have a need for any more. She would have been content

Dalton's Pit

with Neal even if he were poor. Now with Neal gone and no family left to speak of she found herself lost. She was very lonely and when it came to simple things like paying the bills, she was a novice. Neal had always handled everything. She had to learn at her advanced age how to do some of the most basic things that people do in life. It had been 15 months since Neal's passing and she was no better off mentally than the day he left her. In fact, she was worse. Every Saturday true to their routine, Violet would go into town to the Hillside Cafe and have Saturday afternoon brunch. Prior to his death every weekend for the past 20 years, Neal and Violet would go into town and spend the afternoon having brunch at Hillside and then taking a leisurely walk in the park just across the street. They would watch the children in the playground or some of the older kids playing softball across the way. It was their time to imagine what it would be like had they had their own children. It was a sad game of pretend for them to play, but it was all they had at that stage of their lives. Violet now being all alone would retrace her steps and sometimes even talk with Neal as if he were still by her

Ultra Violet

side. She only knew one way of life. She only had one best friend and now he was gone.

One Saturday afternoon on her walk alone, she was so entrenched in her pretend conversation with Neal she accidentally stumbled over a knapsack left in the pathway. A young woman sitting just off the cement path in the grass reached up and prevented Violet from falling right on her face.

"I'm so sorry I shouldn't have left that out in the open like that. Are you okay? Please accept my apology," said the woman.

"That's okay, dear, I'm fine," Violet replied. Violet quickly walked away, appearing a little embarrassed maybe even a little dismayed. *Did this woman hear me talking to Neal?* she mused. *Maybe she thinks I'm crazy?*

Violet briefly glanced at the woman sitting in the grass and noticed that she was filthy. She looked like maybe she was on drugs and it seemed as if she hadn't had a bath in a while. The woman had a carriage next to her filled with what appeared to be all her possessions. Just a few yards away playing in the field was a little boy who

Dalton's Pit

couldn't have been more than three years old. He was playing with a ball all by himself, rolling it back and forth in the dirt. Violet, clearly a bit spooked, decided to walk in the opposite direction to avoid further conversation with the woman.

As she turned to walk away she heard the woman say to her son, "Come on, Thomas, it's time to go. Play time is over."

By that time Violet was maybe 20 yards away and couldn't help but think of Billy Dalton and his last words to her. 'You can pay me back by helping the next person you find that's in need of help just like you were.' Now feeling a little guilty, Violet carefully walked back to where the woman was sitting and said, "Excuse me, miss, but is there anything I can do for you?"

The woman looked up at Violet with shame in her eyes. "Thank you, we're just fine." Violet then heard the woman's son in the background, "Mommy, I'm hungry."

The woman picked up her son, placed him in the carriage amid all her other things and started to walk away.

Ultra Violet

"Please, miss. I would like to help you. Please come with me. I know a place we can go and enjoy a great meal for you and your son. My husband and I used to go there all the time."

The woman now with a tear in her eye said, "I don't need your help, lady. We are just fine. Come on, Thomas, we have to go now."

Violet just stood there as the woman quickly sped off and disappeared down the path and onto the street. Violet continued her walk but appeared somewhat bothered by the conversation. Was this woman on drugs? Maybe she was a prostitute. Either way it didn't matter now, she was gone.

Violet finished her walk about 10 minutes later and returned to her car. She buckled in and was about to pull out of the parking spot when she noticed the woman's child sitting on a bench across the street near a row of stores. The store on the end had a sign which read Angelo's Bakery. Violet just couldn't seem to shake Billy Dalton and what he'd said to her out of her head. Just then wave of emotion then came over her. She

Dalton's Pit

turned the car off and walked across the street to the little boy.

"It's Thomas, right?" she asked.

Thomas just looked at her without saying a word.

"Thomas, where's mommy?"

Thomas simply pointed to the alleyway on the side of the bakery.

Violet grabbed Thomas by the hand and proceeded to walk down the alley into the small courtyard behind the row of stores. There was the woman fishing through the dumpster behind the bakery with what appeared to be a plastic bag filled with day old bread and bagels in her hand. Violet walked up to the woman and touched her on her shoulder as she waded through the pile of garbage.

Jumping back, the woman, seeing it was Violet said, "I told you to leave us alone; we are fine." She grabbed her son's hand and started to walk away again.

Ultra Violet

Violet blurted out, "I just lost my husband. I have no one. Please let me help you. Let me at least buy you and your son a good healthy meal."

The woman, facing the alleyway exit, stopped walking. Violet walked to her and she turned around. The woman burst into tears and sank her head into Violet's shoulder.

"I can't do this anymore, I just can't," the woman said, sobbing uncontrollably.

"Come with me, my dear," Violet said. "It will be okay. What's your name, sweetheart?"

"My name is Rose and this is my son Thomas."

"Hi, Thomas," she said.

Thomas gave Violet a smile and then looked down and continued to play with his toy truck. Over the next few hours at the Hillside Café, Violet learned all about Rose. Rose was not on drugs, nor was she a prostitute. Rose left home at the age of 15 and ran away with her boyfriend Tom. She married him at age 16 when she became pregnant with Thomas. She told Violet all

Dalton's Pit

about her husband Tom Sr., how he turned out to be this really bad guy. She had no idea he was a drug dealer until after they were married. She also told Violet how he used to beat on her whenever he pleased. Rose, now 19, left Tennessee 4 years ago, because her parents forbade her relationship with Tom. Now too ashamed to go back, she decided to live on the street instead. Only 3 weeks ago she landed in a hospital after one of his beatings. He had punched her in the face so hard he'd left her with a broken nose and two black eyes. She fell and hit her head on the tile floor and ended up with a concussion as well. A few hours after Tom left the house, she walked into the local hospital emergency room all bloodied and dazed. She spent the next 3 days in the hospital.

Tom visited her every day as if nothing happened. Probably just to make sure she didn't tell anyone about the beatings. Instead of squealing on him she made up a story to the hospital nurses about how she was mugged. She was scared to death of Tom and she knew if she didn't get out of there soon he would eventually kill her. The day of her release from the hospital with Tom and Thomas waiting for her in the lobby, she knew

Ultra Violet

she had to make a run for it. The hospital nurses brought her down to the lobby in a wheelchair even though she was able to walk just fine. When she arrived in the lobby the nurses told her husband to pull the car around and they would wheel her out to the car when he pulled up. As soon as he left to get the car, Rose told the nurses, "I need to go to the bathroom. Thomas, come with Mommy."

Rose quickly pushed Thomas's carriage toward the bathroom down the hall. Across from the bathroom was the emergency room exit; Rose immediately ran towards it without looking back. As soon as she got outside, she took off for the train station and caught the next train, not caring where it was headed. That was two weeks ago; since then she had been sleeping in bus terminals or the local park. She also had been hanging around restaurants scrounging for whatever she could find to feed herself and Thomas. Violet at this point was clearly ashamed of the way she had looked upon Rose when she first met her. Now feeling the need to further help Rose, Violet offered to give her some money and a place to stay. Rose accepted a few dollars, but declined her invitation to stay at her house.

Dalton's Pit

"Thank you so much for your help, but Thomas and I are trying to get to San Antonio. I have an old friend who lives there who Tom doesn't know. She agreed to take us in for now."

"Nonsense, where will you sleep tonight? Let me help you. Please, I could use the company as well."

"OK, Violet. But only for one night, then we must be on our way."

Violet then drove Rose and Thomas back to her home for the evening. Rose and Thomas got all cleaned up and had a good home cooked meal. Something they hadn't had in quite a while. Then it was Violet's turn. She told Rose all about Neal and her college swimming records. She also told her how she could never have a child and how lonely she was since Neal passed away. You could say that Violet needed Rose's company just as much as Rose needed her hospitality. They stayed up half the night just talking about Neal and Tom and anything else that came to mind. Violet, for the first time in her life felt like a mother. She had someone she could take care of. It was something that she had coveted more than

Ultra Violet

anything else in life. A daughter of her own and a beautiful grandson. Even if it was only for just one night. The next morning Rose was up bright and early. With tears in her eyes she hugged Violet. She thanked her for everything she did for her and for her son.

Violet then asked, "How will you get to San Antonio?"

"The money you gave us yesterday should be enough for two one-way Amtrak tickets. Thomas and I will walk to the station from here. It's not that far; it's only about half a mile. Thank you so much, Violet; I will never forget your kindness."

Violet was sad to see her go. Just 24 hours before she didn't even know this woman and now she needed her to stay. She needed to take care of her.

"Wait Rose, take this." She handed her an envelope and said, "Here are a few dollars and my phone number. Please call me and let me know how things work out for you. Come back and visit me anytime." Then she took the keys to her husband's beloved car out of her purse and said, "Rose, here. Take my husband's old car; you need it more than I do."

Dalton's Pit

Rose now weeping like a baby, said, "How can I ever repay you?"

Violet, thinking back to Billy Dalton's words, turned to Rose and said, "You can pay me back by helping the next person you find that's in need of help just like you were. A young man told me that a while back when I was stuck with this very car on the highway and I never forgot it."

Rose then gave Violet the hug she had been yearning for since Neal passed away 15 months ago. An embrace of love, of family. Something that had been missing in her life for a long time. She then said, "I will never forget you either, Violet." Rose then packed Thomas into the car and off she went.

Rose was both excited and nervous at the same time. She had a chance to start her life over somewhere where nobody knew who she was. An opportunity to re-create her entire existence. She couldn't wait to get to San Antonio and get started. She merged onto the parkway at the next entrance and set out on her journey. In addition to her excitement she was also very frightened. What if Tom found them? She knew he had

Ultra Violet

friends all over the place. She had to make sure that when she arrived in Texas she stayed off the grid as much as possible. Maybe she should change her last name. She didn't even have a high school diploma. What would she do to make money? How would she be able to take care of Thomas? How long could she expect her friend to let her stay at her house? So much to think about and so many questions to answer. For now, though, she was just happy to get away from him and from her life.

It was almost 10 p.m. and Rose had been driving for most of the day. She was beginning to get tired and noticed that Thomas was fast asleep, sprawled out in the back seat. She saw a sign up just ahead that read *Skyway Motel 1 mile up ahead* and decided she would exit the highway and pull into the motel just off the exit. Her first thought was to sleep in the car, but she was tired since she had spent most of the night before talking with Violet. She felt she'd rather get a room at the motel and get the good night's sleep she needed. She parked the car in the lot and with Thomas still asleep, carried him in her arms into the lobby and up to the front desk.

Dalton's Pit

"Can I get a room for the night for me and my son, please?"

"Sure thing, miss. It's $45 for the night. Will that be cash or charge?" said the man at the desk.

"Cash." Rose reached into her purse and pulled out exactly $45. "Here you go, thank you."

Rose still had the money Violet had given her at the park when they first met. It was just about enough to cover the cost of the room.

"Ok. Name, please?"

"Excuse me?" said Rose.

"I need your full name for our log book," he said.

Rose was a bit hesitant. She didn't want to give him her last name. She wanted to stay off the grid. She stumbled for a second and then blurted out the first thing that came to mind. "Dawson, Rose Dawson."

The front desk attendant looked up and smiled. "Rose Dawson? Really? I saw that movie too."

Ultra Violet

The man at the front desk winked at Rose and said," Okay, Ms. Dawson, please sign here."

Rose realized how stupid that was, considering Titanic was one of the biggest movies of all time. She gave a weak smile and signed the book Rose Dawson. She knew she should have come up with a better name than that. She carried Thomas up to the room, laid him on the bed and within five minutes they both were fast asleep. The next morning, she woke up early, cleaned Thomas up and grabbed a few breakfast rolls at the convenience counter then immediately headed out onto the road. When she got in the car, she realized she was almost completely out of gas. She had spent almost everything that Rose had given her yesterday at the restaurant. The motel and the fast food they had last night cost her about $60. As she pulled into the gas station she remembered the envelope that Violet handed her when she left yesterday morning. Hopefully there was enough gas money inside to get her to San Antonio. She had another full day on the road before she arrived there. Now at the pump she pulled out the envelope from Violet and opened it. In there was $5,000 in cash with a note that read,

Dalton's Pit

Dearest Rose

I am so blessed to have met you. I have more money than I could ever spend in my lifetime. Please accept this and begin your new life with Thomas Jr. If there is anything you ever need please let me know. I consider you the daughter I never had.

Love,

Violet Harrison

1-313-555-2387

P.S. Stay in touch

Rose just sat in the car in disbelief. Violet hardly knew her. Why would she do this for her?

Just then the gas attendant knocked on the window and asked, "Fill 'er up?"

Rose, wearing a huge grin on her face said, "Yes, please."

Chapter 5

The Corporal

New York City was bitterly cold that Christmas. The snow on the ground was frozen rock solid as the temperatures dipped into single digits for the first time in a year. The smoke was wafting off people's heads like a log cabin chimney. Everyone was rushing around doing last minute shopping before their company arrived. This year's holiday rush was in full swing. The tree in Rockefeller center looked more majestic than it did the last time Billy visited Hannah. The ice skaters were all flying around the frozen rink just below the tree. Billy had forgotten how beautiful New York City was around Christmas time. This type of excitement was not that easy to find in his home state of Kansas. It was almost as if he were thrust inside a Currier and Ives picture postcard. *Pip would love this*, he thought. The truth was, however, she was getting worse and if this was a motion picture, it wasn't going to have a good

Dalton's Pit

ending. Would she ever be able to see the tree again? He fretted as he stared at the skaters down below.

Just then Travis exited the deli across the street and walked over to Billy by the tree. "Here's your coffee, kid. Hey, whatcha thinkin' 'bout, little brother?"

"Thanks Travis, I was just thinking about how much Hannah would love this. She always loved Christmas and the tree. We had to have come here at least five or six times over the past few years. She loved to watch the skaters. She always imagined herself skating under that tree, but somehow deep down she knew it would never happen. I wish I could have taken her at least once. Life just isn't fair sometimes."

"You just never know, kid. Maybe she can do it next year. Stranger things have happened. Let's go see her."

"Actually Travis, I need to make a stop first before we head uptown.

"Ok, no trouble at all, Bill; whatever you say. Where we goin'?" he asked.

The Corporal

"I would like to head downtown and visit Ground Zero. I spoke with my friend Jimmy's wife Lilly last week and I told her that when I got here I would go down there and pay my respects to my friend."

They hailed a cab and headed downtown. After the few mile trip, they tipped the cabbie and exited right onto the west side highway. It didn't seem as if either of them were prepared for what they were about to experience next. Ground Zero was reminiscent of what Germany must have looked like at the end of World War II. Billy had been in the World Trade Center buildings a few times in the past, but was now completely humbled by what he saw. On one side of the street businesses were just reopening and people were going about their daily activities as usual. On the other side, it was pure chaos. There were cranes operating in the middle of this giant hole of twisted metal and ash. Trucks were lined up carrying scrap metal to the local heaps. It was hard to imagine that just a few months ago, two buildings, both over 100 stories each, stood in its place. How did they not tip over and destroy the businesses across the way? The sheer magnitude of this tragedy now hit home. Over three thousand innocent people didn't

Dalton's Pit

make it back home that night, including his good friend Jimmy. He had seen the footage on television many times over the past few months and had done his best to prepare himself for what he might encounter. Instead he just stood there with a somber look and a tear in his eye thinking of all the people who lost their loved ones that day. He thought back to Jimmy and the late nights back in school preparing for exams. They were inseparable for quite a few years during school.

Whenever they would get together they would always talk about one crazy night in particular. It had to have been his junior year of medical school. Jimmy's roommate Nick had just broken up with his girlfriend after having a huge fight. Billy and Jimmy took Nick out to a local bar to cheer him up. After about an hour of drinking, both Jimmy and Nick were feeling good when Nick started getting loud and acting stupid. Billy, always the cautious one, wasn't drinking as he quickly realized he needed to have his wits about him given their condition. Billy had just stepped outside the club and was on the phone talking with Karen when Nick made the mistake of hitting on some guy's girlfriend. If that wasn't bad enough, after she rejected him he called her

The Corporal

a bitch and dumped his beer over her head. When her boyfriend returned from the bathroom all hell broke loose. The guy grabbed Nick in a head lock and threw him across the floor and into some tables where people were sitting quietly enjoying a few beers. Jimmy jumped in the fray and was immediately cracked in the face by one of the guy's friends. By the time Billy could get back through the crowd to help his friends, he heard a single gunshot. Everyone immediately froze in their tracks. The shot was fired by one of the off-duty police officers who just happened to be at the bar. He was simply trying to restore some order. Nick and Jimmy were promptly cuffed and taken outside to the squad cars. Billy had to put his thinking cap on and get his friends out of this mess or else they would be booked and sent to the local jail overnight. He was afraid it could affect not only their graduation but also their careers. He had to think of something and fast before they were escorted down to the station. Just then he realized he had his white lab coat in his trunk along with a doctor bag filled with the instruments he used in class. He quickly ran to his car and put all his gear on, including his stethoscope and name tag. He ran back to the police

Dalton's Pit

car where the officers were holding them and without missing a beat walked up to the sergeant and said, "Sergeant, thanks so much for finding my patient. Had he slipped away that would have been dangerous for all of us."

"Excuse me, but get out of my way or I will have to arrest you as well, Doc," he replied.

"You don't understand, sergeant, he has to be released into my custody immediately, the other one as well. Surely you must recognize him?"

"Recognize him? No, who the hell is he?"

"This is Jimmy Nelson. He is the youngest recipient of the Congressional Medal of Honor. He was awarded the honor by President Bush himself for his bravery under fire in Iraq. Surely you've seen it on the news? He suffers from severe Post Traumatic Syndrome. I must return him to the institute immediately. Sergeant, I implore you; he is a very dangerous person. You must release him into my custody. "The sergeant was now smirking. "Kid, I don't know who the hell you are, but that was some hell of a story. Now take these two idiots

The Corporal

and get the hell out of here before I change my mind. And by the way your name tag says Vet student ID. Tell your buddies to go sleep it off and beat it, *Doc.*"

The sergeant now realizing that these were just stupid kids out drinking who meant no harm took off the cuffs and pushed them toward Billy.

"Thanks, Sarge." Billy ushered them into the back seat of his car and pulled away. Disaster averted, but a story to tell for the rest of his life.

Billy couldn't help but muster up a smile for his friend Jimmy and all the good times they had in college. He realized that the story he had told so many times before when they were together now had a different meaning. They would never laugh together about his Congressional Medal of Honor again. His smile quickly changed to sadness. He now remembered all the stress and pressure they put on themselves during their time at school. What was it all for? It just didn't seem fair. He didn't understand. Then he began to think about Hannah again and what it was going to be like when she

Dalton's Pit

left. He then knelt and said a quick prayer for his friend. Then he rose back up and wiped the tear from his eye.

Travis put his arm around his little brother. "Sorry, kid. Sometimes we just need to be happy for the time we have. We just never know what's gonna happen tomorrow."

Billy realized in that instant that his brother was so right. One would never look to Travis for advice on life, that's for sure, but this time he'd nailed it. Enjoy each moment, you never know what tomorrow will bring.

"Thanks, Travis. Now let's go and see Pip. I miss her."

Travis then grabbed him by the neck and gave him the business as usual. They grabbed a cab and headed back uptown.

The ride uptown was a reunion of sorts. Travis showed Billy pictures of the kids while Billy talked about Lucky Dogs and the old house. They also talked about Mom. But mostly they were passing the time trying not to think about Hannah. How would she look this time? Would it be the last time they would see her alive?

The Corporal

Although Billy was in the medical field, the veterinarian world was a bit different than real life. He always felt uncomfortable when entering hospitals. This was especially true when it pertained to Hannah. The ride up in the elevator was a bit anxious for both Dalton boys. Neither of them had seen Hannah in a while. How was she doing? What would the doctors say? Finally, the elevator reached the 32nd floor. It was time to find out about their little sister. The doors opened to a lobby that looked like the North Pole. There were decorations covering every wall. The stockings were all lined up with patients' names on them. Gifts were under the tree in the corner of the room and the girl at the front desk was smiling with her Santa hat on. The name on her hat read Donna.

Although Billy was pre-occupied with his concern over Hannah, he couldn't help but notice that Donna was quite attractive and had this amazing curly black hair. Donna just happened to be the nurse on call that day. As they approached the desk, Donna was wrapping up a call with one of the doctors and had just stood up. Billy meanwhile tried to hide his admiration of her slender physique. Donna was easy to admire since she'd spent

Dalton's Pit

most her free time jogging around New York City keeping in shape. She even ran the NYC marathon in just under four hours a few years back. Donna's real talent, however, was her ability to add happiness to an otherwise dreary place. Her smile and soft personality was so well received by her patients. She had a heart of gold and everyone loved her. She made the patients feel special. She was one of those people who thought of everyone else before she thought of herself. Over the past few years she had spent quite a bit of time getting to know Hannah. When Hannah first arrived at the facility they used to go for walks together down by the Hudson River on the east side. It was only a few blocks walk from the hospital and easy to get to. Sometimes they would spend an entire lunch hour just sitting by the water talking about their lives. Donna was only a year younger than Hannah and somehow, they'd hit it off right from the start. Perhaps it was because when they were growing up, neither of them had a sister of their own. Not only was Donna an only child, but her mom passed away when she was only two years old. Her dad raised her by himself until he became ill and passed away only a few years back. On their walks together

The Corporal

Hannah and Donna shared so much of their life stories and innermost secrets with each other. Hannah shared with her all about her family and Cooper's death and her mom dying a few years back. She told her about how Billy had to leave Boston and his life for her. She also told her about Lucky Dogs and all the commercials she was in.

All throughout Hannah's life she never had a close girlfriend her age that she could talk to. It was only either Billy or her mother that she could just unwind with. There are just some times when you need a friend outside the family, someone to share secrets with. This was all new to Hannah. Donna in the meantime also shared her story with Hannah. She told her how her mom passed away when she was a baby and how she took care of her dad for the last few years of his life. She also shared with her that at one time she was engaged to be married to her boyfriend who she met in college. She met David in her freshman year at New York University just about 10 years ago. They dated all throughout college and got engaged two years after graduation when they both settled into their jobs. They found a place down in Greenwich Village for a decent

Dalton's Pit

rent and even adopted a rescue dog named Harry. One day due to a schedule change at the hospital, Donna got off work early and came home to surprise David and found him in bed with her best friend and future maid of honor Jennifer. If Donna had a personality flaw it was that she was always too naïve and trusting. Until that moment Donna had no idea that David and Jennifer were screwing around behind her back. She grabbed Harry and walked out. She was devastated. That was the end of David. It had been a bit rough on Donna since then. The only family she had left was her father who was getting up in age and he lived in Philadelphia where she grew up. She thought about returning home, but she loved her job so much she didn't want to leave. She decided to stay in New York and go it alone. She found a small apartment in the Park Slope section of Brooklyn and commuted every day to the hospital in Manhattan by train. She had gone on a few dates over the past few years, but nothing to write home about. There were also several married doctors in the hospital who constantly flirted and propositioned her pretty much on a daily basis. That was just not Donna's style. She decided instead to put all her energy into her job. The

The Corporal

running began a few years ago as an outlet to release her stress.

Billy stood in front of her at the front desk. "Hello Donna, Hannah Dalton's room, please."

"Oh, you must be her brother Billy. She has been talking about you for so long I feel as though I know you already. It's so very nice to meet you. She is in 11b, down the corridor, last door on the left. C'mon, I'll take you."

"Thank you. This is my brother Travis."

"Hello, brother Travis," Donna said with a smile.

Travis smiled and looked at Billy, giving him a nudge. Billy quickly pushed his brother's arm away and gave him a look. The three of them proceeded down the hall toward Hannah's room. Travis lagged a bit, carrying a three-foot teddy bear he bought in the gift shop downstairs.

Donna reached the room and approached her door. "Here we are. I'll give you some privacy. Call me if you need anything." She then leaned over, looked through

Dalton's Pit

the door and waved to Hannah with a smile, then left down the hall.

The boys entered the room and there she was. Hooked up to about 100 machines, all making their own different beeping sounds. As she slowly opened her eyes, that same Hannah smile appeared across her face. She almost jumped out of the bed with excitement and a few of the machines started beeping uncontrollably. As they approached her bed she couldn't stop hugging her brothers. She was so excited to see them. Her appearance though was a bit startling for Travis. After all, he hadn't seen Hannah since their mom's funeral. She no longer looked like the kid he would take for ice cream after school. She looked frail, almost ghostly. Sadness filled the room very quickly as the realization of her situation set in.

Hannah looked at her brothers. "What do you say we sneak out of here and head down to Sprinkles for a milkshake? C'mon, maybe we could even take Donna with us? Hmm, Billy?"

The smiles returned to their faces if only for a moment.

The Corporal

Billy softly said, "Merry Christmas, Pip. How are they treating you? When does the doctor come check on you? I'd like to speak with him."

Hannah sat up in her bed smiling. "Billy, let's just have fun today. Screw the doctors just for tonight. I want to hang out with my two favorite brothers."

The hours flew past as the three Daltons kids just sat around and reminisced about the old neighborhood. They talked, of course, about Travis's six touchdowns, walking home from school, hanging out in the barn, among other things. They also talked about mom and about Cooper. Then suddenly out of nowhere, Billy felt the urge to relieve himself of something that had been bogging him down for years. He finally confessed to them about what happened the night Cooper died. How he heard his brothers' plan while sitting under the porch and how he tried to stop Cooper from going. It was the first time he broke his silence about that night to anyone. If anything, he felt like maybe it would bring the three of them closer together. He also needed to get it off his chest. It was a release a long time coming for Billy. He had been holding onto this secret for so long,

Dalton's Pit

he didn't even know where to begin. He told them how he ran to see Travis at the station after the twins had sped off and how he had just missed him. He told them how he then ran over to Dr. Clifford's and he had just closed the office. Then he spoke about his last conversation with Cooper and how he thought Cooper understood what he was about to do was wrong. He explained to them how he could see in Cooper's eyes that he wanted nothing to do with the robbery and how he felt pressured by Austin. Cooper just simply didn't know how to say no to Austin. It was almost as if he didn't want to let him down. Like it was his obligation to obey everything Austin said. He could see the sadness in Cooper's eyes, like he was trapped or something. That was the relationship they had. Cooper had always sought Austin's approval and it ended up costing him his life. He then told them how Austin walked out onto the porch and shot him right below the eye point blank. This time he'd looked in Austin's eyes. He saw a kid completely disconnected from feeling, he saw a sociopath. There was such a calmness within him when he shot Billy; it was as if he were simply handing him a glass of water. Very nonchalant, very subtle. It was very

The Corporal

scary how easy it was for him to shoot Billy. *What causes someone to have so little feeling?* he wondered.

Billy, with a tear in his eye said, "I could have stopped it. If only I'd had more time, Cooper would still be alive."

Sitting there with his head in his hands he whispered, "If he were still alive we'd all still be together: Mom, Dad, Cooper even Austin."

Most of the time Travis would drift in and out during heavy conversations, but this time he was once again spot on. "Billy, if it weren't for you we wouldn't be spending this great Christmas together. Let's enjoy the family we still got. I'm here, Hannah's here."

Hannah's IV drip was dry and the machine started to beep, so Donna came in with a fresh bag and started to disconnect the empty one. *Perfect timing,* Billy thought.

Hannah smiled and said, "Donna, did you meet my brother Billy? Good looking guy, huh?" Billy, now embarrassed, gave Hannah a look.

"Yes Hannah, we've met. You're feeling good tonight I see."

Dalton's Pit

"Yes I am. I have my three-favorite people in the world with me: my two brothers and my best friend. Oh, and by the way, this is my other brother Travis. He's married."

"Thanks a lot for noticing me, Hannah," Travis said.

The hours passed and the sun was beginning to creep up from behind the incredible Manhattan skyline. Billy and Travis had spent the entire night at Hannah's bedside talking with her. The plan now was for them to go back to the hotel, get cleaned up and steal a few hours of sleep. Then they would come back a little later in the day. They were hoping to take Hannah outside and maybe even see a few sights and grab some Christmas dinner; although, the doctor didn't seem to share their enthusiasm about Hannah leaving the hospital.

As they were walking out, Billy saw the doctor and spoke briefly with him.

"Doc, when we come back in a few hours we would like to take our sister out for a walk and a quick bite for Christmas, if it's okay with you."

The Corporal

Doctor Nazir was almost apologetic. "I am afraid not, Mr. Dalton. Hannah needs to be medically supervised at all times just in case anything goes wrong."

Travis then blurted out, "I have an idea, Doc. What if Nurse Donna came out with us? Then Hannah would be safe, right? I'm certain Nurse Donna would know what to do. Right?" Billy gave Travis the same look he'd given Hannah earlier, grunting slightly.

"Ok, when you come back we'll see how she feels and maybe you can go outside for a walk with one of the nurses for a half hour or so," the doctor replied.

Travis, now grinning said, "You mean Nurse Donna, right Doc?" Doctor Nazir smiled, rolled his eyes and walked away.

The boys returned to their hotel, showered, had something to eat and planned to take a quick nap. They would meet at 6 p.m. and head back uptown to take Hannah out for a walk and maybe even Christmas dinner. Billy tried to get comfortable in his room, but just couldn't fall asleep. He gave Dr. Clifford a call just to check up on the office and a few of his animals.

Dalton's Pit

"Hey Tim, how's everything going? Any issues?"

"Not really, Bill," he replied. "Just a normal week. Mrs. Seaver brought her Lab in again today. She said he was breathing funny. Talk about a hypochondriac. This is the fourth time in three weeks she's brought him in. Other than that, it's been business as usual."

"Tell me about it. She also called three times last week about his heart worm medicine. If you ask me she's the one who needs medication."

"How's Hannah doing?"

"She didn't look very good today, Tim. She seems to be getting weaker all the time. I am afraid she may not have much time left. But on a good note, she was so happy to see us. It was like she came alive the minute we walked in the room."

"Okay Bill, well you take care of her. I have everything covered over here. In fact, you can stay longer if need be. I have everything under control. I even went by the house to check on Lucky Dogs. The two college boys you hired are good. They have everything under control.

The Corporal

"Thanks, Tim. I'll give you a call either tomorrow or the next day."

Billy hung up the phone and decided he would rather take a walk around the city to clear his mind than take a nap. He put his jacket on, left the hotel room and exited the front building entrance. "Maybe I'll walk over to 42nd street," he quipped. "I haven't been down to Times Square in a while." He took out his wool ski hat and put it on, realizing just how cold it was out there. He walked about six blocks over to Times Square in the freezing cold weather. Despite the frigid temperature he saw everything that makes New York the greatest city in the world. He saw a guy jogging in shorts and a tee shirt in five-degree weather on one corner. Just across the street was a woman sitting on a folding chair playing the violin with a change box in front of her. She could have been a famous violinist for all he knew. What talent. He saw a man dressed as Santa Claus outside of a toy store shaking hands with a few of the children walking past. Then there was a guy selling pretzels right next to a woman pushing fake Louis Vuitton handbags. *This city is so alive. Alive with crazy people,* he thought to himself. Finally, he reached the corner of 42nd street

Dalton's Pit

and 7th avenue which is often referred to as "The Nexus of the Universe" because this is where everything happens. As he looked up to cross the street, he noticed a small shop two stores off the corner nestled between a Modell's department store and the entrance to the subway. Of all things to be there was an ice cream and malt shop. Immediately he thought of Sprinkles Ice Cream Shop and of Hannah. He went in and ordered a vanilla for himself and of course a strawberry for Hannah. He figured he would surprise her later when they picked her up for dinner. As he was leaving the shop he stopped in his tracks and did a double take. He saw a young family sitting in the corner sharing some ice cream. It was a husband, wife and 2 children, a boy and a girl. At first glance he thought the wife looked exactly like his ex-wife Karen. A bit frazzled, he walked out of the store and headed around the other side to get a better look from the street through the side window. As he rounded the corner he leered into the large window right where they were sitting. It looked exactly like her, but after a few seconds he realized it was someone else. Am I losing it? Is something missing in my life? He started thinking about how things would

The Corporal

have turned out differently had Flo not taken her own life. Would he have children now? Would he be sitting in a malt shop with his family? It's crazy how one event could alter the path of your life to the point where it is not even recognizable.

He couldn't get Karen out of his mind as he began walking back to the hotel. He hadn't thought about her in a long time. Mostly because he saw her true colors back when he needed her most. At times, it was still very difficult for him to deal with divorce and loneliness. When you have nothing to compare it to, sometimes what you lost appears to be magnified in a more positive way. Hindsight vision usually shows the good times clearly. The bad times often get fuzzy and you start to wonder if you made the right decision. He wondered if she ever remarried or if maybe she had her own family to care for now.

Now totally consumed with thoughts about Karen, he walked the entire six blocks back to the hotel in a mild stupor. As he approached the hotel he noticed directly across the street a homeless man holding up a sign. The sign read I used to own my own home but lost my job and

Dalton's Pit

my family and I ended up here. Please help me with any donation you could spare. He thought back to the words he'd said to Violet back on the highway in Kansas. He also felt like maybe he'd lost *his* family when he left Karen. Probably it was more likely that he was just in the mood to do something nice for someone. He walked across to the man who could not have been more than 60 years old and started a conversation with him.

"Having a rough go of it?" he asked.

The man who sported a grey handlebar mustache across his callous face and a dog tag around his neck that read "Mickey" just looked up and smiled nodding his head yes.

"I would love to help you. I really would, but I'm curious, how did you end up here? You seem like an able-bodied person. What happened to you? Do you need money because you have a drinking or drug problem? Is that why you're out on the street?"

"No sir, I used to be a happy family man. I worked in an office and had a beautiful family. I lost everything that

The Corporal

mattered to me. My wife took the kids two years ago when I lost my job. Since I don't have much education to speak of, I couldn't find another job. After that I just gave up on life. Now it's just me and Mickey.

"You must be freezing out here. Is that your dog?" he asked.

"Yes, this is my dog. My best friend Mickey. My only friend, actually."

"He looks to be about 18 months old or so, right?" Billy inquired.

"He just turned two. I brought him home the week before I lost my job. Two weeks later I lost everything. He's all I got now."

"He looks a bit malnourished. Has he had his shots? I am veterinarian. I'd like to help you and your dog if that's okay with you. The first thing you need is a good meal. Both of you."

Billy now really feeling the urge to help this man and rid himself of the bad feelings he had, said, "Come with me, sir, I will help you. What's your name?"

Dalton's Pit

"The name's O'Rourke. Charlie O'Rourke Corporal 2nd class, United States Army, Division 3679, Vietnam. What's your name, son? Where are you from?"

"My name is Doctor William Dalton. I'm in New York to see my sister Hannah at the hospital uptown. The one on 72nd street. I'm from Kansas."

Charlie responded, "Well it's very nice to meet you, Doc. Most people just pay me no mind and walk on past. I appreciate the conversation. Kansas... hmm, that's pretty far from here."

Billy was now feeling even more determined, learning that Charlie had served our country. He walked with him across the street to the hotel and spoke with the woman at the front desk.

"I would like a room for my good friend here, Corporal Charles O'Rourke."

The woman at the front desk looked Charlie up and down. It was clear he hadn't had a bath in some time. He had a filthy knapsack on his back overflowing with what looked like everything he owned. He wore a

The Corporal

dungaree jacket with a ripped army battalion patch on his sleeve. She turned to Billy and gave him a look. "Sir he's a—"

Billy cutting her off, said, "He's a friend. I would like a room for two nights for my friend Charlie, here and his dog. Please put it on my account; you should have it on file. Also, give him whatever room service or other amenities he needs and put it on my account as well."

As it turned out Charlie was no bum at all. In fact, he was a real force to be reckoned with when he was younger. He wanted to change the world. He enlisted in the army on his own and was sent to Vietnam just before his 19th birthday. While all the other kids his age staged demonstrations or waited anxiously for their numbers to be called, Charlie decided on his own what was right or wrong and enlisted on his own accord. He was brought up to never question authority or his country. Whether that was the correct philosophy remained to be seen. Nevertheless, six months after graduating high school there he was on the frontlines and in the forefront of the war. On May 10, 1969, just short of one year overseas, Charlie and his platoon

Dalton's Pit

came upon enemy fire in what would be later known as "The Battle of Hamburger Hill." For ten days they were holed up in South Vietnam as per orders from above. Out of 37 in Charlie's platoon only 6 survived the battle, with Charlie being one of them. This battle caused a lot of stir and outrage back in Washington and was considered the turning point for the U.S. within the war. Many felt it was a pointless battle since it was of little strategic value and that led to an uprising and internal revolution back in the States.

One day, a few days before the battle, Charlie and 3 of his bunk mates made a pact that should any one of them outlive the others, he would make sure to bring the deceased's belongings back to their loved ones. The four of them had a slogan "All four one and one four all." Eddie Johnson was the oldest at 28 years of age. He was married with two young girls back home in Mississippi. Tim Burke from Oklahoma was a newlywed who pushed up the wedding a few weeks and got married the day before he left for Vietnam. And then there was Charlie's best friend Mickey from Brooklyn. Mickey Fischetti was only a year older than Charlie.

The Corporal

Mickey was an Italian tough guy from Brooklyn, New York. He was an immense man, standing about 6 foot 5 and weighing about 275 pounds of solid muscle. They hit it off right away and quickly became close friends. They often talked about what they would do after the war was over, maybe go into business together. A few days later with the battle well underway and many of their platoon already gone, the 4 of them found themselves trapped between 2 lines of enemy fire. Gunfire was hailing over them like a rain storm. As soon as Tim lifted his head up from the foxhole, he was immediately torn to shreds by gunfire. There's an old saying that service men spend 99% of their time bored out of their minds and the other 1% in sheer terror. Well sheer terror was an understatement. Charlie was scared to death. Over the next half hour nearly their entire platoon was wiped out. Eddie was blown to pieces by a mortar shell while running back to base camp for backup and Mickey's leg was severed right below the knee by a hand grenade. The only reason Charlie survived was because he used Tim's body as a shield and played dead in the foxhole. A few other platoon members managed to get away when rescue copters

Dalton's Pit

finally arrived and scattered the enemy. Charlie and Mickey were the only ones who remained alive at the scene when the helicopter touched down. As they loaded Mickey onto the stretcher and into the helicopter he turned to Charlie and said, "Charlie, make sure you visit my mother in Brooklyn and tell her I love her." Charlie wiping his tears replied, "You can tell yourself, Mickey, when you get home." Mickey smiled. Five minutes later he was gone, died in the helicopter from significant blood loss. He never made it to the hospital. Charlie was then immediately merged into another platoon before he was eventually discharged and allowed to return home for good in late 1970. It was only after he returned home that he learned of Mickey's death. Upon his return home Charlie found much had changed in the States. People shunned him and he couldn't understand why. He was brought up in a military family. His dad had fought in World War II and was extremely strict with Charlie when he was a child. In fact, Charlie had called his dad sir up until the day he died. Charlie got married a few years later to a local girl and found an office job at a small advertising firm. He had two children, a boy and a girl, and tried his best to

The Corporal

live a normal life. He saw a therapist for a few years upon his return to cope with the depression and anxiety due to the things he witnessed in Vietnam. He tried his hardest to block out these memories but unfortunately often slipped up and thus turned to drinking heavily. This eventually cost him his job and his marriage. Where was the country he loved? Why couldn't someone help him work his way through his depression? He felt so alone and misunderstood. Because of his erratic behavior and binge drinking, his wife finally threw him out and divorced him after years of marriage. With nowhere else to go and no other family to speak of, Charlie was lost and alone. All these years he tried his best to block out his Vietnam experience and look where it had gotten him. Nowhere. *Maybe it is time to embrace it instead,* he thought. He knew there were VA support groups throughout the United States, perhaps it was time to deal with his pain in a different manner— head on. It was then that he realized what had been bothering him all these years. He needed to honor his commitment to Mickey and visit his mother in Brooklyn. So off he went 35 years after his promise to see if she was even still alive. All he had was Mickey's name to go

Dalton's Pit

on. Michael T Fischetti, private first class from Brooklyn, New York.

Charlie grew up in Maine and had never been to New York before. So, at the age of 54, now 35 years after Mickey's death, he needed to have some closure in his life. He needed to find Mrs. Fischetti and tell her of Mickey's last minutes alive and how much he had loved her. Charlie packed up his belongings and set out for New York with only one suitcase and his beloved puppy, aptly named Mickey by his side. His first stop was to the local army base where he did a trace on Private Fischetti and his last residence. They provided Charlie with his last known address and he quickly hopped on a bus and headed to New York. Just like that the next day there he was, standing on Emmons Avenue in Sheepshead Bay Brooklyn in front of Mickey's childhood home. He tied Mickey to the fence and was extremely nervous as he walked up the 5 steps to the stoop and approached the front door. He had no idea if his mother still lived there or if she was even still alive; nevertheless, he needed to honor his commitment to his friend. Just maybe if he could see this through it would give him some closure in life. Once he reached the top step he rang the bell

The Corporal

and stepped back, waiting for an answer. A moment later an elderly woman answered the door.

"Yes? Can I help you?" she asked.

"Umm... hello, Mrs. Fischetti? My name is Charlie. Charlie O'Rourke," he replied.

"Yes, what can I do for you, young man?"

Charlie was a bit relieved. "Well this may be difficult for you to believe, but I was best friends with your son, Mickey. We served in Vietnam together," he said.

Mrs. Fischetti's eyes immediately welled up. "My Mickey?"

"Yes, ma'am."

She opened the door wide and asked him to come in. Over the next two hours they shared stories of Mickey with each other. Charlie then relayed Mickey's message to his mom. Mickey was an only child and his father had left his mother when Mickey was a baby. His mother was all alone for so many years since Mickey died. All she had were some pictures and a few letters from

Dalton's Pit

Mickey that he wrote while in Vietnam. She didn't even have anyone to talk with about her son. She cried a good cry as the memories of Mickey came flooding back to her mind as they talked. Charlie had given her a day to remember. Mickey hoped perhaps it gave her some closure as well. After all she never knew how he died, all she knew was that it was in combat. She was so happy to find out that someone else loved Mickey. After they had lunch, Charlie began to say his goodbyes. Mrs. Fischetti kissed him on the cheek, thanked him and said, "Just give me a second; I'll be right back."

She went into the other room and returned a minute later with Mickey's dog tags and said, "Charlie, I don't have much time left; I want you to have these. I have no one to leave them to and I know you will take care of them."

Charlie took the tags and placed them around his neck as he wiped a tear from his eye and went on his way. He felt good for the first time in a very long time. Even though he had no idea where he was going or what his next move in life would be, he felt great. He untied Mickey from the fence and they went on their way.

The Corporal

That was six months ago. Since then Charlie had rented a room to sleep for a few dollars a month on the other side of Brooklyn. He had a small army pension that was barely enough to keep a roof over his head. After a few months, he left his lodgings because he could no longer afford the expense, especially with the expense of taking care of Mickey. He would rather have Mick by his side than have a roof over his head. So now he lived on the street in New York City, begging for food or whatever else passersby would give. Everyone has a story and Charlie certainly had his. A war veteran who always did the right thing by everyone, who now lived on the streets of Manhattan with a bed made of cement. Sometimes in life the ball can bounce away from you and when it does if you are not careful, it can just continue to roll downhill. Only when it stops rolling can you get up and assess your situation. By then it's often too late. Sad, really. When Charlie's ball stopped rolling he found himself living like a bum on the street with nothing. Nothing but his companion Mickey, that is. Billy, feeling somewhat emotional, turned to Charlie and handed him all the cash he had on him. Just about $65 and said, "Good luck, Charlie. I'm proud to know

Dalton's Pit

you and thank you for your service." He then handed him his Vanilla malted and with a huge smile said, "Enjoy your stay, Corporal O'Rourke."

"Thank you, sir," he said. He gave Billy a salute as if he were his army commander. Charlie looked down at Mickey and said, "This is our lucky day, Mick, our lucky day. Let's go get warmed up and get us something to eat."

Just like that Billy erased the negative feelings he had about Karen and replaced them with a feeling like no other. The kind you get by helping someone just for the sake of helping them. Knowing they can never pay you back and more importantly, knowing you didn't do it for any reason except to feel better about yourself. What a feeling. He headed to the elevator bank and returned to his room holding Hannah's strawberry malted in his hands and a satisfied grin on his face. Billy may have been in a giving mood, but no one gets Hannah's milkshake. Not even Corporal O'Rourke.

Just about two hours later Billy was getting ready to leave and head back to the hospital when his phone

The Corporal

rang. *Maybe it's Dr. Clifford*, he thought. It wasn't. It was a call from the hospital.

Donna was frantic on the phone. "Billy, hi... it's Donna from the hospital. Please come to the hospital right away, your sister is not doing well. I went into her room to check on her and she was non-responsive. The doctors are with her now. Hurry, please come here as soon as possible."

"On my way," he said, hanging up the phone abruptly and racing across the hall towards Travis's room.

Billy frantically knocked on Travis's door. "C'mon. Donna just called; Hannah's not doing well. We need to go right away." They rushed out to the front of the building and hailed a cab uptown. Billy was filled with so many emotions. *This can't be happening, not now. Not on Christmas Day.* They reached the hospital, gavethe cabbie his fare and rushed through the main entrance to the elevator bank. As soon as the elevator doors opened on the 32nd floor, Billy flew past the front desk to Hannah's room. The room was empty and Billy in a panic ran back to the front desk.

Dalton's Pit

"Where's my sister? Where's Hannah Dalton? Where's Donna the nurse?" he shrieked.

Donna, exiting the elevator, said, "Billy, thank God you're here; follow me. We had to move her immediately downstairs to ICU."

"What does that mean? Is she still alive? Please tell me she is still alive."

"I don't know; the doctors are working on her now. I came back up here to find you."

They took the elevator down to the 20th floor. The doors opened and the sign read: Pulmonary Intensive Care Unit. Doctor Nazir was standing there waiting for them.

"Right this way, gentlemen," he said.

Billy and Travis at that point were unable to catch their breaths, fearing the worst. They sat down in the two chairs adjacent to the doctor's desk. Donna, who was also very nervous, was holding on to Billy's hand.

The doctor sat on the front edge of his desk and said, "Your sister has slipped into a coma and her heart is

The Corporal

extremely weak. There is no telling at this point when or even if she will ever come out of it. I suggest you start preparing for the worst."

"That makes no sense. She was fine before," said Travis. "Can't you fix this, Doc?"

Billy lumped over in his chair with Donna still holding on to his hand." Give it to me straight, Doc, how long are we looking at?"

"If she comes out of it at all, 3 months' tops. It probably will be less than that. I am sorry, Mr. Dalton."

"What about the heart transplant? Is that still an option?" Billy asked.

"I am afraid not. In her condition, she most likely would not survive the surgery."

"Most likely? On one hand, you're saying she is certain to die in 3 months or less, but on the other you're saying she might not survive the surgery? We need to find a donor right away." Billy leaned into Donna with his head down and exhaled. Donna stroked his hair as she tried to comfort him.

Dalton's Pit

The reality they faced was that they had already been down this road before. No one would donate a heart to a 32-year-old woman whose life expectancy was a few years, let alone a few months. Billy appeared utterly exhausted. There are some people in life who always seem to keep it together during challenging times and Billy was one of them. To see him beaten down like this was alarming to Travis. Usually Billy had the solution to the problem but this time, unfortunately, there were no answers to be found.

The week that followed was not an easy one for the Dalton boys. They came to the hospital every day to visit with Hannah. Most of the time alternating shifts so that she wouldn't be alone if at some point she should awaken. When she was alone for a while Donna was sure to pick up the slack. As the week wore on Billy reached out to every possible connection he had, searching against all odds for someone to help his little sister. He called every hospital that he had delivered dogs to. He also called every person in his alumni directory in search of a donor. He then scripted a few words and called Dr. Clifford who was more than willing to create a 30 second TV commercial on behalf

The Corporal

of Hannah. Donna, meanwhile, reached out to everyone she could as well. She called the NYU medical department in hopes of something, anything. All their efforts were to no avail. Same as always, no donors.

Given the circumstances Travis decided to catch a flight the morning of New Year's Eve so he could spend New Year's Day with his wife and sons. He missed them a lot. Plus, since there was nothing left for him to do in New York, he knew he had to get back to work on Monday. He wanted to settle back in at home before the new week started. He gave his little brother the biggest of bear hugs he could and said his goodbye. He then visited Hannah one last time and told her he loved her before returning home to his family back in San Diego. Billy stayed for the holiday and had a scheduled flight for the following morning to return to Kansas. He called Dr. Clifford to inform him of his flight information and assured him he would be back at work on Jan 2nd. Having a few hours to kill before heading back to the hospital, Billy decided to visit a few of the sights he and Hannah had frequented over the past few years. He walked up Broadway and

Dalton's Pit

visited a few of the stores he and Hannah always liked. He walked past Madison Square Garden and went all the way up to the theatre district on 47th street. Then he stopped by the tree one last time and watched the skaters do their thing on the ice below. He spent almost 3 hours just walking around Manhattan getting in touch with the New York way of life before heading back over to the hospital. As he was crossing over to the other side of the street he noticed there was a little hole in the wall of a drug store with a sign that read, Champagne 2 for $15 dollars. He entered the store and bought two bottles. He placed a twenty on the counter, grabbed his bag of champagne and said, "Keep the change and Happy New Year."

The counter person replied, "Thanks, man, you too." Billy figured he would toast Hannah in the hospital with the first bottle, hang out until the ball dropped and then head on back to the hotel and finish off the second bottle by himself. He wasn't much of a drinker but he was in the mood to be different tonight. Even if only for one night. After all, it may be the last time he would see Hannah alive. He wanted to cherish it for as long as he could. He put the paper bag under his jacket

The Corporal

and entered the hospital. He didn't think the hospital would be so accommodating if they saw him smuggle alcohol into a patient's room. He wanted to toast his sister one last time. It was not the ideal way to ring in 2002 but it would have to do. It was only 8 p.m. and he had a few more hours to kill before midnight. He met with Doctor Nazir, who was leaving for the night, just to thank him for all he'd done for Hannah. The hospital was completely empty, or so it seemed. He guessed everyone else was ringing in the New Year with their families. Billy realized next year he wouldn't have Hannah to celebrate with and with Travis on the other side of the country, he wondered where would he spend New Year's or any other holiday for that matter. Again, he thought about Boston and Karen and the life he gave up a few years back. As the hours passed Billy fell further and further into a place he never was before. A place of depression.

Finally, he popped open the first bottle and held it over his head while looking down at Hannah.

"Here's to you, my baby sister. You are the light of my life. Dalton's Pit will never be the same without you."

Dalton's Pit

Just then Billy looked up and saw Donna standing in the doorway wiping the tears from her eyes.

"Can I get some of that?" she said in a tearful voice, pointing to the bottle.

Billy, a little embarrassed, said, "Sure, but I don't have any glasses."

"Not to worry. The bottle is just fine with me," she replied.

Billy handed her the bottle. She took a swig as they both sat back in the chairs alongside Hannah's bed. They spent an hour or so just talking and getting to know each other. Initially the ice breaker was Hannah. It was a subject they both knew about very well. Donna already knew a lot about Billy since he was all Hannah talked about for years. Hannah had told Donna many times that Billy would be perfect for her. Donna was now starting to understand why. Billy was honest, genuine and he loved his family. All the things in a man that Donna never had. Yet they both felt right now wasn't the time; it was not their moment. It was Hannah's. Their moment would have to wait a while.

The Corporal

This was all new for Donna. In her whole life, she had never met a man who put someone else's needs before his own. Her experiences with men like David and most of the doctors in the hospital showed they were purely self-absorbed. It was only what they wanted and when they wanted it. She started to wonder what her life would be like with a man like Billy. As the time drifted off the clock, the bottle of champagne was finally empty. They were now struggling to keep the conversation going and both seemed to be completely exhausted.

Donna scrambled for words. "Can I ask you a question, Billy?'

"Sure, anything."

"So what's Dalton's Pit?"

Billy smiled. "Well I am not sure I can tell you that. We will just have to wait for Hannah to get up to see if it's okay with her."

"I can live with that," Donna said.

Dalton's Pit

The voice on the TV in the other room could be heard. *Three, two, one… Happy New Year.* Donna looked over to Billy and said, "Happy New Year."

"Let's hope so," Billy said.

Donna, staring back at Billy, was thinking the same exact thing.

The following morning Billy returned to Kansas. The flight went as scheduled and Billy was back in the old farmhouse by 8 p.m. He checked his messages and there were some. He unpacked his bags and conked out on the couch within 15 minutes. What a week he'd had. The fact remained, though, that he was sorely needed at his practice as well as Lucky Dogs. After a good night's sleep and a good breakfast the following morning, he went out back to visit all his dogs in the compound. He walked by the stream and was greeted by many of his four legged friends. It was where he wanted to be more than anywhere else. He just wanted Hannah to be there with him. A few times he turned to the side expecting to see Hannah in her chair behind him along the path, only to realize she wouldn't be coming back here again.

The Corporal

As he was walking back to the house, he felt the urge to go visit someone he hadn't visited in some time. Someone he missed tremendously. He went back in the house, cleaned himself up and then jumped in his car and drove off. A few minutes later he parked the car and walked along the grass near the path. It was very quiet and peaceful where he was. He walked about 50 feet off the path and stopped. He knelt in front of the stone that read

Cooper Dalton

Born May 3, 1961

Died September 27, 1978

He noticed a fresh set of white lilies on his brother's grave with a note that read

Taken too soon. Rest in eternal peace

Billy wondered who would visit his brother's grave. Was it Dad? Maybe it was Austin. Could he still be lurking around here? He also noticed that the area in front of the headstone was impeccably groomed as well.

Dalton's Pit

Someone had been taking care of the grounds. But who?

He sat back on his heels and started a conversation he felt was long overdue. The last conversation they'd had was on the porch on that fateful night.

"Cooper, I am sorry it's been so long since I visited you. I am sorry I couldn't help you more than I did. I miss you so much. I miss Mom and Dad too. I hope you can find it in your heart to forgive Austin wherever you are. Our lives have changed so much since the day you left us. Dad disappeared, Mom passed away and Austin is who knows where. Hannah doesn't have much time left either. She's very sick and will join you very soon. I can no longer protect her. I hope that you are there for her when she arrives. I hope you can protect and look after her. I know you will. It comforts me to know that when she leaves me she will be joining you and Mom."

"I also wanted to thank you. The other day when Travis and I we were talking in Hannah's room he reminded me of what you did for me when I was a little kid. I had forgotten about that story but Travis reminded me of

The Corporal

everything you did for me that day. Now all these years later I understand how important what you did for me was and how it changed my life."

Apparently when Billy was about five years old there was a tornado watch in Spring Hill one September afternoon. Everyone in the family had run for cover in the storm shelter in the back yard that Dad had built a few years earlier. The shelter wasn't very big and it barely fit everyone in the family. That day after the sirens went off, everyone headed to the back yard and into the shelter. As they were getting ready to close the metal door, Billy realized that their dog Bugsy was still in the house. How could they have forgotten him? Without hesitation, he immediately jumped out of the storm shelter and back into the house to find him. After a minute passed and he did not return, Cooper jumped out as well and ran after him. As they were making their way back to the shelter after finding Bugsy, the winds picked up dramatically and swept them across the yard like rag dolls. When they got up from the grass, they saw a massive wind funnel directly in front of them. It had moved Dad's pickup truck off the road and onto its side on the front lawn. Ernie also saw it and yelled to his sons

Dalton's Pit

to hurry back. As he tried to get to them he was immediately blown back into the shelter as the winds were just too powerful. You could hear Flo's screams as the door of the shelter slammed shut above them due to the powerful turbulence. Cooper quickly grabbed both Billy and Bugsy and ran under the front porch for cover. Cooper had Billy and Bugsy nestled between him and the house while under the porch. The next few minutes were completely harrowing as the winds howled around them. They remained huddled together waiting it out. They watched the tornado's swirl not knowing if at any minute they would be sucked up into its eye like lint into a vacuum cleaner.

By the time the ordeal was over the whole yard was destroyed. Tables, chairs, the swing set, everything was in pieces. Even part of the roof had blown off. As soon as the storm passed Ernie and Travis immediately opened the shelter door and ran toward the house in a panic. After quickly scanning through the house and fearing the worst, they heard a faint cry from Bugsy underneath the porch. Travis crawled under and saw the three of them huddled in the corner with Cooper hovering on top. Billy was scared to death and clinging

The Corporal

to Cooper as tight as could be. During the whole ordeal Cooper kept telling Billy, "Don't worry, Billy, I will protect you. I won't let anything happen to you. Just stay with me." Imagine if Cooper hadn't followed him out? He most certainly wouldn't be alive today.

That's the crazy thing about life. One incident or event changes our entire trajectory onto a different path. We all have a story from our past that, had it played out differently, would have completely altered our lives forever. If you could live your life twice, it would be impossible to replicate it the second time. Too many random variables. You might end up in a different town with a different job and different wife and children and still be the exact same person. It's scary if you think about it. That's why it never makes sense to live in the past. All the things you wish you had done differently would most certainly have created a completely different path for you. Would you be willing to give up all that you have for all that you ever wanted? Mistakes are a vital part of life and place you exactly where you are today. Billy wiped the tears from his eyes, rose to his feet and said, "I love you, my brother, until we meet again."

Dalton's Pit

He walked back to the car, started it up and pulled away. It was time to return home and begin life once again. It seemed like every few years he had to restart his life again. First with Karen and now with Hannah. When was it going to get better? When would he have a family again? When would he receive a call from thehospital? Oddly enough he immediately thought of Donna.

Somehow in our moments of deepest thought the things we care about most come to mind. He just realized that he wanted Donna. He needed to hear her voice. She was so amazing. The only time he felt good about himself was when she was around. It was so clear now. Maybe Hannah knew it all along. After all she was smarter than Billy when it came to matters of the heart, that's for sure. He loved her. He loved both of them, that is.

Chapter 6

Best Friends

Rose had been living in San Antonio for two years when Thomas started kindergarten. Her childhood friend Joanne had taken her in when she arrived back in the year 2000. The past few years had been very difficult for her. She was only 19 years old when she arrived, she had a young son and very little money to speak of. The money Violet gave her was helpful early on, but that money was now long gone. Still, Rose had this confidence about her and she firmly believed that nothing was going to defeat her. She was an extremely strong willed person. Despite all her struggles and money issues, she was so happy to be rid of her prior life and Tom Sr. that nothing seemed insurmountable. Nothing, that is, except her husband Tom finding her. She enrolled in some nursing school classes after obtaining her GED last year. She went 3 nights a week

Dalton's Pit

to the local community school while Joanne helped with Thomas. She also got a part time job as a school crossing guard during the day. Rose, who had just turned 22 years old, didn't have much of a social life, though. Her entire life revolved around Thomas and making his life the best it could be. She had been on a couple of dates since she arrived but nothing serious. This was fine with her, especially since she needed the time to get her act together both mentally and financially. Dealing with romance now would only complicate things further. There was always time for that in the future. Besides, most of the men her age weren't in the market for a pre-made family anyway. Raising Thomas, going to school at night and making just a bit more than minimum wage was the way it went for a while for Rose.

Thank God for her friend Joanne who she had grown up with back in Tennessee. They lived two doors away from each other growing up. Ever since they met at the age of five years old in kindergarten they were inseparable. Their grammar school was only two blocks from their houses so every day their mothers would take turns walking them back and forth to school. When they were old enough they walked together themselves.

Best Friends

Wherever Rose was Joanne was and vice versa. One day when they were about 11 years old they were sitting on the stoop in front of Joanne's house and one of the older girls from the neighborhood jumped on Joanne's bicycle and took off. The girl had to be about 14 years old and was one of those kids who was always up to no good. Rose immediately chased after the girl with Joanne following behind her. Sure enough, the girl rode Joanne's bike into the school yard a few blocks away. When Rose and Joanne entered the school yard they saw a crowd of older girls hanging out smoking cigarettes and laughing with the girl who stole the bike.

Joanne turned to Rose. "C'mon, let's go. Forget about it; my dad will buy me a new one."

"No way, that's your bike," said Rose.

"Yeah, but I don't think she wants to give it back. Let's just forget about it," she said, seemingly shaken.

Rose, undeterred, walked directly toward and into the crowd of girls. "Excuse me, but my friend wants her bicycle back."

Dalton's Pit

The girls didn't even acknowledge Rose; they completely ignored her and laughed to themselves.

Rose tried again. "I said, excuse me but we want the bicycle back." She tapped the girl on the shoulder.

The girl whirled around and flicked her cigarette at Rose, hitting her on the shoulder. "Yeah, what do you want?"

"My friend wants her bicycle back."

"Go ahead, try and take it. I dare you," she said.

Rose looked the girl directly in the face and said, "You don't scare me. Give it back."

Joanne was getting nervous. "Rose, c'mon forget about it."

Rose continued to stare at the girl unfazed. The girl got all up in Rose's face with this angry snarl and just stared at her. Usually this tactic would scare just about any of the other girls in the neighborhood. Not Rose, not this time. Rose just gave the same angry look back to the girl. They were now standing nose to nose. Although

Best Friends

Rose's nose had to be a foot closer to the ground. The entire group of girls gathered around waiting for their next move. Rose didn't flinch for what seemed to be at least 2 clock minutes. Her heart was beating out of her chest, but she didn't show the least bit of nervousness on the outside. The age-old definition of courage maintains that it's the ability to hide the fact that you're scared out of your mind. This was the case for Rose.

Finally, the older girl flinched first and said, "Go ahead, take it. It's too small for me anyway."

Rose now had to pass by all the older girls to get to the other side of the yard where the bike was parked. She flipped up the kickstand, grabbed the bike without saying a word as her heart was pumping like never before. The two of them walked out of the school yard with victory in hand. As they approached the street across the way, Joanne looked at Rose and said, "Oh my God, that was amazing. I can't believe you did that. Weren't you scared?"

"Um no. Just kidding, I was scared out of my mind. I figured though if she beat me up once, maybe she

Dalton's Pit

wouldn't want to bother with me the next time. Maybe she would think that I was too much trouble to terrorize and move on to someone else."

Isn't that the way it is with all bullies? The more you avoid them, the stronger they get. If you just accept the fact that if just once you stood up to them and took a beating, it could simply end there. The fact is most times you won't even have to take the beating because they will back down first. It's basically a game of chicken. It comes down to who blinks first. In this case the bully blinked first and she never bothered them again. Rose may not have been a strong bodied person, given her relatively small stature, but she was a strong-willed person which usually wins out over time.

The girls returned to Joanne's house with a new feeling. A feeling of accomplishment. It also made them closer than ever before. Best friends forever. That's why Joanne was devastated when her mom told her they were moving away.

Joanne's father was a very wealthy recording agent in Nashville and had many of the local country stars under

Best Friends

contract. Unfortunately for his wife and daughter he never met a young female country starlet he didn't fancy. To say that he was a womanizer would be putting it mildly. Joanne's mother Barbara finally had enough one day when she caught him red handed with one of his young hopefuls. Barbara divorced her husband when Joanne was only 12 years old. She then abruptly moved away from Tennessee to start a new life, leaving Rose behind without her best friend. They later found out that her father was arrested for improper behavior with a 16-year-old girl. He went to jail for a 3 to 5 stretch and when he came out his business was destroyed, given his reputation as a sleazy pedophile. Rose and Joanne were so close that they continued to stay in touch despite living in different states. They would exchange letters back and forth all throughout their early teen years. Rose wrote to Joanne when she got married and when she had Thomas Jr. Joanne was also aware of what Rose was going through with Tom Sr. So, when Rose needed a place to stay, the first person she thought of was Joanne. She was the logical choice because she lived in another state and far away from Tom Sr. The other reason was because Tom had never

Dalton's Pit

met her nor did even know who she was. Rose somehow managed to keep Joanne a secret from Tom all these years. It was the perfect way for Rose to stay off the grid. Rose's biggest fear since the day she ran out of that hospital was Tom finding out where she was and what he would do if he found her. It had been over two years since the day she ran away from him and so far, she'd managed to stay hidden from him all that time. She was so scared of Tom finding her that she cut off all contact with her old life and then even changed her last name for fear he may track her down. Still, after two years she was still always hesitant about meeting new people for fear they could be connected somehow to Tom. She often wondered if he was even still alive, since she knew he would stop at nothing to find her and Thomas Jr.

Thomas Jr. was adjusting well and even made a few friends at his new school. Rose had become the crossing guard at his school for two reasons. One was the money but more importantly two was to watch Thomas when he was out in the schoolyard. This way she could make sure Tom Sr. wouldn't show up and snatch Thomas away. Every day after her morning shift she would sit in

Best Friends

Violet's old car outside the school doing her nursing course work. At lunch time, she would come out, cross the children who went home for lunch, then watch Thomas in the schoolyard. When lunch time was over, she went back to the car and waited for 2:30 p.m. when school ended. Then at 2:30 p.m. when the younger children came out she would put Thomas in the old car, lock the doors and finish crossing the children. Thomas was in eye view at all times. When she finished, she would drive Thomas and his friend A.J. home from school. A.J. lived a few blocks away in the mobile home park and Rose would often watch him after school. The boys would do their homework together and when finished usually play some video games. A.J.'s parents both worked and his mom Tricia would come by and pick him up straight after work around 5:30 p.m. A.J. loved hanging out with Thomas. Due to A.J.'s size, though, he was often picked on in school. He was much bigger than the rest of the other boys in their kindergarten class. He looked to be about 3 or 4 years older than all the other students. He was born with a glandular problem which in turn caused him weight issues. This issue also caused growth spurts that

Dalton's Pit

happened significantly earlier than most other children his age. A.J. also used an inhaler and wasn't able to run like the other children. Needless to say, A.J.'s early years were very difficult for him as well as his mother. As early as 3 years of age he was sort of an outcast with other children. The children his age were apprehensive around him, given his size, while the older children similar in stature were obviously much further advanced. The only person he had to play with was his mother. He became very dependent on her and very insecure about who he was and what he looked like.

Thomas didn't care what A.J. looked like. He was his only real friend in the class. They would come home and play Nintendo for hours on end on Joanne's living room TV. Their favorite game was Super Mario Bros. They would pretend to be Mario and Luigi and hop around the house jumping on the pillows and couches pretending they were pipes and ledges. A.J. was always Luigi because he was so much bigger than Thomas. When they weren't playing Super Mario, they would just hide the Nintendo cartridges on each other and play a game of hot and cold. A.J. never wanted to go home when his mom would come to pick him up. He

Best Friends

would always beg her to stay for a while since Joanne's house was so much nicer than theirs. Joanne's house had an upstairs, a basement and a nice big yard. It also had a big screen TV and the new Nintendo game console that A.J. wanted.

Some nights A.J. would convince his mom to let him sleep over Thomas's house. One Saturday night Tricia and A.J. had come over to eat dinner. After dinner was over the girls decided to hang out on the back porch and have a glass of wine while the boys played their video games in the living room. Rose and Joanne became much closer friends with Tricia that night. They shared with Tricia about their childhood and how they were best friends growing up. Joanne shared the bicycle story and how brave Rose was as a child. Tricia then shared her story. She told them how her dad was an executive in a large company back in San Antonio who had a lot of money. She also shared with them that her dad didn't like her husband, disapproved of their marriage and how she hadn't spoken to him in years. Tricia needed a night like this. She was lonely since her husband was always on the road working. In fact, that's the one thing all three of the women shared. They were lonely and

Dalton's Pit

needed support from each other. Rose however held back her story about Tom Sr. She was too afraid to share this information with anyone new. In fact, that night Tricia was the first one who had ever asked her about Thomas's father. She grew to like Tricia, but when she asked about her child's father she lied.

"So now you know my story, what about yours? Are you divorced?" Tricia asked.

Rose seemed a little uncomfortable and looked over at Joanne.

"Well my story is complicated," Rose said.

"Isn't everyone's?" Tricia replied.

"Well yes. Okay... Umm."

Rose quickly tried to conjure up a story, but panicked and blurted out, "I am a widow."

"Oh, I am so sorry. Please forgive me; I had no idea."

"That's okay, I don't like to talk about it, but my husband died a few years ago. He was accidentally shot

Best Friends

one night while trying to break up a fight. He was a good man," she said. "Always thinking about everyone else."

Joanne cut in and said, "Hey, let's go inside, the mosquitos are coming out. Trish, would you like another glass of wine?"

Rose felt horrible about lying to Trish but knew she would never risk Thomas's safety for anyone. After all she'd only known Trish a short time. She couldn't possibly trust her with this information. Just then she looked over at the boys hopping around in the living room and saw how happy Thomas was. That was more important to her than anything.

Several hours later the wine bottle was empty and the boys were fast asleep on the couch. Before they knew it, the clock said 3 a.m. Trish, now a bit out of sorts, ended up sleeping on the couch after they brought the boys up to bed. Rose had Tom Sr. on the brain. She couldn't shake it. The always tough Rose was crying in the bathroom upstairs when Joanne walked in.

"Hey? What? Why are you crying?" Joanne asked.

Dalton's Pit

"I am just scared."

"Scared of what?"

"Of everything."

"Impossible, you're the one who always told me never to be scared. You can't be scared. You're the rock. You're my protector. Come here."

Rose leaned her head into Joanne and said, "What if he finds me? What if he finds Thomas? I am scared he will kill us. I don't know what to do. I can't trust anyone but you. You're all I have."

"He won't find you. You did everything right. You moved away; you changed your name. He will never find you." Rose smiled and hugged her best friend and just nodded her head.

Yes, Rose did change her last name, and not to Dawson. She changed it when she enrolled Thomas in school last year. She thought long and hard about it and changed it to the only logical name she could think of. Harrison. After all Violet Harrison was the only person besides Joanne who helped her when she was down. She

Best Friends

figured she owed it to her. They were now Rose and Thomas Harrison. She even contemplated changing Thomas's first name as well but she was afraid that would affect Thomas in other ways. The reality was that he was just a baby at the time and didn't know what happened between his mother and father. In fact, he hadn't brought up his father in a long time. She thought it best to leave it alone.

One day after school just a few weeks later Rose had this strange feeling that someone was following her home. At every light, she would look in the rearview mirror, but no one would be there. This feeling continued for several days. Now her mind started to wander. She feared that maybe Tom had found her. Maybe he was following her and was going to kill her or come in the house at night and kidnap Thomas. The mind can be a dangerous weapon sometimes and will play tricks on you if you allow it. Paranoia was now getting the best of her. This feeling persisted for several weeks, causing Rose to become a different person. Joanne sensing something was going on, questioned her.

Dalton's Pit

"What's wrong with you lately? Everything okay?"

Rose decided to open up. "I just can't get the feeling out of my head that Tom is following me. I feel his presence. I am afraid he will take my son away."

Joanne assured her it was only in her mind and that there was no way Tom knew where she was. Rose wasn't convinced and shared with Joanne that she was thinking about moving again. She didn't want to take the chance that Tom was on to them and knew where she was.

"Why don't you let me look into Tom's whereabouts? After all he doesn't know who I am. Maybe I could check him out and once we know everything is fine you can relax again. He shouldn't be very hard to find. I know his name and I know where he lived. I can do a search on the computer and then check him out. What do you say?"

"I suppose it couldn't hurt, but I'm still thinking of moving on. I just can't take any chances. Thank you so much for everything, Joanne. I don't know where I would be without you."

Best Friends

They sat down for dinner and Joanne mentioned a police sergeant friend she had dated a few times who might be able to look Tom up. She said she trusted him completely and figured he could pull up any file the police might have on him. Rose agreed and then seemed a bit more comfortable after their discussion.

"Ok, maybe that's an option. I just need to know. I can't risk losing my son. Please call him tomorrow if you can."

"First thing tomorrow; don't worry, I promise."

A few days later while still waiting on Joanne's friend for the results, Thomas had come down with a low-grade fever. Although Thomas had to stay home from school, Rose still had her job to do. She still had to go to the school and cross the children. Joanne stayed home with Thomas while Rose reluctantly left her son and went off to school. She kept calling Joanne throughout the day to make sure everything was fine.

"How is he? Everything okay?" she asked.

"He's fine, will you stop worrying," Joanne replied after the third phone call.

Dalton's Pit

"Are all the doors in the house locked?"

"Yes. Rose you must relax. Me and Mom are here and everything is fine. He is playing his game on the couch."

"Okay. I will be home by 3:30."

At 2:15 p.m. Rose was almost done for the day. She crossed A.J., put him in the car and locked the doors like she always did. She left the back window open just a crack so A.J. could get some fresh air. She then walked back to the corner to finish her shift and cross the remaining children. One of the older classes was being held after school for bad behavior so Rose had to wait a few extra minutes for them to be released. When she returned to the car 10 minutes later her heart was in her throat. The driver's side rear door was wide open. There was no sign of A.J. Panicked, she immediately knew. It had to be Tom. He must have been following her all week. She didn't understand, though; why take A.J.? She gathered her thoughts for a moment and surmised that maybe Tom hadn't seen his son in a while and just grabbed A.J. thinking he was Thomas. If he had been following her he would have known that she made

Best Friends

Thomas sit in the car at that time every day while she crossed the older children. The window itself was open about halfway now. Maybe he pushed the window down or somehow got A.J. to open the door, then simply grabbed him without looking. She now became more worried as to what would happen to A.J. when Tom realized he wasn't Thomas. Would he dump A.J. off somewhere or worse, would he even harm him? Rose remembered when Tom used to get angry and the irrational behavior he would exhibit. One time Rose had spilt milk on the kitchen floor and Tom put his fist through the sheetrock wall in the kitchen because she didn't clean it up fast enough. He had this incredible mean streak that could be set off at any time, by almost anything. What would he do when he figured out A.J. wasn't Thomas?

She ran back into the school to find Principal Spitzer. She explained to him what happened and how someone opened her rear driver's side window and must have taken A.J. Principal Spitzer immediately called 911 and informed the police department. He then grabbed all the remaining teachers in the school and created a search party for A.J. Rose then had to make the most

Dalton's Pit

difficult call of her life. The one every mother including herself dreads receiving. She called Tricia on her cell phone.

"Tricia, A.J. is missing. I was crossing the children at school and he disappeared.

"What? He disappeared? How? Oh, my God, I'll be right there." Tricia hung up the phone and headed out from work in horror.

Rose was now thinking to herself, was it Tom? Maybe it wasn't? Maybe her mind was just imagining that it was Tom. Maybe it was someone else. Should she tell Tricia her thoughts? Could Tom be tracking her? Did he think Thomas was the kid in the car? If it was him then he knew where she lived. As soon as he realized it wasn't Thomas, would he go back to their house? She had to get home right away. She jumped into her car, sped home and raced into the house. Thomas was playing on the couch and Joanne was just starting to prepare dinner. Joanne noticed the look on Tricia's face.

"OMG, what's wrong? Did something happen?"

Best Friends

"Someone broke into my car and A.J. is missing. I think it may have been Tom."

"OK, calm down, Rose. How could it be Tom? Why A.J.? That doesn't make any sense."

"Maybe he saw a kid in my car and assumed it was Thomas. Maybe he has been tracking my movements the whole time. I am scared he will come here next. I have to leave this place right away."

Rose ran upstairs grabbed a suitcase and started throwing clothes into the case. She then ran back down and grabbed Thomas. Not thinking clearly at this point, she told Joanne she had to get out of the house.

"Slow down. I think you are imagining things. How do you even know it was Tom?" Joanne asked.

"I just know. I can feel it," she replied.

"What about Tricia and A.J.? You can't just leave. A.J. is missing. She needs your help to find him."

Dalton's Pit

Rose was about to walk out the front door when she realized that Joanne was right. She stopped in her tracks and started to cry.

"Come sit down here. Think about it for a minute. If this was Tom and he was following you, wouldn't he know that Thomas was home sick? And wouldn't he know his own son? After all, A.J. and Thomas look nothing alike. Don't you think your imagination is getting away from you a bit? Let's wait for Tricia and then figure out what do to. We must find A.J. Also, don't mention anything about Tom to Tricia yet, since we have no idea if it was him."

Thomas walked in from the living room. "What's happened, Mom? Did you say Daddy's here? Where's A.J.? What's going on?"

"Don't worry baby, everything is fine. Daddy is not here. A.J. is fine. Go back inside and play your game.

Thomas left and jumped back on the couch to continue playing his game. Just then Tricia rang the bell and quickly entered the house.

Best Friends

"The whole town is out looking for him. I just came from the police station. Tell me what happened," Tricia asked.

Rose now crying hysterically said, "I always put the boys in the car for about 10 minutes, lock the doors and finish crossing the rest of the children. I can always see the car from where I am standing on the corner.

For some reason, I must have looked away for just a moment and when I came back to the car, the back door was open and A.J. was gone. I am so sorry."

Guilt was now consuming Rose. Even if it wasn't Tom who had taken him, it was still her fault A.J. was missing. Rose was afraid to mention her fear that it might be her ex-husband, so instead she said, "C'mon, let's go out and look for him. I promise you we will find him. He couldn't have gotten very far."

Rose got behind the wheel of the old car with Tricia in the passenger seat and they set out to look for A.J. Joanne and Thomas stayed behind just in case A.J. came wandering back to the house. Tricia with anguish in her

Dalton's Pit

voice started rambling on about A.J. and how the bigger kids would always pick on him in school.

"I bet it was one of the older kids who pick on him because of his size and awkwardness. He told me last week that a few of the fifth-grade boys were throwing stuff at him in the cafeteria and calling him names. One of them even pushed him to the floor. We need to get their names from the school and go to their houses. I think one of the kid's name is Murphy. Steven Murphy."

"I know where the Murphy's live. It's only three blocks from here," Rose said.

She immediately turned the car around and headed toward the Murphy residence.

"Let me do the talking, Trish. You don't know if they have anything to do with this." Tricia just sat there nodding in agreement.

They approached the Murphy's front steps and rang the bell. The boy Steven opened the door and said, "Yeah, what do you want?"

Best Friends

"Steven, my name is Rose. I am Thomas Harrison's mom from the first grade.

"So. Who cares? What do you want, lady?" he replied.

"We are looking for A.J., Thomas's friend."

"Oh, the fat kid. He shouldn't be too hard to find," he added with a chuckle.

Tricia standing by the car, heard Steven's remark and approached the house in a fit of rage.

"Hey, you little jerk, where is my son? You pick on him all the time. If you don't tell me where he is, I will beat you up myself."

Upon hearing the screaming outside her house, Mrs. Murphy came to the front door.

"Excuse me, but who the hell are you yelling at?"

"I am yelling at your son. He is a bully and better watch his back," Tricia yelled.

"Oh yeah? You better watch yours, if you know what's good for you. You can't talk to my son that way."

Dalton's Pit

Rose got in between the two women and tried to calm things down a bit.

Rose turned to Mrs. Murphy and said, "Look, Mrs. Murphy, Tricia's son is missing from school and we came here to ask if your son knew where he was. That's all."

"Why would my son know where her son is?"

"Well to be honest, your son has been picking on him a lot lately and we just assumed he may know what happened to him," Rose added.

"Is this true, Steven? Were you picking on this kid?"

"Well, sort of. I mean, Timmy Sullivan usually does it. I just laugh," Steven said.

"Do you know where he is, Steven?" she asked.

"No Mom, I swear. We didn't do anything," he replied.

Mrs. Murphy then smacked the back of Steven's head and pulled him inside.

Best Friends

"I am sorry, ladies. He won't be picking on your son anymore; I'll see to that. I hope you find him."

It was approaching 5 o'clock and A.J. had been missing for about 2 hours already. The women had spent the last hour and a half roaming the area, turning the town upside down. The school principal had called every child's parents in the school to see if they saw anything or knew where A.J. was. Nothing. Rose and Tricia split up and Rose started ringing the doorbells of all the neighbors across from the school. Tricia meanwhile continued driving up and down the surrounding streets. As the sun began to set, the fear began to kick in. Tricia realized that she would soon have to call her husband. He was a truck driver and had been away on a trip for 10 days driving merchandise up to Utah. He wasn't due to return until the weekend. Not only was she worried about A.J. but she was also worried about telling her husband that he was missing. He was a bit of a hot head and would probably blame Tricia. She wanted to wait as long as she could before she had to make that call.

It was 8 o'clock at night. Tricia continued circling around the school area in Rose's car. Rose continued walking

Dalton's Pit

around on foot, feeling guilty. She realized that she may have to tell Tricia about her ex-husband. Suddenly out of nowhere a woman who lived directly across from the school came out of her yard screaming. She was an elderly lady who hadn't been out of her house all day. She had just come out to throw her garbage in the pail when she spotted a leg sticking out between the garbage pails in the back of her house. Luckily Rose was in earshot as she made the rounds. She ran over to the woman's driveway as fast as she could and there he was. A.J. was lying unconscious on the cement in the back of the woman's driveway. The woman's house was exactly where Rose parked her car, directly across from the school. How could they have missed this? More importantly, she realized that many hours may have passed since he passed out and that didn't bode very well for A.J.'s well-being. Rose immediately sprang into action and her skills as a nursing student were put to the test. The woman meanwhile ran back in her house to call 911.

Rose worked on A.J., giving him C.P.R. and elevating his upper body. She tried everything she could think of. After a few moments, he opened his eyes and smiled.

Best Friends

"Hello A.J., do you know who I am?" Rose said.

A.J. just looked at her and said, "I'm hungry, Aunt Rose. Can we go to McDonald's?"

Rose just smiled and said to herself, *Thank you, God.*

The paramedics arrived a few moments later and took over. Rose, however, had done her job. She took care of A.J. until they showed up. Rose was even more confused, wondering if maybe it wasn't Tom after all. Tricia meanwhile had pulled up in the car a moment before the ambulance arrived to see her son alive and cradled in Rose's arms. She immediately fell in the grass where A.J. was and kissed her son. She also kissed Rose. The paramedics then placed A.J. on a gurney and lifted him into the back of the ambulance. Tricia rode with A.J. in the ambulance to the emergency room while Rose followed them in her car. A.J. was very groggy but somewhat aware of where he was. Tricia, however, still had no idea what happened to her son; she was just very thankful he was still alive. That was all that mattered to her. That and the fact that she did not have to call her husband. She also was thankful to Rose for

Dalton's Pit

entering her life when she did. She would be indebted to her forever. She sat in the back of the ambulance with a smile on her face and held A.J.'s hand for the entire trip to the hospital.

The medical staff at St. Ann's Hospital were very concerned with A.J.'s vitals and rushed him right into the ER. They connected him to an IV and started to examine him.

"Who did this to my baby? Why would someone hurt him? I want to know who did this to my baby. He is such a good boy," Tricia lamented.

Rose again had the urge to tell Tricia about her ex, but now it seemed less likely that Tom had anything to do with this. Instead she simply consoled her and said don't worry, he will be fine. The nurse then escorted the ladies out to the waiting area as they began to examine A.J.

What seemed like days was only about 20 minutes when the doctor finally returned to the waiting room. Tricia and Rose jumped out of their chairs to their feet.

Best Friends

"How is my baby?" Tricia asked.

The doctor asked both women to come into his office and have a seat. He explained to Tricia that her son had had a diabetic seizure and could have slipped into a coma had he not been found when he was. He said it was a miracle he survived after being unconscious for so long and it was a good thing Rose was there to assist him before the paramedics arrived.

"The work done by Rose prior to the paramedics arriving on the scene was paramount to his survival," the doctor said.

Rose was relieved. She turned to the doctor and said, "So this wasn't a kidnapping? No one took A.J. from the car?"

"A kidnapping? I highly doubt that. A.J. mumbled to one of the nurses that he could not breathe so he opened the back door just to get some fresh air. He stepped out onto the sidewalk and got really dizzy. He walked about 20 yards into some woman's back yard and then needed to lie down. Apparently, he was there the whole time, right behind the fence between two garbage pails."

Dalton's Pit

The doctor then added, "However, I must tell you, A.J. is still a very sick boy. He will need to remain here in the hospital for at least a few days so we can run further tests. His AIC levels are currently through the roof. I assume you know he has a glandular problem. Who is his doctor? I need to speak with him."

"Yes of course, he has been on medication for about 2 years. Let me grab his doctor's card."

Tricia pulled a business card out of her bag and handed it to the doctor. "Here is the doctor's information. If there is anything else, please let me know as soon as possible. Thank you, doctor. Can I see him now?"

"Sure, but only for a minute. He is asleep."

Tricia and Rose were ushered into the emergency room to see A.J. fast asleep in the hospital bed.

Tricia said to Rose, "Look at my baby. I love him so much."

Tricia kissed A.J. on his head then turned to the doctor.

Best Friends

"Please do everything you can to make sure my baby gets better, doctor. Thank you so much."

"You're welcome. It's a good thing your friend Rose was there. Had she not found him when she did, he might not be here today. I am sorry; I will do everything I can for your little boy. I wish I had better news for you today."

Tricia was hopeful but also devastated. She looked up at Rose and sank her head into her shoulder, sobbing as they walked out of the hospital.

On the ride home Tricia thanked Rose for being there for her. She thanked her for everything she had done for her son, from picking him up every day from school, feeding him every afternoon, to now saving his life.

"Where would I be without you Rose? You are my best friend. How can I every repay you?" she asked.

"There's no need to repay me; we are best friends for life. You, me and Joanne, the three musketeers. It's funny, though, I just thought of something. A few years ago, a woman helped me and Thomas when we needed it most. When I asked her how I could ever repay her she simply said, 'You can pay me back by helping the next person you find who is in need of help just like you were.' That statement will stick with me the rest of my life. I am happy that the person I helped was you. Maybe you can help the next person you find just like I did."

"It's a deal," she replied.

Rose was now able to breathe a sigh of relief. Tom did not kidnap A.J. He did not know where she lived. She couldn't wait to get home and tuck her son into his bed. Still, in the back of her mind she felt that maybe it was time to move on. Maybe move out west and start over again. She didn't want to live in constant fear the rest of her life, but that decision was for another day. Right now, she was happy and she just wanted to see her boy.

Rose drove Tricia home and then rushed to her own home to see if Thomas was still awake. She wanted to kiss her boy goodnight. As she pulled into the driveway Joanne was waiting by the door. Rose explained the

Best Friends

whole story of what happened to A.J. to Joanne. She already knew. It was on the local TV station an hour ago.

"Is Thomas awake?" she asked.

"He just fell asleep about 15 minutes ago," Joanne replied.

Rose walked in the house and up to Thomas's room and kissed Thomas on his forehead. He was fast asleep with his Super Mario stuffed toy cradled in his arms. She looked down and said softly to him,

"Yes, Thomas, A.J. is fine and no, Daddy isn't coming home anytime soon." She covered him up and thought to herself, *I need to find out just where Tom Sr. is.*

Chapter 7

Visiting the Past

It had been touch and go with Hannah for several months now. The good news was that she was still around, the bad news was that her health hadn't improved all that much. She had rebounded nicely since Christmas only to have regressed a little bit thereafter. Travis, who was back home in California, checked in with Billy each week on her progress. Billy had been coming up to see Hannah in New York religiously every weekend since the calendar turned to 2002. Some visits were good, others not so good. Some weekends Hannah slept the entire time Billy was there. This didn't deter Billy, though. He talked to her as if she were wide awake and still 11 years old back on the farm. He kept her up to date about how Lucky Dogs was progressing and all the changes he was making to the compound. He also filled her in on all her favorite animals at the compound and how they were doing. He even brought

Dalton's Pit

some pictures he took of the new dogs he added to the compound just in case Hannah woke up. He labeled them by breed and name just like he used to when they were little. He believed with all his heart that she could hear him and when she finally awoke she would remember everything he said. He envisioned they were sitting in Dalton's Pit under the porch and he was describing the frog he just fished out of the lake. Sometimes she would briefly open her eyes just for a moment and smile. He took it as a sign from her that she could hear him. At least that's what he told himself. This was the way it went for a while. This was his life. Billy, however, sensed that things were about to change and that she was nearing the end. There was no way at this point of getting a heart for Hannah, and Billy started to prepare for the inevitable. He kept Travis in the loop every Sunday on his way back to Kansas.

Travis was a different sort of guy. He kept most of his feelings to himself. He wasn't as smart as Billy nor was he the type of guy to lead the charge unless he had to. While Billy was handling everything with Hannah, Travis remained in California and continued to work and coach his younger sons' football team as if everything was

Visiting the Past

normal. Travis's oldest son Mason was now 17 and about the same size as Travis. He had his father's freakish size but unlike his father, he also excelled in school. Something that had eluded Travis all his life. Mason played middle linebacker in high school and checked in at about 6'5 and 250 lbs. or so. When he was on the high school football field he looked like a man playing against children. It almost wasn't fair to the other teams in the league. Several colleges had been scouting him for months now and Travis was eagerly awaiting all the offers. From time to time, he still dreamt of his own missed opportunities as a young man and what could have been. Nothing would please Travis more than to have his son realize the dreams that he couldn't back when he graduated high school.

One day out of the blue, Travis had just gotten home from work and received a phone call. It was from a new coach from a top-level Division 1 college football program.

Travis answered the phone. "Hello?"

"Mr. Dalton?" the voice said.

Dalton's Pit

"Yes, this is me. Who is this?" he replied. Initially Travis had gotten a bit nervous, figuring this had something to do with Hannah.

"Hello, Mr. Dalton, how are you? My name is Bobby Petrino. I am the new head football coach for the Louisville Cardinals out here in Louisville, Kentucky. Do you have moment?"

Travis raised his eyebrows and said, "Sure thing, Coach."

"I would like to talk to you about your son Mason. A few of my scouts have been watching him play over the past few months and are very impressed with his abilities both on and off the field. I was hoping we could meet with you and Mason to talk about the opportunity for Mason to join our fine university and become a member of our football program. We are prepared to offer your son a full academic and athletic scholarship come this fall. Would you be open to talk?"

Travis was never one to mask his excitement "Wow, sure, Coach. We'd love to talk."

Visiting the Past

Coach Petrino replied, "Great. I was hoping both you and Mason could come visit our school next weekend and we could talk some more. I would like to introduce Mason to some of the players on the team and show him our exceptional facilities. How does that sound to you?"

"That sounds awesome. Let me talk with Mason and we will get back to you really soon."

"Okay, once you call me back I will set up a schedule for Mason for next weekend."

"Thanks, Coach, we look forward to meeting you. Woohoo."

"Sure thing, Mr. Dalton. I look forward to your call. See you soon."

Travis could hardly contain his excitement. The call he had been waiting for since he was a teenager finally came through. He hung up the phone, floated into the kitchen and swept his wife Ivy off the ground. He tossed her around like a little girl being swung through the air by her dad.

Dalton's Pit

"Wow. Let me guess. Which school called?" Ivy said.

"Louisville called, that was the coach Bobby Petrino. The Louisville Cardinals, can you believe it? Our son just got a call from the Louisville Cardinals. They're giving him a free ride to a Division 1 school. I can't believe it. I can't wait to tell him. When we come home we're gonna celebrate. Put the dishes away; we are going out tonight."

"I am so happy for him and for you, honey. I know what this means to you." Ivy gave her husband a big kiss on the lips and said, "Go get 'em, honey. Go tell your boy. You deserve this."

Travis was on such a high that he had to sit down for a moment just to catch his breath. He was filled with so many emotions. Elation for his son, sadness for himself, his failures. In the end as expected the excitement for his son's future easily won out over the sadness for himself and he jumped to his feet. "I have to go tell him. I am going to the field right now. I can't wait for him to come home. I have to tell him now." He grabbed his keys off the kitchen table and headed out to his son's

Visiting the Past

high school where the team practice was just about to end.

He let out with another loud "Yeah" as he exited the front door and then pulled out of the driveway as if he were driving on a cloud. As he pulled into the parking lot of his son's high school, he had to park about 30 yards adjacent to the field. He got out and walked around the bend to where his son's team was finishing up practice. Beaming from ear to ear he saw his son Mason standing in his usual middle linebacker spot in the center of the field. His identity could never be mistaken, given his massive size. He looked like Gulliver out there surrounded by all the Lilliputians. He watched for a moment before getting his son's attention. Mason saw his dad and gave him a nod as the ball was being snapped. Just at that moment Travis's mind quickly travelled back in time to 1972 and the state championship game.

The stands were completely packed. He remembered the last series of the game with his Spring Hill Warriors trailing 46-42. It was 3rd and goal from the 6-yard line. Travis had already amassed 32 carries for 254 yards and

Dalton's Pit

5 touchdowns. The quarterback Greg Whipple took the snap from center with just under 30 seconds left on the clock. The whole stadium knew Travis would get the ball. Just as the ball was snapped; however, Greg bobbled it for a moment and then had to fake it to Travis while he regained possession. After missing the handoff, he then tried to bootleg right to find an open receiver or run it himself into the end zone. When suddenly out of nowhere a defender punched the ball right out of the quarterback's hand. Travis could still envision the ball bouncing around for what seemed like forever. Just as it looked like the game was over, Travis wrestled the ball away from the defender at the 3-yard line and bulldozed his way into the end zone carrying 4 defenders on his back as the final gun sounded. Final score: Spring Hill 48, Valley Center 46. He recalled the entire stands emptying out onto the field in celebration. His teammates then lifted him up on their shoulders and carried him off the field amidst a cheering crowd.

He got chills every time he called up those old memories, even now some 30 years later. That play was the last play of Travis Dalton's football career and in retrospect, his last 15 minutes of fame. It was also the

Visiting the Past

greatest moment of his life. Until now, that is. Sometimes our greatest moments happen when we least expect it. We don't often realize how prolific the moment is until much later in life. It could be a simple thing like landing a great job, meeting a best friend or the first time you were introduced to the love of your life. It all just seems so casual and random when it happens. You just never know when an amazing moment will occur. That's why it's always better to be involved in life's little things when they arise. It gives you more chances to have a great moment. Well, this instance would certainly qualify as one of those magic moments. He couldn't wait to see his son's face when he told him he would be a Division 1 college football player. What could be better than that?

As his daydream slowly dissipated and the fog rolled away from his face, he looked up and Mason was standing right in front of him.

"Dad. Dad? Dad?" he said.

Travis, finally coherent, said, "Mase, I gotta tell you something."

Dalton's Pit

"Everything okay, Dad? What's wrong? You look like you've seen a ghost. Is it Aunt Hannah?"

"No, nothing like that, Mase. It's actually great news, son."

"Well are you going to tell me or do I have to guess, Pop?"

Travis leaned forward with his hands on his knees and exhaled as the water started to build in his eyes and said, "Well, I got a call from Coach Bobby Petrino today of the Louisville Cardinals."

Mason's eyes widened. "Serious?"

Travis, who could hardly get the words out, said in a quivering voice, "They want you to be a Louisville Cardinal. Full scholarship."

Mason was so excited he almost tackled his father to the ground.

Travis started bawling. "Take it easy, kid, save some of that for Louisville. Plus, you couldn't bring me down

Visiting the Past

anyway. Did I ever tell you I scored six touchdowns back in the 1972 state championship?"

"Oh my God, Dad, only about a million times." He chuckled.

Just then Mason's coach and half the members of his team who were standing behind him and overheard the news, came closer. One by one they congratulated him and then formed a football circle around him chanting "Mason, Mason, Mason." What a moment it was for Mason. It was a big moment for Travis also, who had moved to stand on the side with Mason's coach.

Coach Willis looked at Travis and said, "Just another step for your boy, all the way to the NFL." Travis simply put his hand on the coach's shoulder, shook his head and reveled in Mason's moment. They caught a flight the following Friday morning and arrived at the Blue Grass airport mid-day. On the flight over, something had dawned on Travis. How did it take him this long to make the connection? It was something that had been gnawing at him for quite some time. Not to mention he had also been feeling quite guilty about leaving Billy all

Dalton's Pit

alone to take care of Hannah. This could be a way to not only help, but to feel better about himself as well. Travis knew his father Ernie had supposedly settled in Kentucky after coming out of prison years ago. Maybe while he was in Louisville he could look him up. Imagine if he could find him and bring him to New York to see Hannah? That would be amazing. But how? Maybe Dad could come visit her one last time and make her happy. Maybe she would be so happy that she would get better. Let's not forget that Travis had an IQ of about 85, so why wouldn't a visit from her father make her heart problems go away? It made sense—at least to Travis it did.

The problem he faced, however, was obvious. Not only did he not have any idea where he lived, he didn't even know if he was still alive. He did know one thing for sure, though. He knew he would have some down time on his hands while Mason checked out the campus. What better opportunity would he ever have to look up his father? Travis was never one for computers but maybe someone could do a search of his father's name to find him? Over the years he always had in his mind to reach out to his dad one day, but he never had a good enough

Visiting the Past

reason to reconnect. Now with the inevitable passing of his Hannah, he felt it was more than reason enough. Just maybe if he came back to the family and Hannah saw him, all would be good again. Just like when they were young. Travis had always gotten along with his dad, especially when they ran the gas station together. He felt all along that his dad wanted to come back to the family but just didn't know how. You know what they say, "Out of tragedy comes triumph." Here was the chance for both of them to triumph.

After their plane landed, Travis headed over to the rental car area and picked up the car he requested. He then picked up the luggage at the baggage claim, loaded up the car and set out to the Louisville campus with Mason. They arrived at the school that afternoon around 3 p.m., and were escorted by one of the attendants to Coach Petrino's office. A few moments later the coach walked in and formally introduced himself.

"Hello, Mr. Dalton, I'm Bobby Petrino, the head football coach for the Louisville Cardinals; it's great to meet you. I hope your flight was okay."

Dalton's Pit

"The pleasure is mine, Coach. Call me Travis and yes, it was a fine flight. Thanks."

"And you must be Mason. I've heard a lot about you from my scouts. I hear you dominated this year. From what I've seen of your game films, looks like you take after your dad."

Travis was a bit surprised. "After me?"

"Yes, Travis. We know all about your incredible 6-touchdown game in the state championship back in '72. That's very impressive. Too bad you aren't 25 years younger; we could really use a fullback."

Travis now beaming said, "Wow, thanks, Coach."

Now Travis knew without question that he wanted his son to attend Louisville, simply because someone on his administrative team took the time to look up Travis's past. Funny sometimes how a little thing like a simple compliment could carry so much weight.

"So Mason, how would you like to see our complex? Several of the seniors are working out today and offered to show you around a bit before our practice. Then after

Visiting the Past

that maybe you could watch our defense practice over at the field by the commons."

"Sure. I'd love to, Coach," Mason said.

"Mr. Dalton, you are invited as well, of course. Would you like to see the campus?"

"Actually Coach, I have an errand to run. Something I need to take care of. Mason can handle it by himself."

"Okay, not a problem, Mr. Dalton. We probably shouldn't be more than three or four hours. I guess we will see you back here later, say ... 7-ish."

Travis thought to himself three hours should be more than enough time to find out if Dad was still around. He was sure he could find someone able to find him by using the internet.

"Great. That sounds like a real plan, Coach. I will come back later, around 7. Let the kid enjoy himself for a while without the old man around."

As he left the campus, Travis's mind was racing a mile a minute. *Where do I begin?* He decided to start by

Dalton's Pit

checking with the local newspaper, the registry and even the local telephone company to see if anyone knew of his dad and whether he was still living locally. If he knew that then it would be easier to find his last known residence. Unfortunately, after speaking with several people, no one had ever heard of Ernest T. Dalton. After about an hour had passed, Travis was running out of ideas and was thinking that although this was a nice idea, it was never going to happen. He was just about to pack it in and head back to the campus when it occurred to him. Dad was in jail for a while, maybe the police station might have a record of him. Perhaps his dad was still on probation for what he did to Mr. Danby. He got back in the car and drove about 15 blocks to the local police station in hopes of finding a lead to his dad's whereabouts. As he entered the station, just to the right was an older police officer standing behind the counter.

The officer looked at Travis. "Can I help yawl?"

"Sure can, sir; I sure hope so. I'm tryin to find my dad. His name is Ernest T. Dalton. He was in a Louisville jail several years ago. I am tryin to find out if he is still alive

Visiting the Past

and if so, where I can reach him. I was hoping maybe you may have a record of him in your files."

"Well let me see here." He walked over to the computer on the desk against the wall. "What's the name again, son?"

"Ernest T. Dalton is his name. He's got to be about 73 or 74 years old by now, I suppose."

"Let's take a look see." The officer scanned the computer then turned to Travis and said, "Nope, I'm sorry, no one by the name of Ernest Dalton. Sorry, kid."

Travis looked dejected. "Darn. Okay, sir. Thanks anyway."

As Travis was walking toward the station exit, one of the clerks who had been listening to their conversation called out to him. This clerk had been responsible for automating the new system a few years back by switching everything over from hard files to computer files.

"Excuse me, sir, but I couldn't help but overhear your conversation. Not all the files from back then were

Dalton's Pit

switched over to the computer. Some of those dormant files are still locked in the file room downstairs. Maybe I can take a look for you. What was the name again?"

"Ernest T. Dalton. Thank you, kindly."

The clerk left and headed on down to the file room. No sooner than five minutes later, he returned with a manila folder that read, Dalton, Ernest T.

"Is this your father? Is this what you're looking for? The clerk showed him the folder.

Travis was very excited. "Yes, that's my dad. Can I see the file?"

"Actually, first I will need to see some identification. I could get in a lot of trouble showing you this file, otherwise. This type of information is not available to the public, but for some reason I feel like helping you. I just cannot give you information on a perp without proper identification."

Travis eagerly handed over his driver's license and after a few minutes the clerk came back. "All checks out, sir. Here's your dad's file." Travis reviewed the file and sure

Visiting the Past

enough, his last known address was there. The problem was that the address was about seven years old. Who knew if he would still be there all these years later?

Travis wrote the address down on a piece of paper. "By any chance do you know where this address is? How far would you reckon this is from here?"

"Oh, that's about 15 minutes away. There's a mobile home park about 10 miles down the road if you head out of the parking lot going south on Maple. You can't miss it. It'll be on your left-hand side."

"Gents, thank you kindly for your hospitality. Wish me luck; I'm going to find my dad."

Even at this point Travis wasn't expecting this to play out the way he had hoped. After all, he still he had no idea what to expect. Did his dad still live there? Was he still alive? Would he even talk to him? Despite his pessimism he got in the car and headed out of the parking lot and onto Maple Street. Just about 15 minutes later he saw a sign on the left that read "Mobile Home City, next left." He made the next left and pulled in to a seedy trailer park parking lot. He saw a

Dalton's Pit

handmade sign with the address and an arrow pointing left toward the trailers. The sign read Easy Street. How fitting that his father now lived at 75 Easy Street. Travis parked his car in the lot and proceeded into the trailer area. *This sure as heck isn't easy street,* he thought to himself. It looked like a scene out of the movie Apocalypse Now. People were sleeping on beach chairs in front of their mobile homes, one being a very large woman wearing a 2-piece bikini bathing suit that wouldn't even fit Hannah. Then there was a guy in a tee shirt sitting with his feet in a plastic kiddie pool with a quart of beer in hand. It was like the freak show at the circus. All that was missing was the bearded lady.

Luckily for Travis, given his size, no one even dared look at him the wrong way. In addition to that because of the way he was dressed, they probably assumed he was a police officer anyway. Finally, he reached a second street sign just about 20 yards in. This sign read Easy Street, Sections 50 through 80 with an arrow pointing left. He walked another 15 yards or so down the path and noticed the address 75 on the left. He took a deep breath, walked up to the trailer door and knocked twice. No answer. The lady in the trailer directly across

Visiting the Past

the dirt path, Mrs. Hibbard, noticed Travis lurking around and came out of her trailer and said, "He's probably out back working on that damn car of his."

Travis gave her the thumbs up and went around the side of the trailer and into the back. His adrenaline was building like a teapot ready to whistle its tune. Was his father just around the next turn? As he made the turn around to the back of the trailer with his body physically shaking, there he stood. He was bent over the engine of his favorite car of all time, the Austin Cooper Mini pickup. This one was a 1978 model. Travis just stood there for a moment, a bit nervous about what to do next. After all, he hadn't seen his dad in so many years. He never believed he would find him. His heart was beating a bit faster as he started to walk toward the car. He could see his father's profile from underneath the hood. Even though he looked old and frail and most of his hair was gone, Travis immediately recognized his father. The same black 10-gallon hat was resting on the bumper just to the side. Travis slowly approached the car and said, "Dad?"

Ernie lifted his head from beneath the hood. "Travis?"

Dalton's Pit

The tears were welling up in Big Ernie's eyes. He stumbled as he walked toward his son, dropping the wrench he had in his hand onto the dirt patch on the ground to his right. He just stood there staring at Travis. He rubbed his eyes, perhaps thinking it was a dream. Maybe he'd had too much to drink last night. This was no dream; however, Travis was standing right in front of him. He just stared in amazement, probably wondering how Travis had found him—and why.

The tears being shed were not only for missing his son, but also for his embarrassment for how he walked away and deserted his family, especially his daughter who needed him all those years ago when Flo passed away.

Ernie looked at his son and took a moment to gather the right words.

"Son, I am sorry. I am so sorry for everything. How did you find me? How is my Hannah? Is she okay? How's Billy?" Sobbing, he repeated, "I am so sorry."

Over the next few hours they sat in the beach chairs behind the trailer, had a few beers and just talked.

Visiting the Past

Travis told him about Hannah being in New York and about all the things Billy had done for her. He told him about his wife Ivy and the kids and about Mason and Louisville University. It was a conversation long overdue. Ernie, however, didn't have much to tell Travis. He did confess to him that he hadn't left the trailer park in over five years and how he was just waiting to die. He told him about how the only friend he had in the world, Benny from across the way, had just recently passed away. Benny Hibbard and his widow, the busybody, Betsy Hibbard, were the only ones who knew anything about his prior life. He also mentioned that since Benny died, his widow the old bag from across the way kept throwing herself at him. "God forbid I'd ever let that woman anywhere near me," he said.

Apparently, Benny and his wife Betsy also had a sordid past they were trying to keep under wraps. When Benny was in his early twenties, he got mixed up with the wrong bunch of guys in a drug deal gone bad and was arrested. To avoid going to jail for a long time, he ratted out some very seriously corrupt people. He ended up having to go underground for a very long

Dalton's Pit

time in the witness protection program. Initially he was placed in Fargo, North Dakota where he met his wife Betsy before relocating to Kentucky. She also had a past well worth forgetting. It seems she grew up in San Francisco in the mid-sixties and was rumored for a short time to be a member of the Manson Family. She even lived in their headquarters at Spahn Ranch back in '68. Although she was never linked to any of the murders, she knew way too much about his group of followers. In fact, she told Ernie a story once of how she sang backup on the Manson family album that was created back in '69, which predicted a chaotic apocalypse and the end of the world. When Ernie heard about her past, despite his closeness with Benny, he decided to stay as far away as he could from Betsy or whatever her real name was. Now that Benny was gone and it was just the two of them, she'd been trying to latch on to him ever since. Ernie made it clear to her many times that he would rather drink himself into a coma than to hook up with her. Despite his obvious rejections of her she continued to try anyway.

He then told Travis that after his release from prison, he had planned to go home, but needed some time to

Visiting the Past

get his act together. Then when Flo passed away, he was so devastated he simply gave up on life and fell further into depression. He'd always meant to reconnect, but the more the days went by, the more difficult it was to face his past. He spent the last few years drinking beer and working on his car. That was his life. He was just waiting to die. He sometimes wondered if God just simply forgot about him. After all, in his mind he was very easy to forget.

"Dad, I got an idea. I want you to come with me to New York to see Hannah. She doesn't have too much time left. You can say you're sorry to her if you want.

She would love to see you. Billy would too. Please come. It would mean everything to us."

"Oh, I could never do that, son. I am too ashamed of who I am. Besides, they would never welcome me back anyway. I'm just better off being forgotten. Just let me be, son. Please."

"Dad, think about it, please. I am goin' to New York City next week to see Hannah. It could be the last time we see her alive. I want you to be there with me.

Dalton's Pit

Promise me, okay, Dad? Please promise me that you will come with me."

Ernie got up from his beach chair and just stood there with his now much frailer body and thinly spaced white hair. "I hope so, son, I hope so." They hugged one last time and Travis said, "I'll be in touch soon, Dad." Travis then left the mobile home park and headed back to his car. He had been gone a good three hours and had to get back to the campus to meet with Mason to see how everything went with his visit. The drive back to campus was a complete blur to Travis. What was normally a half hour car ride, seemed to last only five minutes. All Travis could think about was reuniting his father with Billy and Hannah. He replayed the conversation over and over in his head, thinking, *did that really just happen? Did I just have a few beers with my dad? Will Billy believe me?* He knew he had to make sure that his father was on that plane come the following weekend.

On the flight home, for the first-time Travis told his son Mason about what happened to his Uncle Cooper when they were little. He felt his son was finally old enough to know the truth about his family. He told him about

Visiting the Past

Austin and what happened the night Cooper died. He then told him how their family fell apart once his grandmother died. He poured his guts out about every last Dalton secret. Mason, at 17, was a man. It was time he knew about his family.

Meanwhile back in Kansas, Billy was preparing for what was coming. He was sitting at the kitchen table of the old house when his phone rang. "Hey brother, I just booked a ticket to NYC. I will see you there next weekend."

"That's great Trav, Hannah will be happy. I can't wait to see you. How was the trip to Louisville? Did Mason like the campus?"

Travis was tempted to tell Billy about their father, but decided to hold back. "Yes, he loved it. I reckon he will decide pretty quick. I think he's decided already. You can't appear too anxious, if you know what I mean. Anyway, I should arrive Friday, early afternoon. How's she doing? Any change?"

Dalton's Pit

"Nope. She's the same, Travis. I am getting things in order over here. See you next weekend; if anything comes up I'll call you."

"You got it, bro; see you there," he replied.

The plans were set. Travis had a flight scheduled to land in Louisville on the following Thursday morning. He would spend the night with his dad at his place and then head out to the airport early Friday morning for the trip to New York to surprise Billy and Hannah. Dad still had not agreed to go, but Travis booked everything anyway. Billy, in the meantime had spent the last few weeks working every media channel he could think of to find a heart donor for his sister. He created flyers and had them posted all over the place in local stores in the NYC area. He created an online ad on the Veterinarians Association website. He called all his contacts in the medical field; he even took out a 30 second spot on a television station. Money was not an object to him. He had plenty of it to go around. No matter what he did, though, the story was the same. It just wasn't worth using such a valuable commodity as a heart on someone who had such a short life expectancy.

Visiting the Past

The following Thursday Travis landed at Louisville Airport around 11:00 in the morning, picked up his bag from the baggage claim and headed out to Easy Street and his father's trailer. He spoke with him on Wednesday and told him he would be there mid-day. This time being a little bit more prepared than last time, Travis was unfazed by all the characters hanging out on Easy street. There were a few meth heads who scattered as Travis walked toward his father's place. Travis, however, didn't even acknowledge his surroundings, he simply proceeded to the trailer. Upon reaching the trailer he saw a note on the door which read:

Travis, I am sorry but I've caused enough pain to our family, I can't go with you. Please forgive me. Take care of yourself. Please understand, I love you son.

Travis, extremely frustrated, ripped the note off the door, crumbled it and threw it to the ground. Then he dejectedly leaned his head on the door. He slumped down onto the two-step ladder that served as the trailer's stoop and hung his head. What to do now? His flight out to New York wasn't until tomorrow. Maybe he

Dalton's Pit

could wait around and see if his father came back. He checked around back by the car, but Ernie was nowhere to be found. Travis waited for an hour or so and started to become restless. He was tired and hungry. He decided that instead of leaving, he would rather go out back and work on the Austin Cooper. He'd pick up where his father left off just to keep himself occupied. Then it dawned on him. Dad said he hadn't left the trailer park in five years and Mrs. Hibbard was the only one he spoke to. He had to be hiding out in her trailer. In addition to that she hadn't come out of her trailer once since Travis arrived. That was not like the nosy Mrs. Hibbard. Travis came back around to the front of the trailer and muttered to himself, "Ok Dad, I give up," and then walked back to the main road. He figured if his dad was in there he wouldn't come out of Mrs. Hibbard's trailer until he knew for sure that Travis was gone. Travis left the park and then quietly returned through the woods behind the trailers about 15 minutes later. Sure enough he heard Mrs. Hibbard's trailer door open and out came Ernie wearing the same black 10 gallon hat he wore 15 years before. Ernie, believing Travis had gone, entered his trailer, sat down and

Visiting the Past

cracked open a beer. He tossed his hat onto the table and flipped on the television. A few seconds later he saw a huge shadow standing behind him.

Ernie was not terribly surprised. "Son, I knew you would come back. I just can't go with you. I've made my decision; please understand and respect my wishes. I beg of you, son."

"Dad, I forgive you, but Hannah really needs you. Please come with me."

"I want to see them, son, I just don't know. Look at me. Look what I've become. Why would they want to see me? Why do *you* want to see me? I am not the same man they remember from years ago. I pale in comparison to him. All I am now is what you see. A drunken fool who abandoned his family and is not worth anyone's time."

"Dad, we've all done stupid stuff, we all miss Mom and Coop. We just want to be a family again, especially for Hannah in the days she has left. We need you now more than ever, Dad. You could make up for everything you feel bad about just by coming with me. Please, Dad,

Dalton's Pit

come with me. We love you. We need you. Please, Dad."

Ernie now stammering shook his head up and down. "Ok, son. I will go."

Travis and Ernie spent the remainder of the day and night talking about Kansas and the good old days. Ernie kept talking about his beloved Flo's cooking and how her meatloaf was the best thing he ever tasted. He talked about Cooper and how he missed him. Surprisingly he even talked about Austin. He spoke of him for the first time in a long time in a fond way. After all, they were all his kids. He shared with Travis the guilt that weighed on him for everything that happened. How back then he never spent any time with his children. He was always too busy working or drinking at Farley's Pub. It was the first good cry he'd had in years. He missed his old life. He knew he couldn't get it back, but maybe seeing Hannah before she died was a message from above. He realized there was nothing more he wanted in life than to see Billy and Hannah and tell them he loved them. It was the best night's sleep he'd had since Cooper's death. The best day as well.

Visiting the Past

The following afternoon when they arrived at the airport, Billy had been there for about an hour. His flight landed a short time earlier and he figured he would wait by the gate for Travis. He had no idea his father would be with him as well. Travis told his father that Billy would be there waiting at the gate and the closer they got to the terminal the more terrified Ernie became. He was so nervous getting off the plane that Travis had to help him walk down the ramp. What was once a 6 foot 4 inch, 275-pound man now looked to be a shriveled up 180 pounds at best. When they walked out of the gate, Travis scanned for Billy but didn't see him at first. Ernie certainly wouldn't recognize him and there was a good chance Billy wouldn't recognize his father either. Except of course for the hat. He would recognize that ragged hat anywhere. Billy had just stepped away for a moment to use the restroom and was thumbing through a magazine over by the newsstand. Just then he happened to look up and he immediately saw both Travis and his father as they walked out of the gate. He was stunned. He lost his composure for a moment when he was paying the cashier for the magazine and left his

Dalton's Pit

change on the counter. He walked toward his father with his eyes welling up.

"Dad, is it really you?"

Ernie was so overwhelmed that he fell into Travis's arms for a second before composing himself. "Hello, William. It's been a long time, son."

No other words were spoken. Billy walked over to his dad and hugged him tightly. Ernie just collapsed into his son's arms and cried. No apologies needed to be said. They both knew how the other felt.

Billy then turned to his big brother and said, "I don't know how you pulled this off, but thank you, Travis. This is the greatest gift you could have ever given me."

"Hey, I do what I do, kid. What can I say, little brother, I am the man. Then with a smile he said, "I'll tell you everything later. It took a while to convince him, but I think he finally realized just how much he needed to see you and Hannah."

The three Dalton men were finally together again for the first time in a long time. Travis gathered the bags

Visiting the Past

and Billy walked with his father as they headed out of the airport and hailed a cab to the hotel. Just a quick respite on their ultimate destination to see their Hannah. After all was said and done, Hannah was really the one thing that brought them all together again.

Chapter 8

Ultimate Sacrifice

Tricia made the very difficult decision to move A.J. to a hospital across town that was more suited for his condition. One that specialized in adolescent thyroid and diabetic issues. So, every day Tricia would leave work a little earlier and head across town to the hospital. When she wasn't sleeping, she was either at work or at the hospital. It got to the point where she didn't even know what day it was because they were all the same. To make matters worse, since she didn't own her own car, each night after work she would have to stop by Rose's house to pick up her car then drive all the way across town to see A.J. Then at night she would drive the car back to Rose's house and walk home. Since her husband was always on the road, Tricia was essentially on her own when it came to dealing with A.J. and his illness. At least she had Rose and Joanne whom she could count on for help when it was needed.

Dalton's Pit

Rose on the other hand was in a much better place mentally once she found out about Tom Sr. Joanne's friend did some investigating and found out that her husband was incarcerated last year for armed robbery and attempted murder in a drug deal gone wrong. He was sentenced to 25 years in prison without the opportunity for parole. For the first time in a long-time Rose felt safe in San Antonio, free from the stress of being worried that one day Tom would just show up. The only thing that she concerned herself with was A.J. and her dear friend Tricia. A.J. wasn't getting any better; in fact, he was getting worse. One day after getting off from work, Tricia arrived at the hospital like she always did. Upon entering the lobby, she was immediately greeted by one of the head nurses and informed that the doctor needed to speak with her about A.J.'s condition. Tricia was then escorted directly to the head surgeon's office and she waited there patiently for him to arrive. The next five minutes were without question the most gut wrenching minutes of her life. Tricia received the news that every parent dreads more than anything else in the world. A.J. had slipped into a diabetic coma and had to be put on life support. The doctor informed her that his pancreas was beginning to shut down and he had to be put on a machine that fed him insulin directly into his bloodstream. Without the insulin, he was sure not to survive very long.

Throughout all of A.J.'s health issues there was never a time when Tricia believed he wouldn't survive. It was incomprehensible to her. She just looked at the doctor, at first, wondering if he knew who he was talking to. *He must be referring to some other child*, she thought. The cold reality, though, was that he knew very well who he was talking to. After coming out of her quick denial, Tricia stood up from the chair and let out a scream. She wasn't prepared for this conversation and was completely blindsided. She couldn't handle it and fell to her knees. She felt every hair on her body stand on end at once. It was almost as if she were dreaming. How could this be? Then as she tried to stand up, she immediately got dizzy and fainted, falling back onto the tile floor and hitting her head. The nurse came running over and helped her come to and sat her up. After that she just sat there in disbelief. She was at a complete loss

Dalton's Pit

as to what to do next. Overwrought, she called the only person she could.

Fighting through tears, Tricia said, "Rose, my A.J. is going to die. He is in a coma and they just told me he most likely will not come out of it. I don't understand how this could happen. Why would such a beautiful young boy have to go through this? It's just not fair. It should have been me, not him. He has so much more life to live. Why can't they just take me instead? I don't want to live without my baby. I can't go on without him."

Rose responded with a lump in her throat, "I am so sorry, my friend. I am here for you for anything you need. I love you."

Tricia then called her husband and gave him the horrific news. They cried together on the phone and he told her he loved her and that he would leave his deliveries and come to the hospital as soon as he could. For the first time in their relationship they had a strong connection. The love for their son became more powerful than any of their petty differences.

Ultimate Sacrifice

As the week progressed the news on A.J. was not any better. He was still on life support. Tricia had been at the hospital nonstop every day. Rose would come by with a change of clothes for her each day and would stay by A.J.'s bedside so Tricia could have a brief respite here and there.

Tricia had been sleeping by her son's side for five days straight with no change whatsoever. She expected her husband home shortly. He had called from the road and said he would be there early the next morning. The boredom of the nights and the sounds of all the machines were getting the best of Tricia. She was at her wits' end when a commercial appeared on the TV.

"Hello, my name is Dr. Clifford. My associate's sister Hannah suffers from Microcephaly. This disease causes severe stunting of a person's growth. Hannah is in need of a heart transplant from a child between the ages of 5 through 10 or she will die very soon. If you or a loved one is a donor and would like to save a life,

please call 1-800-555-1234. If you have ever been helped by someone in the past think about helping

Dalton's Pit

someone in need like you once were. There's no feeling like it in the world."

Tricia just stared at the screen. *Is this my calling? Am I supposed to help this girl? The words he used are the same words Rose said to me a few weeks ago. Maybe this is how I can make sense of A.J. dying. Will my husband allow it? Am I crazy?* Tricia scribbled the name of the doctor and the number on a piece of paper and put it in her pocket. She then spent the rest of the night lying next to her son and crying herself to sleep. In the morning she couldn't help but think more about the commercial she had seen the night before. A few moments later when the nurse came into the room to adjust one of the machines, Tricia asked, "Excuse me, but how would I go about having my son become an organ donor?"

The nurse replied, "It's actually a very simple process, dear. I can get the paperwork for you. I will come back with it and explain to you how it works."

Ultimate Sacrifice

"Thank you, nurse. I'm just curious at this point. I would have to speak with my husband first before making any decisions," she replied.

The nurse returned 15 minutes later with all the necessary paperwork and spent the next half hour explaining the process to Tricia. She explained to her that if she signed, it wouldn't mean she had to go through with it and that she could still speak with her husband and decide later. Tricia nervously signed the paperwork and handed it back to the nurse.

"So basically this gives me the option to donate his organs without committing right now?" she asked.

The nurse replied, "That's correct. You can discuss it with your husband when he comes and then decide later.

Tricia thanked the nurse and said, "I will let you know for sure after I speak with my husband later today."

About an hour later her husband finally returned from his cross-county deliveries and proceeded directly up to the hospital to be with Tricia. Tricia told him that

Dalton's Pit

the doctor said it's only a matter of days and that they had better start preparing. She also told him about the commercial she saw about this woman in New York who needed a heart transplant and just maybe they could save her life by donating A.J.'s organs. It was a bit much for him to handle all at once. At first he said, "No, absolutely not." Tricia then proceeded to explain why she felt this was a message to them from God. She told him the whole story about Rose and A.J. and the car incident. After listening to his wife and then speaking with the doctor, he finally realized that his son was going to die. He reluctantly agreed to donate his son's heart. Upon hearing this Tricia hugged him tightly and immediately called the number she had scribbled on a piece of paper the night before. She needed to find some good in A.J.'s death; she was also hoping it would give her and her husband at least some comfort.

"Hello, is this Doctor Clifford? My name is Tricia; I saw you're commercial on TV last night and wanted to talk with you further. I have a son . . ."

Billy, a bit surprised, said, "Umm commercial, yes? Wait what?"

Ultimate Sacrifice

"I saw your commercial on television last night. This is Doctor Clifford, correct?"

Billy, a bit more coherent, responded, "Yes, well actually, he's my partner. Can I help you?"

"Well, my son is on life support and he only has a short time left with us. I saw his commercial last night about your sister. And well, I think I may be able to help you."

Billy was speechless. *Maybe this is a prank. Why would anyone help a woman who had a projected life span of maybe 3-5 years at best?*

"Is this a joke?" Billy asked.

"Certainly not. You are Doctor Clifford's partner, aren't you?"

Billy quickly realizing this was no joke, responded, "Yes, I am."

"Well my son A.J. is on life support in San Antonio General Hospital. The doctors tell us he likely has less than a week to live and for some reason, I believe I'm supposed to help you and your sister."

Dalton's Pit

Billy felt like he was dreaming. "Okay Tricia, is it? I just arrived in New York to see my sister. I don't know what to say. Shall I have my sister's doctor send you her current prognosis? You see she was born with Micro-"

Tricia quickly interrupted him. "You don't have to tell me now; we can discuss this tomorrow."

It was Billy's turn to interrupt her. "I can make arrangements for you and your son to be moved here immediately. Please give me your phone number. I will have my office call you right back with the details and have a helicopter ready for you and your son. There is something you should know about my sister, though."

Tricia, unwavering said, "Don't worry about that now."

Billy replied, "You have no idea what this means to me and my family. I will never forget this kindness. How can I ever repay you?"

Tricia was now smiling through the phone. "A good friend of mine once told me, 'You can pay me back by helping the next person you find that's in need of help, just like you were'."

Ultimate Sacrifice

Billy was stunned. That's exactly what he'd told Violet years before. That's exactly how he lived his life.

Billy then said, "God bless you. I will be in touch as soon as possible." After he hung up he sat there just staring into his phone asking himself, *did that just happen? Am I over-tired or did that just happen?*

Billy experienced an adrenaline rush like he hadn't had in months. For the first time in a long time there was a reason to be slightly optimistic. At least there was a small chance. *Would this work? A young boy willing to sacrifice for his beloved Hannah?* He couldn't wait to get to the hospital and tell the doctors and Hannah. He was so excited he forgot to tell Travis and his dad who were in a hotel room just across the hall. He immediately went downstairs to the front of the building and hailed a cab and headed directly to the hospital. Upon his arrival, he headed directly toward Hannah's room to tell her the great news. He had hoped she was awake or at the very least aware of his presence. When he arrived, however, the room was empty. The machines were gone. The bed was made. "Oh God," he murmured. He

Dalton's Pit

immediately feared the worst. Billy ran full speed down the hall to the nurse's station.

"Where is Hannah Dalton? She's not in her room? Did something happen?"

"I know the doctor was trying to reach you; I will have him come see you right away. Please have a seat," the nurse replied.

"Please, tell me, what happened. Did she . . .? Where's Donna?"

"Please have a seat, sir. The doctor will be with you shortly."

Billy suddenly realized he forgot to tell his brother and father about the child in San Antonio and the phone call he received. He had to call and tell them that Hannah may be dead. Billy took out his phone and called Travis.

"Travis, I am at the hospital; please come right away."

"What's happening? Why'd you leave? Is Hannah alright?" Travis asked.

Ultimate Sacrifice

"I don't know. I'll explain when you get here. I'm waiting for the doctor to come in. Plus, I got this phone call from this woman about her son. Just come here now, Dad too."

Billy hung up with Travis just as the doctor walked in. Billy's heart was beating rapidly as he followed the doctor into his office.

"Doc, where's Hannah? Is she…?"

"Billy, we had to move her. She does not have much time left. Her heart is failing and we think she won't survive the next day or two. I am so sorry."

"It's okay, Doc, she's going to be okay. I found a heart donor. He can be flown here tonight. She's going to be fine," Billy replied.

"I don't think you understand, Billy; it's too late. She won't survive the surgery at this point. It's over. It's just her time, son."

"You're wrong, Doc, she will survive. She's a fighter. It's not going to end like this. I have the donor. It was meant to be."

Dalton's Pit

"I am sorry, Billy, but it's not going to happen."

Billy was undeterred at that point. "Whether in this hospital or not, Doc, it will happen. We didn't come this far to let her die now. If you can't accommodate her, then I will have her flown to another hospital tonight."

Travis and his father arrived at the hospital a few moments later. Billy filled them in on Hannah's status and the possible donor and how if the hospital wouldn't allow the transplant to happen, they would have to move Hannah. Billy then said, "Let's go see her. She is in Room 2035 on the other end of this floor."

The three of them walked to the other end of the hall and entered the room where they moved Hannah just an hour before. Ernie was so afraid. He just wanted to see his little girl. He wanted to talk to her and apologize to her. As they entered the room, suddenly the realization hit them, especially Billy. The doctor was right. She wouldn't survive the operation. She was motionless. It looked as if she were already lying in a coffin. The three of them started to cry. Ernie collapsed

Ultimate Sacrifice

the chair with his head in his hands. "God, forgive me. Hannah, forgive me. I love you, girl," he cried out.

Just then Hannah's eyes opened. She gave a big smile to her dad. Then her eyes closed again.

In that instant Billy's cell phone began to ring.

Billy walked out the hospital room doorway and into the hall. "Hello?"

"Hello, this is Tricia again; we spoke earlier. Well, I had my son's doctor reach out to your sister's hospital and my son is being transported by helicopter tonight. The surgery can happen first thing in the morning."

Billy stumbled. "Okay, but how—"

"My husband and I have already left and are driving up in my car. If our calculations are correct we should arrive just in time for tomorrow's surgery. See you then."

"But there's something I should tell you, Tricia," he replied.

Dalton's Pit

"I know. Don't worry about anything just tell me about it in the morning. I'll see you tomorrow." She then hung up the phone.

After hanging up, Billy proceeded to tell Travis and his father about Tricia and what she was willing to do for Hannah. As he was explaining the situation, the doctor walked into the room.

"Well Dr. Dalton, it appears as though my colleague in San Antonio is transporting a young boy here, willing to donate his heart to your sister. As I said, she is not likely to survive the surgery, but this young boy will likely not survive much longer either and his mother is adamant about trying to help your sister. My colleague explained Hannah's age, situation and prognosis and regardless of what he said, this woman still wants to help her. We are scheduled for surgery at 8 a.m. tomorrow. His parents have already left and should arrive in time for surgery tomorrow morning."

"I wish Hannah the best of luck tomorrow, Mr. Dalton," he said.

"Thanks, Doc."

Ultimate Sacrifice

That night seemed to last forever for the Dalton boys. *Would Hannah survive the surgery? Would she even survive the night? And why are these parents being so nice to us? Perhaps it's an act of God.* After all, Hannah deserved a break in life also. As expected Billy couldn't sleep, so like he always did when he needed time to think, he decided to walk around the city. He had no specific destination in mind this time so he just wandered around the city making his usual rounds. He started out uptown to 42nd street, walking past his usual pit stops. He eventually ended up near the spot where he had met the corporal a few years back. He even remembered his name. Corporal Charles O'Rourke. He wondered what ever happened to him. The fact that he wasn't in the spot he saw him in a few years ago was a good sign, he figured. Or was it? Was he still alive? What about his dog Mickey? Billy spent the next few hours just sauntering around Manhattan enjoying the nice weather wondering what tomorrow might bring. What did God have in store for his Hannah? Only time would tell. In just a few hours all his questions were sure to be answered. By the time he got back to the hotel the sun was starting to peek out behind the

Dalton's Pit

buildings across the way. It was just a matter of time. Either way he would know very soon.

A few hours later both A.J. and Hannah were being prepped for surgery. A.J. was being given his last rites in one room with his parents who had just arrived, standing by his side. Hannah was in the room right next to his. After driving all night Tricia and her husband began to argue in the hospital room. Apparently, her husband had a change of heart and no longer wanted to go through with the organ donation, believing his son somehow would come out of the coma.

Tricia said to him, "How can we back out now? This girl and her family need us. We can't go back on our word."

"Our word?" he replied. "Who gives a shit about those people? This is my son. I don't care anything about those people. You're the one who came up with this stupid idea, not me. I said no and that's final. I am bringing him back home; call the doctor now!"

Billy, Travis and Ernie were standing in the hallway outside both rooms and couldn't help but overhear the argument when Tricia stepped out of his room in tears.

Ultimate Sacrifice

Tricia hadn't realized that she had company at first and then looked up a bit startled.

"Are you Billy? Hannah's brother?" she asked.

"Yes I am. Are you Tricia?"

"Yes I am, but we have a little problem. My husband is having second thoughts about helping your sister. I am sorry, but I can't go against his wishes. He is a very difficult man and when he makes a decision it's final."

Billy's face fell. "Perhaps I can speak with him. Maybe I can convince him."

"No, he will just get mad and blame me. I just said my goodbyes to my A.J. and I don't want to make my husband any angrier. I had hoped that my A.J. could somehow live on through your sister. He was such a good boy," Tricia said as she started to cry.

Billy's shoulders sagged as he reached out to comfort Tricia and gave her a hug. "Thank you so much for your efforts. I would still like to speak with your husband, if that's okay," he added.

Dalton's Pit

Tricia, not even acknowledging Billy's last statement, blurted out, "Here, I want you to have this. I brought this picture of my son for you and your sister to remember him by. This is my beautiful boy. My shining light. My A.J."

Billy looked at the photo and saw A.J. in his kindergarten portrait. A big boy with a full head of orange hair and a face loaded with freckles. On the bottom of the picture it read Austin Dalton Jr, Kindergarten Class 3.

Billy's brow furrowed in confusion. "Wait. Why does it say Austin Dalton Jr. on the bottom of this photo? Your last name is Dalton?"

"Yes. My son is Austin Jr., and I am Tricia Dalton."

Billy still could not quite grasp what Tricia was saying. "Wait. Your son's name is Austin Dalton?"

"Austin Dalton Jr., actually he's named after his father. That's why we call him A.J."

Billy, Travis and Ernie were now looking at each other trying to comprehend exactly what was happening. All

Ultimate Sacrifice

three of them were just staring at Tricia in stunned disbelief. It couldn't be. Could it?

The rollercoaster of emotions was just too much for Ernie to handle. Without so much as an afterthought he pushed past Travis, Billy and Tricia and stumbled with incredible anticipation into the room where A.J. and his father were. As he burst into the room his heart was pumping like never before. There was Austin hunched over the bed sitting in a chair with his head in his hands. Tricia, Travis and Billy followed him into the room.

Tricia spoke immediately. "Honey, I'm sorry, but these nice people wanted to talk with you. This is Hannah's fam—"

Austin lifted his head up from his hands and wiped away his tears. He snapped at Tricia, "I said no; didn't you hear me? I don't want talk to anyone. Now get out of here, all of you before I hurt someone."

Then he spun around as if to lunge at Tricia and stopped in his tracks. He scratched his head, confused as to what was happening. He just kept staring in eerie disbelief.

Dalton's Pit

"Austin, is that really you?" Ernie finally blurted out.

"Dad? How? Who? What's happening here?"

Suddenly Ernie felt like he had the strength of Samson. He walked right over to his son Austin and lifted him off his feet, giving him a huge hug. The next few moments were the most epic and humbling moments of their lives. Austin couldn't control his emotions and broke down weeping. It was as if his whole life had culminated in this one moment. He looked at Travis and Billy as if they were not real. He walked over just to touch them. He saw the scar under Billy's left eye from when he shot him with the BB gun and mumbled beneath his tears, "Billy, please forgive me," as he touched his face. "I don't know what…, how the…, wait, what's going on here?"

Travis walked over to his two brothers with a huge grin and embraced them both in one of his bear hugs. It seemed to last an eternity until finally Austin pulled back to make sure this was really happening. After the initial shock wore off and all the tears and apologies were exchanged, they explained to Austin about

Ultimate Sacrifice

Hannah's situation. And how she was the person in need of the transplant. And that she probably wouldn't survive the operation.

Austin turned back to his dad. "Dad, I don't know what to say. I am sorry about Cooper and about Mom. I never should have left. I was afraid to stay, knowing it was my fault. I've caused so many problems in our family. Now Hannah. I just can't believe this is real. I can't believe I am sitting here talking to you."

"Son, we've all made mistakes, including me. Let's not talk about the past right now. We're just lucky to have a second chance together. We will have time to discuss the past one day, not now, though."

Tricia meanwhile was caught completely off guard and had no idea what was unfolding before her eyes. Especially since Austin had never discussed his family before. She didn't even know he had brothers. She just realized she had been pushing all this time to save her husband's sister. She turned to Austin and before she could say a word, she noticed something very different about him. He no longer had that irritated look on his face. He was humbled for the first time in his life. Perhaps his anger was directly related to his estrangement from his family. He looked like a boy lost in a department store looking for his momma. She walked over and sat down next to him and put her head on his shoulder. He looked at her and said, "Thank you for being my wife; thank you for dealing with me. I know I am a difficult person and I am sorry. I love you. Thank you for finding my family and giving me the opportunity to save my sister." He then stood up and walked with his wife over to his son's bedside. They kissed A.J. one last time and cried together as they walked out of the room.

Hannah's surgery was about to get underway. The incredibly invasive surgery was scheduled to last for just over eight hours. Billy asked Austin if he would like to see her before the surgery started. He agreed and the two of them entered her room while everyone else walked out into the hallway. Billy remained at the door while Austin slowly inched up to her bed and knelt beside his sister with his hands clasped as tight as could be. He just stared at her and then hung his head. He realized in that moment all that he had missed while he

Ultimate Sacrifice

was estranged from the family. In his mind, he could hear Hannah's voice. He could see her smile. He wanted so badly to go back in time. To go back to that night at the Food way. He now realized that Cooper wasn't the only victim that fateful night. Every single member of the Dalton family was a victim. Even the innocent, like Hannah. Sometimes in life though you only get one take at a scene. One hand dealt to you. If you misplay it, you must live with the consequences. After a few moments, he wiped his eyes and lifted himself up off his knees. He kissed her forehead and turned to Billy standing by the door. Billy put his arm around his brother and said, "I am happy you're here, Austin. It's all going to work out."

Now it was simply a waiting game for everyone. When the initial shock of reuniting with Austin wore off, and the stress of Hannah's surgery was temporarily on hold, a cold truth permeated through everyone's mind. It's a terrible thing to say, but with all that was going on, it initially seemed like an afterthought. Austin and Tricia had lost their only son this morning. Billy felt a bit guilty for the oversight.

Dalton's Pit

Billy turned to Austin and said, "Austin, I am really so sorry about A.J. I can't possibly imagine how you feel at this moment."

Austin looked at Billy. "Losing my son was an act from above, Billy. If I can use his death to save Hannah, then there was a reason he was taken from us. Saving Hannah would be closure for me. It's now in His hands."

Billy responded, "Austin, don't worry. Hannah will be fine. I just know it. She's a fighter and there is a reason Tricia saw that commercial. I'm sure of it. It was meant to be. I am just so happy we are all together again especially for her."

After all the anticipation and the hours of waiting, their Hannah was finally in surgery. Would it work? Would this be a storybook ending? The odds were still not very good. They still had several hours to kill while waiting for Hannah to come out of surgery.

Billy said he needed to clear his head, so everyone decided to go outside and get some fresh air. They walked out of the waiting room into the elevator and down to the hospital lobby. They headed around to the

Ultimate Sacrifice

back of the hospital and into the parking lot. The stress level was pretty high at this point for everyone. Tricia then asked, "Is anyone hungry? We have a few hours to kill."

It had been a crazy night for everyone and food sounded about right, so everyone nodded yes.

Billy said, "There's a diner only two blocks from here. Let's head over."

They all agreed and started walking when Tricia said, "Give me a minute I just need to get my sunglasses out of the car."

Tricia walked about 10 yards over to the car and opened the driver's side door. Billy noticed it right away. It was as if he'd had a flashback. There it was. The purple violet emblem on the trunk of her car. How could that be possible?

Billy ran over to Tricia who had just closed the car door and exclaimed, "This is Violet's car. I know this car."

Dalton's Pit

"Actually Billy, it's my friend Rose's car. She lent it to me to travel back and forth to see A.J. while he was in San Antonio General."

"There's no way two cars could have the same violet emblem on the trunk. I know the prior owner of this car. Her name is Violet. I helped her one day when the car broke down alongside the highway in Kansas a few years ago. I will never forget this car and that violet on the trunk. Her husband Neil put that violet on the trunk so whenever he was on the road he felt like she was with him. I even remember what I told her when she wanted to pay me for helping her that night in the rain several years ago. I told her, 'You can pay me back by helping the next person you find that's in need of help just like you were'."

Tricia's jaw dropped. "Billy wait, Rose told me the exact same thing. She said that a woman in her past who helped her out when she was down told it to her also."

Billy stood there in disbelief, now realizing that by helping Violet that night in the rain he was paid in full and then some. What an amazing revelation. If you do

Ultimate Sacrifice

something to help someone without any expectation, it can come back to you when you least expect it. This was proof to Billy that everything we do has future consequences one way or the other. Now he believed more than ever that Hannah would survive the surgery. This was too much of a coincidence for it all to fall apart in the 11th hour. He knew that everything that had happened up to this point was a setup for this and not a setback. It just had to be, there was no other explanation for it. It was the culmination of luck, destiny or whatever you wanted to call it. He just knew she would be fine.

As they walked on down the block to the diner, Billy reached up and grabbed Travis by the neck and started giving him the business and said, "Today is going to be a great day, big brother."

Chapter 9

Entering the Game

It was getting late in the day. He hadn't realized he had been playing video games for as long as he had. It must have been six or seven hours straight of clicking away at the controllers. Finally, he shut the console off and got up from the couch. He was looking around a house that seemed oddly quiet today. *Mom must be outside hanging the laundry,* he figured. He walked into the kitchen and grabbed a few low sugar cookies from the cabinet above the microwave. Then he went to the fridge and poured himself a glass of milk and started dunking. He called out, "Mom, I'm tired I'm going up to bed."

He cleaned up his mess in the kitchen and headed on upstairs, brushed his teeth and got into bed. He popped on the TV and within minutes, drifted off to sleep. The next morning, he woke up, came downstairs and breakfast was already on the table. He sat down in his

Dalton's Pit

usual spot at the table and scarfed down his favorite breakfast. He had waffles with some toast on the side. After he finished he called out to his Mom. "Mom, where are you?"

He heard a voice. "Come outside into the yard."

He put on his sneakers and wandered out into the yard while still eating his last piece of toast. Across the yard he saw the shadow of a woman through a sheet hanging on the clothesline. He walked up to her and said, "Hey Mom, can we go over to Thomas's today?"

The woman looked down at him and smiled. He was startled to see that it wasn't his mom.

He got really nervous and ran back into the house and up to his room, closing the door behind him. The woman followed him up a few moments later and knocked on the door.

"Can I come in? I didn't mean to scare you. I promise I won't hurt you. I just want to talk to you." She slowly opened the door and saw his feet sticking out from under the bed. He was cowering in fear.

Entering the Game

"You can stay under there if you like; it's okay. I just wanted to introduce myself to you. My name is Florence. I am your grandmother on your father's side." Now he was even more nervous. He certainly didn't believe her. He didn't have a grandmother. His dad told him that his grandmother died a long time ago. Flo could hear the boy crying underneath his bed and said to him, "That's okay, A.J. I will go back downstairs and clean up the dishes. When you feel like it, come down and we can talk about your dad and where you are. Take your time."

Flo went back down the stairs and into the kitchen to clean up the breakfast dishes. About a half hour later she heard noises coming from upstairs. Maybe A.J. was ready. Sure enough she could see him from the corner of her eye, carefully peering down the stairs. She pretended not to notice for fear of him running back upstairs. It took about another 15 minutes for A.J. to finally come all the way down. Again, Flo stood in the kitchen, pretending not to notice. A.J. finally got his courage up.

Dalton's Pit

"You're not my grandma. Dad says my grandma died a long time ago."

Florence smiled. "Come here, A.J., come sit beside me. I have a story to tell you."

A.J. was still a bit anxious, but he walked over and sat next to her at the kitchen table.

"A.J., it's true what your father said, you know. I have been here for several years now. I came here especially so that I could meet with you. Can I show you something?"

A.J. nodded.

"Here, look at this." Flo pulled out an old family picture she kept with her always. It was of the entire Dalton family. It was taken way back when Travis was a senior in Spring Hill High School at his homecoming game.

Flo looked over at A.J. "Come here, sit on Grandma's lap. A.J., look; here is your dad. He couldn't have been more than 11 or 12 at that time."

Entering the Game

A.J. couldn't help but look and noticed his dad when he was a boy. "Wow, he looks like me, but who are all these other people?"

"Here's your grandpa on the left, then that's me, then your uncles Billy and Travis and your aunt Hannah. And then—"

"Who's that next to my dad?" he asked.

"That's your uncle Cooper. He is your dad's twin brother. They were best friends when they were little. They were always together."

"My dad has a twin brother? How come I never met him? I don't believe you. I think you're trying to fool me."

"It's true, A.J., he left before you were born. Would you like to meet him?" she asked.

A.J. nodded his head yes and said, "Can I ask you a question?"

Flo smiled and said, "Of course you can, my child. Anything you wish."

Dalton's Pit

"Where are we now? Where's Mommy and my dad?"

"Let's take a walk, A.J., okay? I want to show you something," she replied.

Florence grabbed A.J.'s hand and asked him if he was ready. A.J. nodded and they exited through the front door and out of the house. A.J. looked around with a surprised look on his face and realized that he was no longer outside the trailer home where he lived.

"Wow, where are we?"

Flo turned to A.J. "What's the last thing you remember, A.J.? The last thing before you were playing your video game yesterday on the couch."

"Well, I remember sitting in the car after school waiting for Rose to finish. I remember lying on the grass with Rose and Mommy."

"Is that all you remember? Do you remember the ambulance that took you to the hospital?" A.J. shook his head yes.

Entering the Game

"Well son, the ambulance that you were in that day drove you here to see me, so you wouldn't feel bad anymore."

"Well, what about Mommy? When is she coming to get me? I want to see my mommy. She takes care of me. Besides, she has to give me my medicine, you know. Every night at 6 o'clock I have to take my medicine."

"Mommy won't be here for a while, she asked me to look after you for the time being. Is that okay with you, A.J.?"

"Okay, but don't forget to give me my medicine. Mommy always told me when I had to take my medicine. It makes me feel better, she says."

"Don't worry, A.J. I won't forget. C'mon, let's go for a walk."

After walking for about ten minutes, A.J. turned to Flo and said, "Wow, I don't feel tired or anything. I feel like I can run all around. Can I run for a little bit?"

"Sure, you can run if you'd like," she said.

Dalton's Pit

A.J. then sprinted ahead about 20 yards, as fast as he could. Then looked back with a huge grin on his face. "How did you like that? Did you see how fast I ran? And I'm not even out of breath."

Flo smiled. "Wow, you are fast, A.J., really fast."

Flo caught up with A.J. and the two walked for a while, talking and getting to know one another. When they eventually stopped, they were standing in front of the old brown farmhouse the Daltons grew up in.

"A.J., this is the house your dad and uncles grew up in. Would you like to go inside?" A.J. nodded and said, "Sure would."

They stepped onto the porch and that old creaking sound immediately brought a smile to Flo's face. It had been a long time since she'd heard that creak. It immediately brought back so many memories of her family time. We never know exactly when something will trigger a memory from our past. Sometimes it's a picture or a smell, other times it's simply a noise that can transport us right back to the best times of our lives, if only for a moment. That creaking sound made her

Entering the Game

think of her children and the better days of her life. If only she'd known just how great those days were, maybe she would have enjoyed living them just a little bit more than she had. I guess to some extent everyone can say that. We often worry so much about tomorrow we forget to enjoy today.

Flo opened the front door of her home as the flashbacks engulfed her very being. As they walked in she turned to A.J. and said, "Would you like to see something really cool, A.J.?" Again, he shook his head yes.

They walked over to the couch, sat down and she said to him, "Watch this."

She snapped her fingers and the television screen popped on. "How would you like to see your dad when he was a little boy? How about your aunt and uncles?"

"Wow, that would be really cool," he said.

Over the next hour or so Flo showed him on the screen a complete rerun of many of the Dalton family highlights. The TV screen showed her marriage to his

Dalton's Pit

grandfather and the birth of his dad and uncle Cooper. It even showed the six touchdowns his uncle Travis scored in the 1972 championship game.

A.J. just sat there mesmerized. He saw his dad and uncle Cooper when they were his age. He saw uncle Billy and aunt Hannah playing with a frog under the porch as well. To him it was like he was watching a favorite video game. Flo didn't see the need to go any further than that about Austin and Cooper. There was no need and A.J. was too young to understand anyway. She then pointed at the screen again and it fast forwarded right to A.J. playing a game of hot and cold with Thomas in Thomas's living room. A.J. was smiling ear to ear.

"Hey, that's my friend Thomas. He's my best buddy, Grandma."

Grandma. That's the first time she had ever heard anyone call her Grandma. She looked at A.J. with such admiration. He was her grandson and she was his proud grandma.

Entering the Game

"Look, Grandma. I hid the game good on Thomas and he can't find it. I hid it good." He chuckled. "I can't wait to show him where I hid it. He's never going to find it."

They finished watching television and then Flo stood up and asked, "Did you like that, A.J.? Wasn't that fun?"

"Sure was, Grandma."

"I think you're going to like this even more, then," she said. "Come with me."

They walked back outside onto the front porch. Flo escorted him down the dirt path all the way to the right of the yard until they reached the back of the barn.

"Okay, are you ready, A.J.? Are you ready to have some fun?"

A.J. nodded yes. Then Flo pulled open the barn doors and stepped inside with A.J. by her side. When the doors closed behind them, A.J. nervously grabbed onto Flo's hand tightly. He was startled. It was pitch black and he couldn't see anything in front of him.

Dalton's Pit

"Don't be scared, A.J.; stay with Grandma. Trust me, you're going to love this," she said.

They looked to be in a dark tunnel of some sort. It certainly wasn't a barn. A.J. could now see slightly better. He looked at Grandma a little nervously. "Okay," he said.

As they walked a bit further it appeared they were being sucked into the tunnel and up. A.J. was even more distressed; he squeezed his grandmother's hand and then all of sudden, *Pop.*

It was as if they were shot out of a cannon and onto the road. As he looked to the left there were trees and flowerpots all over the place. Just to the right of them was a very low brick wall that he could easily jump on. On top of the wall were all these ledges and boxes to climb on. Some had large question marks on them. As he climbed up onto the next ledge he saw a row of pipes ahead as well as a huge mushroom. He then looked down at himself and saw that he was now dressed in red and blue. He would recognize this place anywhere. He proceeded to run around and jump as high as he

Entering the Game

could while screaming "Yippee." He was in his favorite place in the world. He was in Super Mario World.

A.J. turned to Flo and said, "Hey Grandma, this is my game from back home. Make sure you stay away from those bombs over there. They might explode on you."

Flo smiled from ear to ear at her grandson. "I'll be careful, A.J."

They walked up and climbed down every ledge in the road hopping around from place to place. They went in one tunnel and came out the next, hitting every coin they could find. Finally, A.J. stopped. He stood in front of a big castle with a huge flagpole right in front. Just ahead was a huge row of ledges for him to jump up on.

As he climbed up the ladder of ledges, he commented, "Wow, Grandma, this is the best day of my life."

Flo smiled and said, "A.J., after you grab the flag and pull it down, let's go inside the castle."

"Oh boy, really Grandma? Watch me jump and get it," he said.

Dalton's Pit

A.J. hopped up onto the highest ledge, jumped higher than he was ever able to before and pulled the flag down. He then looked at his grandma with a huge smile. "You see how high I jumped, Grandma? Can we go inside the castle now?"

As soon as they walked through the castle door, they were once again transported into another world. This one looked a little different, though. This one didn't have any flowers or ledges or coins. It looked to be a small tunnel or bridge of some sort.

"A.J., follow me; I would like you to meet someone."

"OK, Grandma," he said.

Flo and A.J. walked to the end of the covered bridge and Flo looked up to the roof of the covering and said, "Can you come down, son? I'd like to introduce you to your nephew A.J."

"Sure thing, Ma," he said.

This time Cooper didn't jump off the bridge like when he was little, he just shimmied down the side onto the

Entering the Game

ledge and jumped the remaining five feet of the way down onto the bridge.

"Hello A.J., I'm your uncle Cooper. I'm your dad's twin brother. I am happy to meet you."

"Hi Uncle Cooper I'm happy to meet you too. How long have you been here?"

"Well let's see now, I've been here for almost 24 years now, A.J. Would you believe I have been looking for someone to play with the whole time. Would you like to play with me?"

"Sure thing, Uncle Cooper. What would you like to play?"

"Follow me. Just jump up here onto the roof with me; I'll show you how. First crouch down and then jump up as fast as you can and yell "Yahoo!"

They both crouched down together then jumped up yelling "Yahoo!" and did a backwards flip, landing onto the roof of the covered bridge. They then slid down what looked like a small chimney and just like that they were thrust back into Super Mario World. This time

Dalton's Pit

Cooper was in all green like Luigi while A.J. was once again in red and blue like Mario. The next few hours they shared an amazing adventure. They dodged bullets, climbed in and out of pipes and mazes. They met Yoshi, Donkey Kong and Toad on their journey. They even saved the Princess from the evil Bowser.

A.J. had always had confidence issues during his life on earth. He could never jump or run like the other kids and was often ridiculed by his classmates. For the first time in his life he felt proud of who he was. He was no longer tentative. He no longer felt inferior. He felt he could do anything he wanted and wanted everyone to see.

The reality is that regardless of what our beliefs are on earth we see what we want to see when we die. A.J. wanted to see his favorite video game and that's what he saw. That was his favorite place. When Cooper arrived years back he wanted to see his grandmother and taste her apple pies so that's what he saw. Everyone's entryway into the next life is to experience, for one last time, the things they loved to do the most on earth when they first cross over.

Entering the Game

When Florence arrived several years ago she entered through her childhood days back in Kentucky. She was greeted by her twin sister Sienna who she'd missed terribly. Sienna walked her through their early life together in the backwoods of Kentucky. She was able to see all the hardships her mother went through for them as a single parent with no money. Flo's mother Helen became pregnant with Flo and Sienna at the age of 14. One afternoon a friend of her father's saw Helen working in the fields alone and approached her inappropriately against her will. Three months later when her father found out she was pregnant he disowned her despite her story about what his friend did to her against her will. She was sent away by her father in disgrace. She had the twins in an old lodge house for single mothers six months after she refused to have an abortion. They lived on the premises for 16 years until Flo met Ernie and left. When Helen died a few years later from a botched surgery, her sister Sienna was all alone and one day just disappeared from the lodge, never to be heard from again. It wasn't until Flo arrived here that she knew what happened to her twin sister. Sienna ran away from the lodge at age 18

Dalton's Pit

and married. She died in childbirth 2 years later in Arizona at the young age of 20. She never got the chance to reconnect with Flo.

Flo explained that prior to coming to heaven people have only been privy to seeing life through one vantage point. The one to which we were born. When we finally arrive here we get to see the world from all vantage points. It not only teaches us that things are not always as they appear but also allows us to heal from any disappointments or misunderstandings that happened during our stay on earth. The biggest thing that we learn when we arrive, however, is that all the people who left before us on earth are here waiting to greet us. If only we knew that prior to our arrival; imagine how differently our lives on earth would be spent. There is no longer a need for money either. So, all that money people are saving as they age is wasted. No one cares what your status or title was before you came over either. It was all simply a test. The fact is that all of us flunk the test in some way or another. The good thing is that despite it being a test, no one fails in the end. We just learn and then all is forgiven.

Entering the Game

After defeating Bowser and meeting all his favorite characters, A.J. was getting tired. So, Cooper and A.J. slipped through the final tunnel and were right back on the bridge. Standing there waiting was Grandma.

"Did you have fun, A.J.?" she asked.

"It was the best day of my life, Grandma," he replied.

"You look tired. Let's head on home. Say goodbye to your uncle for now."

A.J. gave his Uncle Cooper a big hug and said, "Thanks, Uncle Cooper. I'll see you tomorrow."

Flo and A.J. began walking back to the house when A.J. asked, "Grandma, tell me more about my dad when he was little."

"Well let's see. Your dad was a born leader. Ever since he could talk he always took control of things. His friends always looked up to him and he was the leader of his group. He had the gift of persuasion. He was so confident he believed he could do anything."

Dalton's Pit

A.J smiled proudly. "Grandma, why is Uncle Cooper here?"

This one was not so easy to explain to A.J., so after she thought about it for a while she put it in a way that would be easy to understand.

"Well A.J., when Grandma was married only a few years, I had a baby girl named Charlotte who you will meet soon. She got sick as a baby and had to come here all by herself. She was very lonely since no one was here to play with her. One day God decided that someone from our family needed to come here to be with her. So, he thought about it for a while and decided that your Uncle Cooper should be the one to come."

"Well, why Uncle Cooper and not my dad?" he asked.

Grandma thought about it. "Well, if your dad was chosen to come here then you would have never been born. He had to stay on earth so that you could be born and so I could be here to wait for you."

Entering the Game

A.J. smiled from ear to ear. "Wow, it's a good thing, right Grandma?"

"Right, A.J. You're a very lucky boy to have a dad like yours," she said.

"What about the rest of our family? When are they coming? I want to meet them."

"Well I am not sure exactly when they will come. I do know that someday they will all be with us though. We will find out just before they do and will be here ready and waiting for them when they come."

"Wow, this is such a cool place; I am so happy I am here with you, Grandma."

After all their talking they finally reached the trailer park where A.J. lived with his parents and entered through the front door. At this point A.J. was very tired and drifting off before he even walked through the door. Flo lifted him up and carried him up to bed. As she tucked him in she noticed just how content he was to be there.

Dalton's Pit

She thought to herself about how death is hard only on the people you left behind and not the one who actually died. She thought back to her Hannah and wondered when she would come join her. She missed her so. She couldn't wait until she joined her, knowing full well that she would no longer need treatments and would no longer be confined to a wheelchair. She didn't realize it until just then that what she needed more than anything was to be needed again. A.J. made her realize just how much. She did have Charlotte to take care of and Cooper, but she still felt incomplete. She thought it was funny, back on earth, the worst day of her life was the day that Cooper died. Once she was able to see everything from all vantage points, she realized that it was the best day of his life. Now she just sat and waited for her Hannah. She wanted to walk with her again. She wanted to rock her to sleep like she did when she was a baby. She remembered back to the night she found out about Hannah's illness. How she cried knowing that her life would be different and that it would not last as long as it should. She just sat back and anxiously waited for the call.

Chapter 10

The Reunion

It had been seven hours since Hannah's surgery began. Billy had spent the last hour or so in the hospital chapel with Travis and Tricia after returning from breakfast. Tricia was filling them in on how she met Austin years earlier. While Billy explained to her what happened years before when Austin left. It seemed like several hours had passed while they were getting each other up to speed on each other's history lessons.

Apparently when Austin left Kansas back in 1978 he went to stay with relatives of his friend Tyler who lived in Gainesville, Texas. Austin, who at the age of 18 had no high school diploma, took a minimum wage job at the dairy farm that Tyler's relatives owned. Mr. and Mrs. Stansfield were Tyler's aunt and uncle on his mother's side. Mr. Stansfield was getting up in years

Dalton's Pit

and needed someone to give him a hand on the farm. Up until that point, though the only thing Austin had ever handled around a farm was his BB gun. Nevertheless, he started out milking cows and feeding chickens for four bucks an hour. He didn't care too much about the money. He figured at least it was a place for him to hide out for the time being. He thought he would stay there for a while until things calmed down and that would give him some time to figure everything out before he eventually returned to Kansas. Nothing in his prior life, though, could have prepared Austin for working as a farmer. After all, this was really hard work. Something that Austin carefully eluded for his entire life. He would be up before dawn on most days and then spend the next 12 hours working like never before. He hated it. He kept mostly to himself in the beginning. He had a small room the size of a shed out back, just off the chicken coop. After his day's work, he would shower in the main house then usually join the Stansfield's for dinner and eventually go back to his room for the night. It was as if he'd created his own little prison cell for himself.

The Reunion

For a long time, he couldn't even look at himself in the mirror and was ashamed to be seen in public. He rarely left the farm. The only outside communication he had was the occasional visit from Tyler. Tyler would come by and give him the scoop about what was happening back home with his family and friends. He was Austin's only true link to the outside world. Although he didn't look forward to seeing Tyler himself, he needed the occasional visit just to keep his sanity. He needed to know just how bad it was back home and where he stood in the community. Needless to say, it wasn't good. It went on that way for a couple months. Somehow Austin thought that by some miracle the next time he spoke with Tyler all would be forgiven in Spring Hill. Perhaps being secluded from society began playing with Austin's mind just a bit.

One night about six months after Cooper's death, Tyler decided to pay Austin an unexpected visit in hopes of cheering him up a little. He arrived around 7:30 that night and went directly to Austin's room out back. He figured it was time for Austin to get out and mingle a little bit with the rest of the world. Maybe go to a club in the area and have a few beers just to relax. After all,

Dalton's Pit

no one in the state of Texas knew who Austin was or what he was running from. As he approached the entrance to Austin's room he rapped on the door. No answer. He knocked again. Nothing. He thought maybe he was in the main house talking with his aunt and uncle. It was late March and there were a few remnants of slushy snow remaining on the grass near the path back to the house. As he turned back he slipped a bit before regaining his balance. After cleaning himself off, he came around the left side of the building, walking past the chicken coop and all the way to the front of the house. He knocked on the door and walked in before waiting for a response.

"Hello? Aunt Iris? Uncle Gene? Anyone home?"

Nothing. Not a sound. Now curious he looked around the kitchen and living room, then took a quick glance up the stairs. He walked around the bannister and headed up the stairs now a bit more concerned. Where was everyone? He got to the top of the stairs and saw a light on in the room all the way at the far back of the hallway. As he got closer he heard faint crying. *What the heck is going on?* he mused. He was almost afraid to open the

The Reunion

door for fear of what he might find. Could Austin have done something to his aunt and uncle? He burst open the door, not sure what he expected to find. There was Austin sitting in the corner crying like a baby all muddied up in his overalls.

Tyler turned to him. "Austin, what the hell is going on? Where are my aunt and uncle? What did you..." Suddenly he heard noise coming from the bathroom directly across the hall. He ran to the bathroom door just as it opened.

"Tyler, you scared me half to death. What are you doing here?"

"Uncle Gene. You're okay? What did Austin do? Where is Aunt Iris? Is she okay?"

"I'm fine, Tyler, what are you talking about? Your aunt is out tonight at her church group. Every Friday night is bingo night. What's wrong with you? Are you feeling okay?"

"Umm nothing; so you're okay? Why are you limping?"

Dalton's Pit

"Yes, Tyler I'm fine. We had a little incident tonight."

"What happened? Why is Austin crying? Did he hurt you?"

"No son, he didn't hurt me. It was nothing like that. Just about a half hour ago after your aunt left for bingo I went out to the back to see if Austin wanted anything to eat. When I knocked on his door he must have left it unlocked and it just swung open. I looked in and he wasn't in there. Then I heard a noise coming from the barn so I walked over and there he was. He was standing on the table with a rope hanging from the ceiling. He was about to hang himself. Well, I got so nervous I ran over and knocked him off the table before he could put the noose around his neck. I hurt my leg on the table as we fell to the floor. Thank God I decided to see if he wanted anything to eat or he surely wouldn't be with us now."

Tyler now understood. Austin was his best friend. He would never hurt his aunt and uncle. Austin's issues were much bigger than that. Austin was in so much pain that he didn't want to live anymore. How could he not

The Reunion

see that? Austin certainly didn't pull the trigger on Cooper, but he knew his involvement in all the lives that were ruined that night at the Food way. He also knew Cooper only went along with the plan because of him. Seeing someone else's pain isn't always easy, especially when we are preoccupied with our own struggles. The signs can be everywhere yet we only see them after it's too late. Luckily this time it wasn't too late. Fortune would have it that Uncle Gene decided to go down to the barn that night. Tyler, feeling a bit guilty for his previous assumptions, was hoping for a second chance for his friend Austin.

Tyler peered back into the room and saw Austin again huddled in the corner sobbing. He came in and sat down next to him on floor

"It will get better, buddy, I promise," he said.

"What do you know? You don't know anything. I killed him. I have no one left. I don't want to be here anymore," Austin cried out.

"Listen, Austin, you didn't kill him. It was an accident. You can't blame yourself for the rest of your life. He

Dalton's Pit

made his own decision; besides, he's the one who brought that stupid BB gun with him. It was his fault, not yours."

"I can never go back. I can't. I wish I could make this right, but I can't. I should have stayed after it happened. I should have faced my family. I just wish there was a way to fix this. A way to go back to my family. I just don't know how."

Tyler didn't say anything. There was nothing he could say. He was just there for his friend in his time of need. Uncle Gene had been standing by the door listening to their conversation. He walked in and sat on the bed adjacent to the boys and leaned in.

"Listen Austin, we all go through things we regret. Things we wish we could go back and change. It's okay to grieve our loved ones. Believe me, I know. I lost my only son when he was only 8 years old in an automobile accident. I've played it over and over in my head for the past 25 years, but nothing's changed. 'If only he'd left on his bike five minutes later,' I said, 'Maybe that car wouldn't have made that turn at that exact time'.

The Reunion

There's not a day that goes by that I don't think of that. Eventually, though, you must move on. Otherwise you die with them. C'mon son, let's go downstairs and get something to eat. You must be hungry."

Up until that day Gene Stansfield had never acknowledged Austin. He always kept him apart from his life, apart from his inner circle. Maybe it was because of his own son's death that he refused to have parental feelings again for another. Who knows? Now, though, Gene Stansfield began to feel a great deal for Austin Dalton. He let him in. Maybe this was a healing for Gene as well. Finally, perhaps he could accept the tragedy that hit him 25 years earlier when his son was killed in that automobile accident. Maybe he needed a project. Maybe it was Austin. It was pretty evident by now that Austin needed him.

Everyone has their own timetable for self-healing. Now if Gene could look forward and not backward, perhaps he could help Austin deal with his own self-healing. It certainly was a step in the right direction, a good place to start.

Dalton's Pit

As a result of Gene Stansfield's new, growing fondness for Austin, what started out as weeks turned into months and then eventually into years for Austin. He just did not know how to reconnect with his family. He accepted instead that the Gene and Iris Stansfield would be his new family. So, after a few years of learning the business and helping run the farm, he started helping distribute the dairy products to local vendors. He delivered milk, eggs, butter and various other dairy products that the Stansfield's produced on the farm. He would drive the company dairy truck to local business owners all over Gainesville and its surrounding area selling their dairy. Their market share began to expand as did their territory. Austin, always the persuasive one, found his one true calling. Talking people into doing something he wanted them to do. Just like when he was a kid, just like with Cooper. He could sell anything.

After a while though, Austin started to become bored, and began feeling unchallenged. Selling milk to average bumpkins who owned a local grocery store wasn't very challenging. So, one day Austin scheduled a meeting

The Reunion

all the way in San Antonio with a big supermarket chain. San Antonio was five hours away from Gainesville and was clearly outside of their territory. Even if he could convince them to do business with the Stansfield's, how would they ship out the dairy every day? Austin, as we already know, never worried about details or even consequences. He just wanted to prove that he could do it. Then he would let someone else figure out the details.

He arrived at the meeting late as usual; his tardiness had never deterred him before. He proceeded to take over the meeting and go right into his pitch as to why they should do business with him and his company. The difference this time, unfortunately, was that he was not talking to the local small business deli owner, but instead he was talking with executives of a large corporation. His brash tactics did not go over very well with the white-collar suits like they did with everyone else. In fact, he pretty much made a fool of himself. Needless to say, he couldn't close the deal that day and was abruptly asked to leave.

Dalton's Pit

After being escorted out of the meeting rather quickly by the company CEO, Austin as usual, had a few parting words for the group.

He snarled, "Oh yeah? Screw you guys; who needs you anyway? I'll go sell my stuff to the supermarket down the street. Then you'll beg to do business with me." He then pushed away from the executive escorting him out and left the store. He then stood in front of the supermarket fuming. After belting out a few explicit phrases about his potential customers who remained in the meeting, he turned to his left. He realized he wasn't alone. He saw a young woman smoking a cigarette, leaning against the window in front of the building.

"Tough day?" she said.

"Nah, to heck with them. They have no idea what they're doing. Who needs them?"

"Cigarette?" she said.

"Sure, why not? That guy Davenport, the CEO, really pissed me off. What a jerk. I'll get him back, though. Nobody talks to me that way and gets away with it."

The Reunion

Austin was so caught up in his failure that it took him a few minutes to realize that he was talking to an attractive young woman just about his age. He straightened up quickly as he saw a potential opportunity in front of him. He turned to her and said, "So, what's your name, by the way?"

"Tricia. Tricia Davenport. That jerk is my father."

Austin, looking embarrassed, took a long puff of the cigarette. "That makes sense. That's the way this day has gone so far, I suppose." Then he looked over at Tricia, realizing he had nothing to lose at this point and said, "So, are you hungry? Would you like to grab some breakfast?"

"Sure, why not," she said with a smile.

They walked over to the next block where there was a small diner and sat down at a booth. Since he barely got his sales pitch off in his first meeting of the day, he figured he would use it with her. He told Tricia that he was a business man in charge of distribution at the Stansfield Dairy. And that he was expanding his territory down to San Antonio. He didn't shut up for the whole

Dalton's Pit

half hour they spent eating breakfast. While it was clear he'd struck out with the first Davenport that day, it was even more clear he had connected with the second. The attraction was obvious on both sides. By the time they finished eating, she felt like she had known him her whole life. On the walk back, Austin asked her if he could see her again. She agreed and the rest was history. Fast forward one year later and they were married.

Tricia's father made life very difficult for his daughter. He despised Austin and his antics and never approved of the marriage. He felt Austin was beneath his daughter. He went so far as to forbid her to see him and told her he would cut her off completely if she did. As history has shown us time and time again, when he forbade her to do it, what do you think happened? It only drew her into his arms that much faster. She and her father had a huge fight and she left to start her new life with Austin.

A few years later Austin Jr. was born. Austin continued driving the dairy truck for the Stansfield's but Tricia wanted to stay in the San Antonio area despite her

Dalton's Pit

father. She had her life there and didn't want to move to live on a farm in Gainesville. Austin agreed, but over time the travelling back and forth eventually took its toll on him. He would split the week between San Antonio and Gainesville. The first few years were tough on both of them. Austin was always travelling for deliveries and sleeping at the Stansfield's half the week while Tricia stayed at home with the baby most of the time by herself. Sometimes Austin would spend a whole week in Gainesville and then come home for only few days. Then he would go back again. This routine allowed them to put food on the table, but was taking its toll on their marriage. Many times Tricia was tempted to go to her father for money or for a better job for Austin, but she just couldn't go crawling back. She would rather struggle; so would Austin. Even later on when her father found out she had a son, he never even bothered to called her. From that day on, as far as she was concerned, her father ceased to exist. She was determined to go it alone with Austin.

When they found out some time later that A.J. had some medical issues, though, the responsibility fell squarely on Tricia alone. Poetic justice, I suppose. Just

The Reunion

like his dad, Austin was the provider and Tricia, like Flo, was the one who raised the kids. Austin now realized the responsibilities his father had when he was little and why he couldn't spend much time with him. He didn't want the same for his son; he wanted to be there for him. Teach him right from wrong. Unfortunately, he didn't have much of a choice. He needed to put food on the table and a roof over their heads. In addition, his limited education and experience didn't give him many opportunities to improve himself financially. He knew where he stood with the Stansfield's. They liked him, they trusted him and the money was decent. There weren't all that many people in Austin's life who liked and trusted him. In fact, he couldn't think of one other person. He knew he had to stay where he was.

Billy, intently listened to Tricia's story, could not help but feel sorry for his brother. Despite the misery Austin put the family through, Billy still felt pity for him. Now it was Billy's turn to share. He spent the next hour telling Tricia about Cooper and what happened to the family after he died. She had never heard about Austin's twin brother or any of them for that matter. She never even knew he had a real family. The only people Austin ever

Dalton's Pit

mentioned were his aunt and uncle who owned a dairy farm. Austin had told her he was an only child and his mother had died when he was a baby.

"Why would he hide this from me?" she said. "I'm his wife."

"Don't take it personal, Trish, he was probably embarrassed about his past and didn't want to relive that part of his life over again."

"But I would have understood; I love him," she said.

Billy then shared with Tricia the story of the night he was coming home and saw Violet and her car stalled by the side of the road. Violet needed his help and he helped her. He never would have imagined at that time that by helping Violet it may have saved his sister's life. The two of them were so engrossed in conversation that they just sat and lamented about all the years gone by and all that was missed. He shared with Tricia about Flo and what a great farmhouse they had as kids and that he still owned it. Finally, he told her about his relationship with Hannah and the significance of the wonderful thing that she and Austin did for them.

The Reunion

Tricia was exhausted by then. She had experienced so many emotions in that one day. She lost her only son. She learned so much about the man she married years ago. She may have saved a life simply by scribbling a number down from a television commercial she had seen. She knew it wasn't a coincidence that she saw that commercial. She knew it was more than that. At the time, though, there was no connection whatsoever except a gut feeling she had. Now she fully understood how this all was tied together from the beginning. So overwhelmed with emotions she just sat back and cried. Tears of sadness? Tears of joy? Tears of relief? Maybe all three combined into one. Meanwhile Travis, who had been sitting there the whole hour without saying a word, decided to break the tension with one of his classic statements.

"Hey Billy, you forgot to tell her the most important thing."

Billy was curious as to what Travis was referring to. "What's that?"

Dalton's Pit

Travis turned to Tricia and said, "Did you know I scored six touchdowns in the 1972 state championship game?"

Billy just shook his head and laughed. "How could I ever forget that?"

Austin and his dad meanwhile had been in the grieving room across the hall from the operating room all the while talking with each other. They had spent the last few hours trying to relieve themselves of all their guilt. They had relived all the events that happened since they last saw each other. At first Austin couldn't even look in his father's eyes. He was consumed with embarrassment and pain. He told his father everything about that fateful night. Fighting through tears he begged for his father's forgiveness. Ernie simply grabbed his son in a big hug and cried on his shoulder.

Ernie said, "I forgive you, son. Please forgive me. It was my fault."

"No Dad, it was mine. I was a bad kid back then. I only cared about myself. I used to boss everyone around, especially Cooper. I miss him so much."

The Reunion

"I was not there for you, son. I should have been there more. I am the reason the family fell apart. I am the reason your mother took her own life, not you," he said.

Neither one of them knew how to reach beyond the emptiness. The truth was that other than the Dalton family tragedies, they didn't have much in common. In their entire lives, they had never had a father and son moment. No baseball games, no fishing trips, no life advice. Nothing. They both just wanted to make their pain go away. Then maybe one day they could talk about happy things. Things that fathers share with their sons. Just maybe, if Hannah survived, they could begin the healing together and feel the connection that was sorely absent. It was the one thing they both desperately needed. The one thing that could bring the healing they both wanted. In their minds, they thought perhaps it could somehow make up for all the bad decisions they'd made in their lives.

It was after nine and Tricia, Billy and Travis had returned to the waiting room, awaiting news from the doctor. Billy and Tricia decided to go downstairs to check on Austin and Ernie to see how they were making out,

Dalton's Pit

while Travis stayed just in case the doctor emerged from the operating room. No sooner than 10 minutes later with Travis dozing off in the chair, the doctor finally emerged from the OR. He saw Travis fast asleep in the chair and approached him.

"Travis?" he said.

Travis quickly jumped to his feet. "Yes, Doc? What happened, is she okay?"

"Hannah is extremely weak, but she did survive the surgery without any major complications. We do not know if her body will accept the transplant yet. It may take some time before we know. I guess this is as good as can be expected, but we are a long way from being out of the woods just yet."

Travis breathed a mild sigh of relief. "Thanks, Doc. I got it. What do we do next? Can we see her?"

"Unfortunately no, Travis. The best thing you can do for her now is to pray. If she makes it through the night, it's a good sign, but we won't know until then. This is going to be a long recovery. We hope."

The Reunion

Travis left the waiting room and ran down to the parking lot where everyone was just standing around talking. As soon as he walked out everyone froze in their tracks. Their hearts were beating out of their chests. They were afraid to ask him. They knew he had spoken to the doctor just by the look on his face.

Billy finally spoke. "Tell me."

"She survived the operation but he's not sure if she will survive the night. We can't see her yet. He said so far so good, though."

Billy was relieved he didn't hear the words he had dreaded, but still there was no reason to celebrate. Nevertheless, there was a bit of optimism abounding. Everyone hugged each other but all of them clearly understood what they were still facing. Now they needed to share the somewhat good news with their loved ones. Tricia called Rose, Travis called his wife, while Billy called Dr. Clifford. They asked each of them to pray for Hannah and for her to make it through the night. Austin even called Mr. Stansfield to share the news. During her call Tricia shared with Rose the story

Dalton's Pit

of the car, how Violet and Billy Dalton met years ago and how fate brought Austin's family back together again.

These phone calls were made to the people who had become their family during their times of uncertainty. These were the people who filled the void in their lives when the family had broken apart. They had all come to the realization that day that they were now family as well. If you ever want to know who your real family is, you can figure it out very easily. It's the first person you call to share news. Whether it's good news or bad news. It does not have to be someone with the same bloodline as you. It's simply someone you need to have beside you during life's bumps in the road.

It was a difficult night for all involved, but just like every other day before, the morning sun never lets you down. It's always there to greet you when you open your eyes. This morning, however, the sunrise was different since their lives could be headed down a completely new path. Billy already knew that Donna had spent the whole night by Hannah's bedside. The fact that he

The Reunion

hadn't received a phone call from her throughout the night was a good start.

The sun was shining especially bright that morning when Billy woke up. He quickly got dressed walked across the hall to Travis and asked him to let everyone know to meet downstairs in 30 minutes. He was so nervous. Although he was a very moral person who always thought of others first, Billy was never a praying man. That day, though, was different. He felt he needed to say a few things. He knelt facing the window in his room and asked for only one thing. He asked for Hannah's pain to end. One way or the other. If it was her time, then let it be. If it wasn't, then please take her pain away. It's time for their next chapter. Time for both to walk through the next door in life.

They all met downstairs in front of the hotel and Billy and Travis hailed a cab, while Tricia followed behind in her car with Austin and Ernie back to the hospital. When they reached the front entrance to the hospital they all hugged each other for luck before entering the building. No one said anything. There wasn't anything to say. They all knew how each other felt. They all knew their

Dalton's Pit

hearts were in their throats. They stepped into the elevator and up to Floor 20, not knowing at all what to expect when the doors opened. As soon as the doors opened Donna was standing maybe 15 feet from the elevator bank and saw Billy enter the lobby. She immediately ran over to him and jumped into his arms giving him a huge hug.

She smiled and said, "Billy, she had a good night. She's even awake. It's amazing. The doctors can't believe she's conscious and speaking. They don't know how to explain it."

Billy was so excited he planted the biggest kiss of his life right on Donna's lips. Something he had craved for such a long time. It was just never the right moment. Not until that moment. Donna clearly appeared to have a similar sentiment. After finally unlocking their lips, Donna said, "Would you like to see her now? I believe she already has company."

Billy, mildly embarrassed over the kiss, said, "Yes of course, wait… company? Who is her company?"

The Reunion

"I'm not sure, but about a half hour ago two women were sitting in her room talking with her. They said they were friends of the family; I am not sure who they are."

The entire Dalton family looked at each other. Who the heck would be there so early in the morning the day after Hannah's surgery? How would anyone even know about it to begin with? The truth was, though, that it didn't matter. Who cared? Hannah was awake. That's all that mattered.

Billy led the way to her room with Donna by his side. Everyone was filled with anticipation and maybe even curiosity as well. Who else was in her room?

Billy asked the rest of the family to wait in the hallway at first. He wasn't sure how Hannah would handle all that had gone on with Dad and Austin. How could he possibly even explain it to her? After all, she hadn't seen her father or her brother in years. He was afraid it would be too much for her too soon. Billy and Donna approached the door and opened it slightly. They noticed a young woman sitting in the chair next to Hannah's bed. Hannah, still very weak saw Billy and

Dalton's Pit

Donna enter and that magical Hannah grin appeared across her face. Something that Billy feared he would never see again. As Billy and Donna approached her bedside, the first words out of Hannah's mouth were, "Hey Donna, Billy's cute, huh?"

Donna smiled as she put her arm around Billy. "Yes, very."

Billy with that same embarrassed look, said, "Pip, you have no idea how good it is to see your smile again."

He was so relieved to see Hannah's smile that he momentarily forgot there was a woman sitting in the chair alongside Hannah's bed. He leaned back over his shoulder to look at her. Who was she, he wondered?

And why was she in his baby sister's room at 7 o'clock in the morning?

"Excuse me, miss, but who are you?" he said.

The woman smiled at Billy and said, "My name is Rose Harrison; I am Tricia's best friend. She called me last night and told me all about your sister and about A.J.

The Reunion

Tricia is family to me and I just had to be here for her. I wanted to come and meet your sister as well."

"It's very nice to meet you, Rose. We are indebted to Tricia for what she did for us."

Billy turned to look at Hannah again. "Wow Pip, you see how popular you are? People you've never even met before are coming to see you."

Just then the toilet flushed in the bathroom to the right of Hannah's bed. Billy remembered that Donna mentioned there were two women in Hannah's room this morning. He looked over to see an older woman washing her hands with the door wide open. She came out of the bathroom and said, "Hello, William. It's great to see you again. I am so happy for you and your sister. It's been such a long time."

Billy, at a loss for words, trembled and slid back into the chair next to Rose. "Violet," he exclaimed. He just sat there in amazement. "I can't believe it. How? Why are you here?"

Dalton's Pit

"I am here because of you, William. You're the reason I am here. You changed my life that night in the rain. I wanted to come here and thank you in person. When Rose called me to tell me what happened I just had to come to meet Hannah and see you again."

Billy still did not fully understand what was happening. He heard rustling outside the door. Travis peeked his head in with a goofy grin and Billy snapped out of his stupor for the moment. Collecting himself, he realized that Hannah's whole family was outside the door wanting to see her.

Billy realized how difficult this must be for Hannah to accept. He turned to her and said, "Hannah, I have something I need to tell you. It's very big and I want to make sure you can handle it."

"Oh my God, Billy; you are so dramatic. Tell them to come in already," she said.

"Wait. What? Tell who?"

"Our family. Dad and Austin. And Tricia of course. Tell Travis to let them in already."

The Reunion

Travis, listening all along, opened the door and came in with his father Ernie by his side. Ernie shook his head as he slowly walked up to the side of the bed and smiled at Hannah.

"My Hannah. My angel. My baby. Daddy always loved you."

Hannah smiled. "I know, Dad, I know. I love you too. Always have."

Ernie touched his daughter's hand and kissed her on her head. "I'll never leave you again, my angel."

Billy walked over and helped his father into the chair alongside Rose by the foot of the bed. He then walked out to the hallway and asked Austin to come in.

"You're up, brother. Are you ready?"

"Not really. I'm not sure I can handle this. It's been so long. What would I even say to her?" he asked.

"Don't worry, Austin, you're never at a loss for words, that's for sure. You'll think of something."

Dalton's Pit

Austin was trembling at the thought of seeing Hannah for real. He entered the room with his wife Tricia by his side and before he could say anything Hannah broke the ice.

"Hey Dred, how are you? I see you've gained a few pounds since I saw you last."

The room went from apprehension to laughter in a flash. Talk about an ice breaker. Austin cried with both laughter and sadness at the same time as did most everyone else. He then walked up to Hannah with much more ease than he ever imagined.

"Sis, I just want to say—" Hannah stopped him short. "I know, I know, you were a bad kid and you're sorry. You're forgiven, Austin, now come here and give me a hug. I've missed you."

Billy was totally confused. He walked over to Hannah with a very serious look on his face and said, "I don't understand, Hannah. How did you know they were here? That doesn't make any sense. Did Rose or Violet tell you?"

The Reunion

"Nope, they didn't," she said with a grin.

"Then how?" Billy replied.

"To be honest, Billy, I saw everything that went on the whole time I was unconscious. I saw you, Travis and Dad by my bedside a few days ago. I heard every word you said to each other. It was pretty weird, though. I was looking down at you guys. It was like I was watching you look at me from the ceiling above you. I can't explain it, but I was able to move around freely, like I have never done before in my life. I was also able to move between rooms. I was in the room next door when Austin and Tricia said goodbye to A.J. I then watched all of you waiting for me to come back last night. That's when I knew about Rose and Violet. When we met this morning, I felt such a connection with them even though we had never actually met before. Then after we spoke this morning they felt the same way. Kind of strange, but it all seems to connect together somehow."

Hannah then turned to Rose and said, "Oh by the way, Rose, tell Thomas Jr that A.J. said he hid the Super Mario

Dalton's Pit

cartridge in the bookcase behind the globe just in case he was looking for it."

Rose turned to Hannah. "Wait a minute, how could you know that? He's been looking for it for a long time now. That's impossible."

An eerie feeling permeated throughout the room as everyone looked at each other.

"Well, when we were both up on the ceiling yesterday looking over everyone, A.J. told me that Super Mario was their favorite video game to play and the day he left he forgot to tell Thomas Jr. where he hid it. He said to tell him he was cold not hot," she said.

Chills ran up and down Tricia's arm as Hannah described her encounter with A.J. She then told Tricia that A.J. wanted her to know that he was no longer out of breath, not to worry about him anymore and that he was fine. She also told them that just before A.J. left her she heard a woman's voice calling him. She couldn't see her but was sure it sounded just like her mom Flo. Everyone just sat there in silence. They were all just staring at each other dumbfounded. Could this be real?

The Reunion

Just then Doctor Nazir, who was making his rounds, walked in as the room went silent.

"Hello Hannah, great to see you again. How are we feeling this fine morning?"

Hannah smiled. "Couldn't be any better, Doc. I have my whole family together."

"I see that, Hannah. You must be a popular girl," he said.

"Sure am, Doc," she responded.

Doctor Nazir turned to Billy. "Billy, you were right all along. I don't know how to explain it, but in my 30 years practicing medicine, I have never seen someone rebound so quickly like Hannah did. I am sorry I ever doubted you. I owe you an apology."

"Thank you, Doctor. No need to apologize. Hannah wouldn't be here if it wasn't for you. She owes her life to you."

"My pleasure, William. He then turned around to the rest of the room. "I do still want to caution everyone. Hannah still has a long way to go before she can leave

Dalton's Pit

ICU and return to her old room. So far so good, but let's try to give her some rest. I would please ask that everyone go downstairs and let her sleep for a while. Perhaps later you can come back and visit."

"Ok, Doc," Travis said. "C'mon everyone, let's go down to the diner around the corner. Breakfast is on me this fine morning. As they exited her room, everyone gave Hannah a hug and kiss and headed out to the hallway, except for Donna and Billy.

Donna burrowed under Billy's right arm and looked up at him. She smiled and then gave him a kiss on the cheek.

"What was that for?" he asked.

"That's for being an amazing man. And an amazing brother."

Billy normally very shy and reserved mustered up some courage. "Um, Donna? Would you like to maybe um, go get something to eat with me? I mean like tonight or tomorrow night?"

The Reunion

"You mean like a date, Billy Dalton? Are you asking me out on a date? In front of your sister?"

"Um… yes. Yes, I am."

"Well let me think about this for a minute, Mr. Billy Dalton."

"Um… Okay," he said.

Donna smiled. "I'm just messing with you, Billy. Of course, I will go out with you. I've been waiting for you to ask me out for months now."

"Great, maybe we could—"

Donna interrupted him. "Wait, Billy, there's something I need you to do for me first. It's very important. If you do it, then I'll go out with you."

"Anything. You name it, Donna."

"Tell me what Dalton's Pit is," she said.

Billy laughed. "Soon, Donna, soon. I'll have to ask Pip about that one first."

Dalton's Pit

Donna smiled at Billy and nodded her head in acceptance. They walked out arm in arm. Hannah then lifted her head after pretending to be asleep, thinking to herself, "That's my Billy. Never relinquish the secret of Dalton's Pit. Not to anyone, not even Donna."

Chapter 11

Hannah

The one thing that could always be said about the Dalton farmhouse was that despite all the drama and tragedy, it was a home always filled with adventure. This was especially true around the holidays. Despite all the hardships endured by the Dalton clan over the past few years this year was no different. It had been seven years since Hannah's heart transplant was deemed an amazing success. It had also been seven years since the day that Austin Jr. passed away. It had been quite a while since the whole Dalton clan was under the same roof, sharing a holiday meal. This year they were all looking forward to spending Thanksgiving dinner together at the old farmhouse. Hannah was especially excited to see everyone. It was the night before Thanksgiving and Billy and Donna were preparing for the next day's festivities.

Dalton's Pit

Billy had just come in from outside. "Babe, how many chairs do we need around the table... 15? I'm not sure?"

"Fifteen, I think. No wait... we are sixteen now. You had better get the table extension from the basement if we are going to fit everyone. Wait, I'm sorry you were right the first time; it's only fifteen, plus little Cooper's high chair," Donna replied.

Donna had been cooking since early that morning, since she knew the following day would be filled with mayhem. The kind of mayhem you look forward to. Hannah was sitting in the living room in her wheelchair playing a game of I Spy with the twins.

"I spy something purple in the room," she said.

Harrison (Harry) and Jackson (Jack) were now four years old and adored their aunt Hannah.

"Um... is it the couch pillow, Aunt Hannah?" Harry said.

"Wow, you guys are getting too good for this game. You make it so easy. I'm going to have to make the next one much harder," she said.

Hannah

Billy finished setting the chairs around the table and entered the living room area. "Let's go, boys, you need to get washed up before bed. What do you say we surprise Mommy and go upstairs and take a bath?"

"Dad, I wanna keep playing with Aunt Hannah. Just five more minutes? Please, Dad?" Jack asked. "One more game and then we will come up."

"Boys, your mommy's been cooking all day. I want to give her a break. Let's go. Last one upstairs is a rotten egg," he replied.

"Go ahead, boys. I'll be here when you get back," added Hannah. "And I'm going to make the next one really hard for you."

The boys followed Billy up the stairs to get washed and into their pajamas. Hannah was at that point all alone in the living room. Just at that moment Donna happened to walk by to grab something off the table when she saw Hannah wince a little bit. It was clear that she was having some pain. As soon as Hannah saw her, she pretended it was nothing. This was the third time in the past few days that Donna had witnessed Hannah

Dalton's Pit

wince in pain. She walked in and sat down next to Hannah.

"Hannah, are you okay? I saw you do the same thing yesterday. I need to know if you are okay," she said.

"Yes, I'm fine, Don; just a little stomachache. It's no big deal. I've been through a lot worse. No one knows that better than you. I'll be fine," Hannah said with a smile.

"Okay, Hannah, but I need you to tell me if you're having pains. Okay? Where are the boys?"

"Billy just took them up two minutes ago for their bath," she replied.

"Are you sure you're okay?"

"Donna please, I'm fine."

The truth was that she wasn't fine. She had been having significant pains for the last few weeks, but didn't say anything because she didn't want anyone to worry about her. First it was in her legs, then it spread to her arms and then her head. They were short lived pains, but were becoming more frequent the past few weeks.

Hannah

The last few days the pains sliced through her head like a knife. Through it all, though she pretended it was nothing. She had been looking forward to seeing everyone again for so long she didn't want anything to ruin the day. Hannah was 42. She was already beyond the life expectancy for someone with Microcephaly. In her mind, she wondered if this would be her last holiday with everyone together. Just in case she wanted to make it a memorable one.

The boys finished their baths then came down for a bit to finish playing with their Aunt Hannah. They played a few more games and then went up to bed. Hannah picked up a few of their toys off the carpet and put them in the toy chest next to the television and went out to the kitchen. She said goodnight to Billy and Donna and then retired into her room for the night. Her room was just off the living room to the right. A few years earlier Billy had it completely remodeled. He built Hannah her own back entrance which allowed her access to the back porch directly from her room. It had wheelchair ramps that led to every part of the yard. One ramp fed directly into the Lucky Dogs compound all the way at the end of the yard. She had the biggest room in the

Dalton's Pit

house. Some nights when she wasn't feeling well Donna had to help her get into bed. Tonight, though, Hannah had refused her assistance. Perhaps it was more about proving she was fine.

Donna and Billy decided to relax for a bit and watch a little TV before turning in. Donna sat next to him on the couch and crawled under his left arm to rest her head.

"Billy, I saw Hannah wince before like she was in pain. I am not positive, but I think something's not right with her. This was the third time this past week I saw her look uncomfortable. She is definitely in pain. She tried to shrug me off by saying it was a stomachache but I don't believe her. She is hiding something. I'd like to have her check into Spring Hill for some tests right after tomorrow."

"Ok. Babe, let's see how she feels after tomorrow and if we need to confront her we will."

Billy looked down at his wife and smiled. "How in the world did I get so lucky to marry a woman like you?"

Hannah

Donna just gave him her signature look. She wrapped her arms around him, buried her head in his chest and sighed.

Billy reached over and turned out all the lights in the living room. He then got up, shut off the TV, picked his beautiful wife up off the couch and carried her upstairs.

The following morning Travis and his family landed at the airport around 6 a.m. after taking a red eye flight from San Diego and made it to the old farmhouse just before 8 o'clock. On his way over from the airport he stopped off at the bagel store in town and brought a few dozen bagels back to the house with him. He also brought a malted for Hannah of course, strawberry as always.

As soon as Travis approached the steps out in front of the old house, that old creaky porch started playing its tune. At least they knew no one could ever rob the place. As soon as someone stepped onto the porch, the whole house knew.

Donna, upon hearing them arrive, opened the door in her apron and said with a smile, "Hello, brother Travis."

Dalton's Pit

Travis, Ivy and two of his three boys entered the house and exchanged their pleasantries with Donna. Jacob and Travis Jr., now 21 and 19 respectively were both currently in college in California. Jacob was a junior accounting major at UCLA and Travis Jr. was a biology major at Santa Clara University. They both stood over 6 feet tall, just like their dad.

Ivy moved to the kitchen area and was talking with Donna.

"I am so excited we are all together today. It's been so long. Where are Hannah and Billy?"

"Billy's upstairs dressing the boys and Hannah is in the living room. Come in, sit down. How was the flight?"

"The flight was smooth, the boys slept most of the way. Travis didn't sleep a wink though. He is driving me crazy. He is a complete bundle of nerves. He can hardly control himself," she said.

It was a very big day for Travis. After all, it wasn't every day that your son got to play football on national television. Let alone on Thanksgiving Day. Mason

Hannah

Dalton was the starting middle linebacker for the Detroit Lions. It was his second year in the league but the previous year he didn't get to see a snap all year due to an injury to his left quad. That day though he would be primetime. Travis was a wreck. He had seen so many of his son's games, but this was the NFL. If it wasn't for Hannah and Thanksgiving, he most assuredly would be there in the stands. He chose, however, to be with Hannah and the rest of the family instead, knowing full well that there would be plenty other games for him to see in person. Mason was just starting out and had the world in front of him. Travis, on the other hand had seen his dreams crumble right before him years ago. To have his son fulfill his dream was just as special, if not more special. It was not even 9 a.m. yet and Travis had plopped himself in front of the TV, wearing his number 55 Detroit Lions jersey. The name Dalton was stitched on the back. He was already waiting for the pregame show which wouldn't start for another 2 hours.

Billy came downstairs with the boys and greeted everyone. He helped Donna and Ivy cut up the bagels and put the juice on the table. Travis then walked in from the living room and as usual greeted his brother

Dalton's Pit

with a head lock, causing Billy to spill the juice on the table.

"He loves it, Ivy," Travis said. "Don't you, little brother?"

"Yeah Ivy, I love it. I couldn't wait for this monster to jump on my back," Billy squealed. "Don't worry, I've been dealing with this lunatic my whole life."

Most of the family was around the kitchen table eating breakfast together in full conversation mode. Hannah was in the living room talking with Jacob and Travis Jr catching up on college and all their girlfriends. The rest of their company would be there soon. The last time Travis and the family had come to the old house was last March when his father Ernie passed away. Ernie lived to the ripe old age of 81. He died a very happy man. A far cry from when he was living in the trailer park just waiting to die. He shared with Billy and Hannah just before he died that the last seven years spent together with them were the best years of his life. He was able to see the births of some of his grandchildren and he was also able to help take care of his Hannah, even if only for a while. The frayed 10-gallon black hat he always

Hannah

wore rested on a shelf above the television in the living room along with a model car, a 1978 Austin Cooper mini pickup.

The doorbell rang nonstop. First it was Rose, Thomas Jr. and her new husband Jeff. Then it was Violet Harrison. Then about a half hour later Austin, Tricia and eight-month old Cooper arrived. The whole family was together and just in time for the 12:30 kickoff. Billy was in the kitchen cutting up the bird while some of the boys were in the yard tossing around the football. Travis and Austin were watching the pre-game in the living room with Hannah. The house was filled with love. It was filled with family. Billy looked up from his cutting board and remembered back just eight years ago when he was the only person in the old house. He had Thanksgiving dinner alone that year and to the best of his recollection, ate a turkey sandwich over the kitchen sink and went up to bed by 9 o'clock.

He looked out that day and saw a family, his family. Violet was off to the side looking over the counter and could just feel what Billy was thinking. She eventually caught his eye as he was scanning the room with pride.

Dalton's Pit

She walked over to him and said, "You know this was all because of you. You started this in motion many years ago. It was just one random act of kindness for an old lady like me. Did you ever think this would be the result? You should be proud, Billy. I know your mother and father must be. They are looking down at this old house with huge smiles on their faces. You can't possibly imagine how important you are to each person in this room."

Violet leaned over and gave Billy a kiss on his cheek. Billy smiled sheepishly and said, "Thank you, Violet, I believe you were meant to be stuck on that road for me that night. I believe that life gives us these opportunities all the time. We just don't see them most of the time because we get too caught up in our own issues. We're too focused on the things that aren't perfect in our lives to see all these opportunities around us."

Violet touched Billy's hand. "By the way, did Rose tell you she is expecting?"

"Really? That's so great."

Hannah

"Yes, it's a girl and she's due in May. She asked me to be her grandma. I am so happy I could cry. She's going to name her Hannah. You know she gave me the car back, right? It's funny I've wanted to get rid of the damn thing for so long, but now it's a part of me that I could never let go. Billy, you gave me the family I was never able to have as a young woman. You are the son I never had."

Just then Donna yelled, "Ok everyone, dinner's ready; let's eat." Billy smiled and looked at Violet.

"C'mon Grandma, sit next to me."

Billy stood up to say a few words before the meal. He spoke of how only eight years ago he ate Thanksgiving Day dinner alone standing up over the sink while Hannah was in New York in the hospital. He shared how he never imagined that day would ever come and how life paid him back 100 times over for everything bad that happened in his past. He looked around the room, lifted his glass and simply said, "Everyone look around and remember this day. Life doesn't get any better than this."

Dalton's Pit

Dinner was well underway; everyone was eating and laughing at the table. Billy got up to stretch his legs and stepped into the yard for a moment for some fresh air. He looked across the yard, smiling to himself while he admired his latest creation. A few months back he re-did the archway to the compound to read "**Hannah's Lucky Dogs.**"

Hannah's Lucky Dogs Inc. had become one of the largest nonprofit organizations in the United States. It had shelters in 37 states and was a household name. Although Hannah was no longer active in the company she still would drive her chair into the compound almost every morning to walk with Billy and visit with all the animals. A while back Billy had coffee mugs made for Hannah and himself that said *President* and *Vice President*. He always left the President mug for Hannah. After all, she was the reason it was created. They had a ritual: Every morning they would share their morning cup of coffee on the back porch and then go out and visit with the animals. Billy would walk along the stream and Hannah was always alongside him in her chair on the path just to the left. Their morning walk was Billy's favorite part of the day.

Hannah

Austin and Tricia moved back to Kansas a few years back and Austin became the head of transportation for the entire company. He orchestrated the adoptions as well as the transporting of all the animals to their forever homes. Tricia gave birth to baby Cooper in Spring Hill hospital just last spring. Ernie, prior to passing away had moved back in to the house seven years ago right after Hannah was released from the hospital. He stayed by her side until his passing last year.

As for Billy and Donna they married six years ago and Donna, instead of going back to work, became Hannah's primary caregiver. She loved Hannah so much since the days they used to walk down by the Hudson River. She dedicated her life to caring for Hannah. She gave birth to the twins two years later. Billy meanwhile gave up his veterinarian practice when the twins were born to help around the house and decided to focus 100 percent of his time on Hannah's Lucky Dogs Inc.

Some days when Hannah wasn't up to going out, Billy would walk down by the creek alone just like when he was a kid. He would pick out a frog or some other critter and bring it back to show Hannah. Unfortunately, they

Dalton's Pit

were both now just a little too big to fit into Dalton's Pit. So they would sit on the back porch with their coffee mugs and watch the sun come up, pretending as if they were still 11 years old.

Hannah saw that Billy was outside by himself, so she excused herself from the table. She followed him out in her chair down the ramp.

"Pretty awesome, isn't it?" she said.

Billy looked at Hannah and smiled, wondering if he should mention what Donna told him the night before. "The most beautiful thing I've ever seen."

"We did it, brother. We did what we said we would. Back then in Dalton's Pit."

Billy put his arm around Hannah. "We sure did, Pip; we sure did."

Donna saw them outside and opened the back door. "Billy, we are serving coffee and cake; why don't you guys come in now. By the way, the Lions won. Mason intercepted a pass with two minutes to go and your brother almost lifted the couch over his head with your

Hannah

sons still sitting on it. I think you need to calm him down a bit."

Billy looked down at Hannah. "C'mon, President. Let's go get some coffee. I could use a cup."

Hannah went in first and Billy was about to follow when he saw something in the brush alongside the compound. He told Hannah he would be right in and proceeded down the ramp to investigate. The closer he got he realized there was a person out there with one of his dogs. Could it be a handler coming for a pickup? Everyone knew they were closed. Something wasn't right. *What to do*, he thought? *Should I go back and get Travis?* As he got closer, though, he realized it was an older person talking to the dog. When he was about 20 yards away, Billy snarled, "Excuse me, but this is private property. Why are you here? You need to leave now."

The older gentleman turned around and looked at Billy without responding.

"Did you hear me, sir? This is private property. Who are you?"

Dalton's Pit

Billy reached the entrance to the compound and the man was grinning from ear to ear. "You don't recognize me do you, Dr. Dalton?"

"I'm sorry, sir, but no I don't." Billy thought perhaps the man was crazy. "You have to... Wait, Charlie?"

The old man stood at attention and with a smile said, "Corporal Charles O'Rourke reporting for duty, sir. You remember Mickey, don't you?"

Billy was confused. "How did you find me? Why are you here? This is crazy. How did you get here? I'm confused."

"Well sir, I came here to thank you. Since we last spoke my life has changed so much and I wanted to find you to thank you in person. I have reunited with my children and have since become affiliated again with my old army battalion. I am now working at the local recruitment office in my home town back east. That day when you came to me was my turning point. It's been seven or eight years since then and my life has changed so much for the better. Then when my superior officer told me I had to come to Kansas for a recruitment

Hannah

symposium, I immediately thought of you. I remembered your name and when I googled it, Lucky Dogs compound came up and here I am. I am only here for the weekend and wanted to come by to say hello and thank you personally. You are a gentleman and one of finest people I've ever met. I salute you, William Dalton."

Mickey was now sniffing by the compound entrance as he saw a few of the dogs running around inside. "My friend Mick, here, is still going strong at the young age of nine. He does, however, seem to be very interested in your compound." He laughed. "Well I just wanted to thank you; I guess I'll be on my way now."

"No way, Charlie, you have to come in for some cake and coffee. I want you to meet my family. Please come and follow me."

"What should I do with my Mickey?" he said.

"Don't worry, I'll put him in the compound. He'll have a ball. I have one of my handlers watching the dogs today;

"he'll take care of him."

Dalton's Pit

Billy opened the gate and Mickey headed off with one of the handlers as the two men walked back up to the house. When they entered the house, Billy introduced Charlie to the family over cake and coffee. After a while Charlie got very emotional and told the whole house what Billy did for him that day in New York. How he walked him across the street and gave him a room and food for him and his dog Mickey. With tears in his eyes he let everyone know what Billy's kindness had meant to him. So much so that seven years later he sought him out. Billy had never shared that story with anyone. The funny thing was everyone already knew the man Billy was. This only added to his legacy. Billy was humbled for the first time in his life. He finally understood his value to others. Especially when he looked over at Donna and saw the way she looked back at him. It was hard to explain, but if her eyes could talk, she couldn't have said more about her love for him than she had with that one look.

The rest of the night was storybook. Everyone was getting along, laughing and talking. Jacob was wrestling with the twins on the front grass while Travis Jr. was throwing the football around with Thomas on the side.

Hannah

Charlie and Violet were talking on the porch. *Hmm interesting*. It seemed like no one wanted the day to end, especially Hannah. Unfortunately, though for us, just like you can count on the morning sun to rise, you can also always count on the evening sun to set. About an hour later everyone began saying their goodbyes and planning the next get-together. The twins were fast asleep on the couch and Travis, who still hadn't come down from his football high, was still as loud as ever.

Violet approached Billy to say goodnight and gave him a hug. "Thank you for all you have given me, William. Let's talk again soon."

Everyone was happy. Everyone except Hannah, that is. She didn't want the day to end. She knew that this might be the last time she saw everyone under one roof. She hid her somberness well. After all, it was hidden behind that great Hannah smile.

After everyone had gone, Donna began cleaning up the mess. Billy carried the boys upstairs and put them to bed while Hannah began putting some of the kids'

Dalton's Pit

books back in the bookcase next to the living room television.

Donna walked into the living room with a concerned look on her face. "Hannah, what's going on? You don't seem yourself. Is everything okay with you? Tell me the truth."

Hannah gave in and said, "Actually Donna, I am in severe pain. My whole side goes numb all the time and I'm having trouble moving the fingers on my left hand. I think I am dying."

"Why didn't you tell me earlier? I could have—"

Hannah cut her off mid-sentence. "No Don, I just wanted to enjoy today. I didn't want anything to ruin it. It was very important to me. You don't understand, Donna. I needed this today." Hannah began to cry.

Donna came over and hugged Hannah while Billy stood listening by the steps.

"If this is my time, then I am ready. I do not want to be in the hospital anymore. I want to enjoy the rest of my

Hannah

life. I want to enjoy whatever time I have left. I want to die here with my family, not in some hospital."

Billy walked in "But Hannah—"

"Billy, just don't say anything. I know what I know. I know you guys are the best thing in my life and I know I wouldn't be here without you. I just can't anymore; everyone who looks at me does so with pity in their eyes. I just want to be normal. I want to die like a normal person. Can't you understand that?"

Hannah wiped her tears and said, "Billy, please come in here and sit next to your wife. I have something to tell her and I want you to hear it."

Billy walked in feeling a little uneasy. What could she possibly want to tell Donna? He sat down next to Donna and Hannah moved her wheelchair directly in front of them.

"Donna, I have to tell you something very important. Something I've never told anyone."

"Anything, Hannah. What is it?"

Dalton's Pit

"Dalton's Pit is a small space under the porch that's hidden by some tires my father put there years ago. Billy and I spent a lot of time there when we were little. We shared all our secrets and dreams there. Well, all of my dreams have come true and it's because of the two of you. I wanted to make sure you knew that. Also, because I know Billy would never tell you what it was. You are the best sister in the world and you deserved to know."

Billy, Donna and Hannah all started crying at the same time. Billy wondered if Hannah was saying her goodbyes already.

Christmas and New Year's Day came and went, but everyone had their own things going on. Travis and the family were in California, Rose and Violet were with Joanne in San Antonio and Austin and his family went to see the Stansfield's who were now in their 80's. It was a quiet holiday week for Billy, Donna, Hannah and the twins. Time to ring in 2010.

On the morning of January 3 Billy had gotten up a little earlier to check on one of the older dogs who was sick.

Hannah

He had to administer an insulin shot to him. He put on a pot of coffee then went out into the compound and gave him the shot. He then came back in and poured two cups of coffee for Hannah and himself. *She should be up any minute now*, he figured. He filled his cup and walked out into the yard and out onto the porch. After sitting out there by himself for about 10 minutes, suddenly he just knew. It came over him like a tidal wave. He ran into the house and right to Hannah's room. There was Donna sitting alongside Hannah's bed crying. Hannah had passed away overnight peacefully in her bed. Billy was very sad, he cried right along with his wife. The moment had finally arrived. Oddly though he didn't feel the way he thought he would. He had prepared for that day for so many years. He worried and worried about her dying for what seemed to be more than half of his life. He was surprised to find he wasn't as devastated as he thought he would be. It certainly wasn't because he didn't love Hannah.

He sat down beside his wife and shared his thoughts. "I am just now realizing that maybe Hannah is better off. I did the best I could. We were able to give her so many extra years and memories."

Dalton's Pit

Donna agreed. "Yes we did."

"I'll miss her smile. Yet somehow I feel a bit relieved. I finally have some closure," Billy added. I know her life was very different from most other people's. Was I being selfish for wanting to keep her here with me?"

"You're not the selfish type, Bill. It was just her time."

"Ever since I was a kid she always came first." He worked up a smile. "I remember this one time when we were kids when I was being picked on in the school yard by this bully Peter and how she tried to defend me. What will I do with all my time now? She was involved in every aspect of my life. She did more for me than I did for her, though," he said with a smile. "After all, she brought me to you."

"Billy, none of us are immune to loss. It's just our turn to grieve. We have to now look forward to our next road together and see what's in store. That's how it works, I guess. That's life," Donna replied.

"She taught me so much. I don't know how she kept that positive attitude she had despite the hand she was

Hannah

dealt. If *she* could stay positive, then how could anyone else be unhappy with their life? I am so happy she was able to see the whole family come together again. She deserved that," Billy added.

"She was asked to go through life with a disability. Why? Was she randomly chosen from above? Doesn't seem fair. She learned from an early age to deal with adversity. I am not sure I could have done that."

"Billy, she was born that way, that's all she knew. She learned to live with her disability because she had no choice. She knew it was pointless to feel sorry for herself knowing full well she couldn't change anything.

Years ago, when we first got to know each other, she would tell me that no matter how bad things were in her life she knew there was always someone worse off than her that would be happy to trade places in a second. She learned to appreciate what most people take for granted," Donna lamented.

"I guess in a way she was right. There's an old saying that goes "Let it hurt, let it bleed, let it heal, then let it go. Those are good words to live by," Billy added.

Dalton's Pit

"I think in Hannah's case it bothered everyone but her that she was disabled, all the way up until the very end. There are so many people today who physically are perfectly healthy their entire lives but go through it without enjoying the beauty around them. In a way, you could say they are more handicapped than she was," Donna added.

The funeral was held a few days later and she was buried just a few rows away from where Cooper was laid to rest some 30 years before. The community had changed so much since Cooper's death. The whole town was not present for Hannah's departure like they were for Cooper's. That's what happens when you get older. Everyone raises their own family and drifts away from where they came from. Then they create new families in new neighborhoods. There were some familiar faces from the old neighborhood but not many. A few of the older neighbors who heard came to pay their respects. In fact, Mr. Danby was there. Now 83 years old Mr. Danby had visited Cooper's grave every Saturday for the past 30 years, placing fresh cut white lilies by his headstone. There's a mystery solved. Sometimes in life we forget those who appear to be the less significant

Hannah

people affected by tragedy. Mr. Danby's life had never been the same since that night. Knowing that his actions whether justified or not, carried with it someone's life was a large weight to carry. Mr. Danby carried that weight for 30 years. True, it wasn't his son. True, it also wasn't even his fault. Yet he was never the same knowing that he had taken a young man's life, had taken him away from his family. When he heard about Hannah's death he came to pay his respects to the family. He didn't just come for Hannah, though, he also came for Cooper and for himself. He hadn't spoken to anyone in the Dalton family since Ernie tried to kill him so many years ago. Was it fear? Was it guilt? Perhaps it was a little of both.

As soon as the Dalton boys saw Mr. Danby, all 3 of them approached him with respect and kindness. Now as grown adults they fully understood what he must have gone through all those years ago. Healing takes time they say but understanding sure speeds it up a bit. Mr. Danby had been carrying around this despair for so long he felt as if it was lifted off his chest as soon as they acknowledged him. He hugged all three of the boys and

Dalton's Pit

then continued to Cooper's grave to plant his lilies like he always did.

After visiting the cemetery, everyone came back to the old house. The mood was a somber one but not as bad as expected. Billy got up to say a few words about his beloved Pip.

"I would like everyone in this room to look around at each other. Now I would like you to think back to 10 years ago today. Think about your life back then and what you were doing."

Donna was thinking about her cheating boyfriend, Austin thinking about being estranged from his family and his guilt, Violet thinking about being alone, Rose thinking about her abusive husband and so on.

"Now look where we are today. Our family has come together because of one person. One beautiful angel. If it were not for our Hannah, none of us would be sitting in this room today. I want to thank her for being such a huge part of all our lives. I love you, Pip and I will see you again someday and we will walk along the stream together one last time."

Hannah

Donna walked over and hugged her husband tightly and said, "Come with me."

She took him into the kitchen and grabbed his and Hannah's coffee mugs. She then walked out of the front door with Billy alongside her. She then got on her knees, crawled under the porch moved the old tires and placed the 2 mugs into Dalton's Pit. When she came out from under the porch she stood up next to her husband and whispered in his ear, "Now it's our secret, babe, just the three of us."

Chapter 12

Full Circle

It was a beautiful afternoon; the sun was shining brightly over the front lawn. Billy had just arrived home about an hour ago. This time, though, the trip wasn't a very smooth one. He entered the old house as he always did and checked his phone for messages. No messages today. The house seemed especially quiet this afternoon. He found that odd since usually it was a bit chaotic. He sat down at the kitchen table just for a moment to gather himself. *What a trip*, he thought. *I am glad to be home. I'm glad I can sleep in my own bed tonight.* Unfortunately, the tranquility of the moment was short lived when he heard some rumblings out in the back yard. He sluggishly rose from the table and decided to investigate what was going on. He proceeded out the back door and walked out onto the porch to see what all the racket was. He wasn't in the mood for company. His mild frustration immediately disappeared and was replaced with a huge grin as he walked down the steps and out into the yard. Everyone

Dalton's Pit

was there. They were all scattered about throughout the yard talking amongst themselves. A surprise party? Wow, for me? He couldn't believe it. His birthday wasn't until next week. He was bit overwhelmed by it all and needed to sit down and rest for a moment. His favorite chair was just a few yards off the porch to the right. It was an oversized reclining lawn chair, perfect for napping in the sun. He walked over just to sit for a moment and catch his breath before greeting his guests.

As he sat there he marveled at such a picture-perfect moment. The whole family was together for the first time in a very long time, he thought. His dad was firing up the barbeque and his mom was setting the table on the other side of the yard. His siblings were scattered about talking with friends. Even his little nephew was there, throwing the ball around with the dog. The celebration was about to begin. Just then he looked across the yard and saw his beautiful wife walking towards him. That same chill went down his spine like it did the first time she smiled at him. It was the perfect day. Everyone he ever cared about was there. Everyone, that is, except his boys. He wondered how they were

Full Circle

doing and when they would arrive. They were the only ones he couldn't see. He knew that things just wouldn't be complete until they arrived. For now, though he had to just sit back and wait. He sat back in his chair just to relax for a moment and within seconds he began to nod off.

He woke up just a few moments later. Everyone was gone and the yard was completely empty. He wondered if he had been dreaming. *Wasn't this yard just filled with people?* It was the strangest thing. He got up from his chair and looked around. Nothing. Not a sound. His mind had been playing tricks on him lately; maybe he had imagined it. He walked back into the house and went about his business. Again, he heard a noise in the yard. *What the heck is going on here?* It seemed to be coming from all the way in the back by the barn. He walked down the dirt path past the chicken coop and all the way until he reached the front of the barn. Hearing some muffled noises, he opened the barn door. Sitting there on the loft with a smile on his face and piece of hay straw hanging from his mouth was his brother Cooper. Billy hadn't seen Cooper in 70 years, since he'd passed away. Cooper hopped down from the loft as he

Dalton's Pit

tossed the straw from his mouth and approached Billy. Billy finally realized what had happened. This wasn't his surprise 85th birthday like he'd thought.

"It's been a long time, Bill, great to see you."

Billy was speechless, trying to let everything sink in.

"Relax, little brother, I know this seems crazy. I was freaking out when I got here also. It takes a while to get used to. You will get used it though, I promise."

"Is this heaven?"

"Not exactly. We will be there soon, but first we have some things to do."

"By the way, Bill, thanks for trying to warn me about going to the Food way with Austin that night. I never got a chance to thank you. I think you may have had a point," he said, letting out a big belly laugh.

"Yeah. I wish I could have done more to stop you. I'm sorry, Cooper."

Full Circle

"I wish you were there when we all reunited later in life. Austin changed. He was a good man."

Cooper smiled and said, "Yes, I know, Billy. I never blamed Austin. We've spoken about this many times over the past few years. I told him the same things I'm telling you. Everything worked out fine. It was just my time."

"You have? How?"

Just then Austin and Charlotte climb down from the roof on to the loft and then to the barn floor.

"Hey, Bill it's been 10 years now. How's the compound. How are the dogs doing?"

Billy gave Austin a bear hug. "They are doing just fine. My sons are running the place now. Jack and Harry are partners. I retired a few years ago."

Billy suddenly realized there was a woman standing next to Austin smiling. He looked at her and couldn't decipher her smile. *Who is she*, he wondered.

"Billy, this is Charlotte, our older sister," Austin said.

Dalton's Pit

"So glad to meet you, Billy. I finally have my whole family together in one place. I am so excited. It's been over 90 years we've been apart now."

Billy, a bit overwhelmed, realized his entire family was together. That meant his Donna was there. He hadn't seen her since she passed away four years ago. She had cancer. Her last few years were very difficult for both her and Billy. She suffered from pancreatic cancer and just wasted away at the end. It was so painful for him to bear. He remembered her in the good times though. The healthy times. He remembered her smile; that's what had attracted him to her in the beginning. That very first day at the hospital. He remembered it so well; it was as if he could reach out and touch it.

Billy gasped. "Donna is here? I need to see my Donna. Where is she? I want to see her now. Please, where is she?" Now starting to well up, he pleaded, "I want her. Please take me to her."

Charlotte replied, "I think I already know the answer to this question, but I'll ask you anyway. Would you like me to take you to her now, Billy?"

Full Circle

Billy was completely overcome with emotion. He simply nodded his head and said, "Yes, Charlotte, please take me now."

Charlotte escorted Billy out of the barn and they walked back to the house together. They talked as they walked.

"I am sorry, Charlotte; I know nothing about you. I heard that you died when you were a baby. I am sorry you didn't get to spend any time with our family on earth."

"Don't worry, Billy, it all worked out. I was keeping Grandpa company while I was waiting for you guys. He's a very interesting guy. I got to meet Grandma a while later. I even got to taste her amazing apple pie. Did you know he had to wait for her for over 50 years in your time?

Now they get to be together forever. Just like us. Now it's time for me to finally enjoy my whole family."

Billy, starting to understand a little bit more, gave her a nervous smile. He wondered, *is this really happening? Am I really going to see Donna? Will she be healthy like when she was younger?* Just then he looked down at

Dalton's Pit

himself and realized something odd. He was no longer an old man of 85 years. He looked like he did when he was about 35. His clothes were also different from when he'd first arrived there. His hair was black again. No gray at all. As he stepped onto the front steps of the porch, that same creek he had heard so many times before rang out. He opened the front door and as soon as he walked in he recognized his surroundings immediately. He saw what looked like the North Pole. There were decorations covering every wall. The stockings all lined up with patients' names on them. Gifts were under the tree in the corner of the room and the girl at the front desk was smiling with her Santa hat on. The name on her hat read Donna. As he approached her he realized that he was back to the exact moment when they first met. In the meantime, Donna was looking down writing something in her desk calendar and appeared not to notice Billy right away. He just stared at her in all her beauty. It was as if he was looking at an old photo that had come to life. As he approached the desk, his body was literally shaking. He walked up to the counter and said, "Hello, Donna."

Full Circle

Donna smiled. "Hi you." She walked out from behind the desk looking the way she did the day they met almost 50 years ago. She looked at him the way no other woman had ever looked at him before and said, "I've waited so long for you these past four years, it seemed like a hundred. Please don't leave me ever again." She melted into his arms and put her head on his shoulder.

Billy struggled over joyous tears to get the words out. "Never my love."

Charlotte had been standing alongside them the whole time. Billy hadn't noticed. Finally, he looked up and saw Charlotte and standing behind her he saw something much bigger than her shadow. There was Travis with a big grin on his face. He walked up to Billy and Donna and said, "Excuse me, Donna, but it's been about 15 years since I've been able to do this." He grabbed Billy in a head lock and proceeded to give him the business.

"Just like old times, Billy boy."

"Yes, just like old times, Trav."

Dalton's Pit

Travis turned to Billy and Donna and said, "C'mon, you two; we've got stuff to do."

The three of them left the house one by one and once again found themselves on the front porch. Travis was beaming. Off in the distance you could see the smoke billowing from behind the house. The three of them proceeded out past the tire swinging from the tree, then down the dirt path back into the yard. As they made the turn, they saw Flo setting the plates on the picnic table in the yard. Flo looked up and immediately ran toward Billy.

"Welcome home, son. I've missed you so much. But you should really go in and wash up now; dinner will be ready soon."

Billy kissed his mother on the forehead. "It's great to be home, Mom."

They embraced as Flo rested her head on Billy's shoulder. Billy then looked up and saw Big Ernie firing up the barbeque grill all the way in the back of the yard. As usual he was wearing his black 10-gallon cowboy hat. He simply looked up at his son and smiled. Billy nodded

Full Circle

his head. They both knew what the other was thinking. Nothing needed to be said. Ernie's smile, however, turned into this really goofy grin after a moment. It was almost as if his eyes were pointing to something. Billy just smiled back, at first. Then he realized it. Where was Hannah? All the time he was there he hadn't seen Hannah yet. He walked over to his dad at the far corner of the yard.

"Dad? Where?" he asked.

Ernie, using the barbeque tongs to push up his large hat, pointed to the Lucky Dogs Compound. Billy looked toward the archway and started walking toward the compound entrance where the gate was left open. He entered the compound and initially saw nothing, no one. He looked further in and started walking down the path by the stream. About 20 yards in he stopped, looked up, and there she was. Hannah was standing on the dirt alongside the stream facing the other way. No wheelchair, much taller than she used to be. *Is that really her?* He walked up to her, reached out his hand and touched her on her shoulder.

Dalton's Pit

"Pip?" he asked.

She turned around and there it was, that incredible Hannah smile.

"Hello, Billy, welcome home. I'm so happy you're here. Donna and I have been waiting for you."

Hannah pointed to her legs. "What do you think, Billy? Not bad for a cripple huh?"

Billy just smiled and said, "No, not bad at all. Not bad at all, sis."

Just then a frog leaped out of the stream and landed by Billy's feet. He picked it up and looked at Hannah and said, "Now this is an American swamp frog. It eats mostly mosquitos and can grow to be about 2 lbs."

Hannah laughed at his analysis and said, "We made it, Billy. All those years you worried about me. You always put me first, never worrying about yourself. This is your reward. Look, look over there." Just as he turned his head to look where she was pointing, several dozen dogs came running over and began jumping on Billy,

Full Circle

licking his face and eventually knocking him down to the ground.

"They're all here, you know. All the dogs that never found their forever home. Every last one of them, and you know what? It's much easier playing with them when you're not stuck in a wheel chair, I can tell you that. I run with them every day, I can even climb the trees if I want. Funny thing is as great as this is, it just wasn't the same until you showed up. I mean what took you so long anyway?"

Billy laughed. "Same old Pip."

"So are you ready, Billy?"

"Ready? Ready for what?"

"Just follow me, I'll show you."

They walk out of the compound back up the road to the front of the house. Hannah got on her knees and shimmied under the porch and then looked up at Billy.

"C'mon, Billy. Let's go already and bring the frog."

Dalton's Pit

"Hannah, we can't fit under there anymore; you're crazy. Those days are long gone, we're way too big now."

"Just c'mon already, slowpoke. Get down here."

Billy reluctantly got down on his knees and crawled under the porch. As soon as he did he realized he was much smaller. He was able to fit under there very easily. He then looked down at his hands and feet and realized that he was a kid of 11 again. Then he looked over at Pip again smiling. She was 11 years old again also.

"C'mon Billy, help me move these tires. Let's go."

They moved the tires over and climbed down into Dalton's Pit. *Amazing*, Billy thought. *If I could think of all the places in the world I would want to be, I couldn't think of a better place than here. I guess that's how it works. Maybe this really is heaven.*

Just then he heard one of the sweetest sounds off in the distance.

Flo yelling just like the old days. "Kids, supper time."

Made in the USA
Middletown, DE
17 July 2017